BLUE EEL

by
Lorne Dixon

Cutting Block Books
an imprint of Farolight Publishing,
a division of Farolight Entertainment, LLC
PO Box 1521
Winchester, VA 22604
www.cuttingblockbooks.com

Blue Eel is a work of fiction. Names, characters, places and incidents are products of the author's imagination, or are used fictitiously. Any resemblance to actual persons, living or dead, or to events or locales, is entirely coincidental.

Copyright © 2015 by Lorne Dixon

All rights reserved. No part of this publication may be reproduced in any form or by any means without the prior written permission of the publisher, except in the case of brief quotations embodied in critical articles or reviews.

First Cutting Block Books hardcover edition: November 2015

Inset Layout and Design by Bailey Hunter Cover art © 2015 by Lynne Hansen

LynneHansenDesign.com

Eel images © 2015 by Ivy Landon

Published in the United States of America

1 3 5 7 9 10 8 6 4 2

Library of Congress Control Number: 2015954152

ISBN 978-0-9961159-3-3

BLUE EEL

by
Lorne Dixon

INVOCATION

    Laurie Felston bounced down three short steps off the school bus, waved over her shoulder to Mrs. Kearn and leaped from the last rung onto cracked asphalt at the edge of Mistletoe Road. She skidded across pebbles of loose gravel and giggled when the weight of her heavy backpack shifted, spinning her. Mrs. Kearn hadn't even questioned the change of stop; the bus driver had become accustomed to Laurie delivering books and homework assignments to absent students.
    Curled into a tube held tightly in Laurie's hand were a glossy brochure and the order sheets that'd help pay for her eighth grade class trip to the San Andreas Tar Pits. She knew her parents would write a check even if she didn't sell a single calendar, but the prospect of paying her own way excited Laurie. That would show her father she could handle responsibility. Maybe then he'd agree to a dog.
    She'd already chosen the dog's name. *Cornelius.*
    Lost in thoughts of long afternoons playing catch with Cornelius in their backyard, Laurie made her way down the road until she came to the wooden gate of the Renaissance Trailer Park. A thick barrier of palm fronds made it impossible to see beyond a short length of curving, unpaved road, but she'd been inside once to drop off Jillian Pilson's homework, and the place wasn't completely unfamiliar. Jillian and her parents moved away during the summer between sixth and seventh grade. Drove their whole house away with them, Laurie thought with a smile. That meant there were no kids left in the trailer park unless they were home schooled, and she wouldn't know any of those. The

rows of parked motor homes had seemed immense, and Laurie recalled how easily she'd gotten lost. That was almost two years ago, and as she'd matured since then, Laurie was confident she'd be able to find her way around this time. There were dozens of mobile homes still inside Renaissance Trailer Park. So many doors to knock on, so many orders for calendars to take.

Laurie grinned at the prospect. She opened the gate, slid between the tall wooden slats and into the trailer park. The dirt road inside was a narrow trail of red mud and stagnant water pooled in deep tire tracks. Laurie crept down the edge of the lane, where serrated blades of tall grass brushed against the hem of her skirt as she walked, but there was no escape—the wet soil pulled at her black and white school shoes, tugging at the tips and heels every time she lifted her feet off the spongy ground. She'd have to be careful to clean them before going home. The previous summer, Laurie had been careless enough to run inside after a rain and left a trail of footprints through her mother's kitchen, across the living room, and up the stairs to her room. Mom got loud, used a handful of words Laurie hadn't heard before, and sent her to work cleaning up the mess. That wasn't fun. She'd remember this time.

The first row of mobile homes had porches and peaked roofs. They looked almost like ordinary houses, except smaller. Some sported potted plants hung from rails. It didn't seem like such a bad place to live, in spite of what her dad said when they drove past. "They live like animals in there, rolling in their own filth. They've got toilets right next to their kitchen tables."

Laurie's plan was to start at the far end of the park and work her way back to the front gate. She felt a pang of guilt as she passed by the first trailer. When her teacher had explained the rules of *safe selling* there'd been a serious, demanding look on her face, the sort of expression she usually only wore when announcing the rules for important tests. The very first rule of safe selling was always to have an adult at her side when going door-to-door. Laurie didn't want to disobey the rules—she hated cheats—but her mom needed to make dinner for her dad, who would be tired when he got home from work. They'd promise to help her out *later*, or *this weekend*, or any time that wasn't now. Laurie was too excited to wait. She knew Cornelius was out there somewhere, waiting for her.

The second and third rows of mobile homes were uglier than those you could see from the road. Narrower and plain, color peeling off aluminum siding that was never meant to be painted. She walked faster, listening to her shoes in the mud, the sound evoking the image of a lion licking its chops. The homes became more dilapidated the further into the park she traveled. She approached a trailer with a dented screen door. A sun-bleached POW/MIA flag covered the only window.

"-you stay away, Bobby, you stay good'n away-"

Laurie averted her eyes as she passed. A pale, unhealthy-looking woman in a nightgown stood in the doorway. From the bottom of the stairs a man in a filthy t-shirt and grease-smeared blue jeans tried to wedge himself inside. A uniformed police officer filled the space between them, one hand firmly on the man's chest.

The cop, voice rising, kept a hand on his holster as he addressed the man. "-Sir, sir, SIR, I'll need you to stand back-"

"-just need to talk with my girl, need to-"

"-about that, huh? What about my money?" The woman yelled. "How's is I supposed to pay for the cable? To eat?"

The man waved a pointing finger. "You got enough of my money. Can't hold on to it. Wanna tell me what you use it all for?"

"-fuck you, Bobby, how 'bout *that* instead? H'bout–"

Their voices grew louder, and Laurie walked faster, until two full rows of trailers blocked out the noise. As she traveled deeper into the park, the condition of the trailer homes continued to erode. She'd entered a dark warren of metal boxes with rusting edges, broken screen doors, opaque windows and plastic stepladders salvaged from swimming pools in the place of real stairs. Some of the trailers seemed abandoned and left to the elements. Then Laurie eyed a shirtless old man sitting on an overturned, rusted out refrigerator and knew better. He barely glanced in her direction, curled his lip then spit out a wad of chew. The old man didn't wipe his mouth, ignoring the dark line of spittle that slipped down from the corner of his lip and onto his stubbled chin.

When Laurie's dad first told her they were moving from Arizona to California, she thought she'd seen the last of that sort of thing. She'd been proved wrong more times than she could count. Still, she liked Santa Flora, her school was nice and so were most of her classmates, and her bedroom window looked right out onto the Pacific Ocean. Laurie guessed there were people like the man on the refrigerator anywhere you went.

She came to the final row of homes and stopped. She glanced

back at the path she'd traveled. The trailers she'd passed were old and weathered, but here, in the back corner of the lot, these houses were in awful condition, perhaps unfit for human occupancy. If people lived like this, would they even be able to afford a new calendar? Did they even care what day it was? Laurie's stomach tightened at the idea of embarrassing people by asking them to buy something they couldn't afford. She knew the prices listed in the catalog under her arm. Good calendars didn't come cheap.

It was probably better to turn back, rather than to start knocking on doors. Maybe the trailer park had been a bad idea all along. Laurie's initial vision of a tight cluster of homes where calendars could be sold without competition hadn't been thought out very well, and she wondered if it wouldn't be a waste of time to try. Then Laurie balled her little hands into fists.

No, I will not turn back now, just because these houses are a little scary. I want a dog and I'll earn him. And once he's home, I'll name him Cornelius.

Or maybe Cleveland. Or Paul. Paul the Dog. Maybe.

At the edge of the property, close enough to the jagged tree line to recede back into the shadow of the towering trees, stood one last trailer. Its outer walls were covered in a complex natural lattice of wild vine. It reminded Laurie of stockings worn by older girls she sometimes saw smoking cigarettes when her dad drove across the city to her uncle's house. Laurie stepped up to the last trailer, climbed the short, uneven ladder propped at its side, and knocked lightly on the flimsy door.

At first there was no answer, not even a stirring from inside. Laurie considered that maybe the trailers back this far were unoccupied after all. Maybe the man on the refrigerator lived in one of the trailers farther up but had taken a walk, gotten tired, and sat—

The door of the trailer opened. Laurie jumped from the ladder and stumbled back a half dozen steps, until she stood at the edge of the tree line's long shadow. From the doorway, the long, unshaven face of a man stared out at her with a lack of focus so profound that Laurie wondered if he was blind. The man's eyelids were heavy pockets, leathery and dark. The rest of his face was ghostly pale. Shoots of gray hair sparked at his temples.

"What d'you want?"

She'd memorized a speech about fundraising and class trips, and the value to the community when young people learned responsibility at an early age. It was printed right there on the back of the catalog. To prompt herself, all Laurie needed to do was look down at the curl of paper in her fist. Instead she blurted out, "I'm selling calendars so I can get a dog."

The man's brow furrowed. Confusion swept over his features.

Laurie shook her head. "No, no. I mean, my class is doing a fundraiser—" The man cut her off with a smile.

"I think you had it right the first time."

She smiled back. He wasn't handsome or well groomed, but the man seemed nice enough. Laurie uncurled the catalog from her fist and tried to smooth it out. It rolled back into a tube.

"They got lots of different ones in here. I'm sure there'll be something you like."

"I'll bet I can sure find something." He cocked his head skyward and wrinkled his nose. "But, y'know, it's gonna start raining again real soon. You can smell it in the air. Why don't you come on in so we don't get drenched out here once it starts."

Caught off guard, Laurie froze—except for her gaze, which fell to the muddy tips of her shoes. Her teacher had been very clear: *Never, under any circumstance, go alone into a stranger's house.*

Thunder rumbled overhead.

"What kind of dog you lookin' at getting?"

Laurie lifted her eyes from her shoes. "I dunno. Maybe a big one."

"Like a German Shepherd?" The man stepped down the ladder rungs. They bowed beneath his weight. He stood barefoot on soggy ground, seemingly oblivious to his feet sinking in the wet soil. "Or, I know. One of those Marmadude dogs, what a' they called, great dames?"

"Danes. Great *Danes*," Laurie corrected him.

"That's right," the man nodded. "Had a neighbor once had one of those. Biggest dog I've ever seen. Taller than me, up on its hind legs."

"Here?" Laurie turned her head to survey the park for signs of a Great Dane. In the distance, the old man pushed off the refrigerator, then shambled away along the center of the lane.

"Well, that was a long time back."

Her shadow raced back to her as a dark cloud moved in and blotted out the last bit of open sky. He was right, rain was coming. Maybe a nasty thunderstorm. Laurie hated those.

"What happened to him?"

"The dog?" Before she could answer the man continued. "Funny you should ask. Went missing. A few weeks later my neighbor moved on. Upstate or down, I can't remember. Thing is, that dog showed back up after he'd left. For a while, all the neighbors fed it. Then one day he stopped coming 'round. We all figured he'd just got fed up with waiting for his master to return and decided to go off looking for him."

More thunder. Laurie feared she wouldn't make it home before the storm arrived. Her teacher's warning echoed in her head. "That sounds like a movie I saw once."

"Does it?" The man extended an open palm to the sky. "There it goes. You feel that? Just started raining. Think maybe I should get inside. I'd be happy to look through that catalog of yours where we won't get wet. C'mon..."

Never. Her teacher had said *never*. That word left little room for excuses. Laurie knew whenever her mother or father used that word, they meant it. *Never go into a stranger's house.*

A cold dash of rain hit her eyebrow and cascaded down onto her cheek. A wet splotch appeared on the catalog. Then another. The cheap ink smeared. Without the catalog and order forms, Laurie couldn't sell calendars. Without sales, Laurie's parents would have to pay for the class trip. If they paid for that, then they wouldn't see how responsible she could be and would say *no*, yet again, to a dog.

She thought of a Great Dane named Paul, as tall as her father when the dog stood on its hind legs, and her teacher's words faded into a blur like the printing on the catalog. Perhaps not Paul, after all. At the moment, Laurie kind of liked the name Buster.

"Maybe the rain'll only last a little while?" she said, but doubted there was any way he could know. "Maybe I could come in for just a few minutes..."

"Few minutes won't hurt." The man shrugged.

Laurie thought about the sales speech she'd memorized but failed to use. The very first thing she was supposed to do, before ever mentioning calendars or class trips or anything, was to introduce herself. Just her first name, the teacher insisted, and *Smile when you say it*, which she remembered to do.

"My name's Laurie."

"Pleased to meet you, Laurie. I'm Bruce."

The rain increased from a drizzle to a downpour, until Laurie could no longer feel the impact of individual drops. Bruce reached for her hand. "If we don't get inside, your name will be Soaked Laurie and I'll be Soggy Bruce."

She giggled, took his hand, and let him help her up the ladder and into the trailer. It was darker inside, but her eyes adjusted quickly. Bruce closed the door behind them. Once inside, he shook his head. Rainwater sprayed off his hair like from a wet dog. A Great Dane, in fact.

Laurie caught a whiff of drifting odor. Not unpleasant but difficult to place at first, the sort of smell that arose from a memory forgotten. Or mostly forgotten. Or from a place so out of place she needed to search in order to find it. Then the scent flooded back to her—the trailer smelled like a real Christmas tree, freshly cut then hauled inside. Laurie remembered those, from when she was just a kid. Since moving to California, her family celebrated Christmas around fake trees. That was never the same.

Motion in her peripheral vision drew Laurie's eyes to a small cot set against the far wall of the trailer, a cot smaller than her own bed, but one that looked much less comfortable. A woman with long red hair lay asleep on it, a blanket twisted around her as if she'd been tossed through a marathon of nightmares. Her face was pale and sunken, like the withered skin of spoiled fruit. To Laurie, the woman looked very, very sick.

But that wasn't what sent a shock down her spine.

The woman glowed.

The surface of woman's waxy skin shimmered with a subtle, yet undeniable luminescence that swirled and pulsed.

"That's Heather," Bruce said. He intoned the name with awe and sadness, the voice of a man much in love with a woman and aware that soon he'd lose her. "She's... resting."

Transfixed by the glowing woman, Laurie stepped toward her across the trailer floor, the squeak of loose boards accompanying her like out-of-tune violins. Tears stained Heather's face. When Laurie got very close, one of the woman's eyes slid open, revealing a milky pupil dotted with tiny black cataracts. Heather's lips quivered, then parted as if she tried to speak. No words came out, only a sputtering whimper.

"Are you an angel?" Laurie asked.

This time Heather's lips pursed, and she blew Laurie a kiss. The red-headed woman then drew a deep breath and whistled a thin warbling tune like some distant echo of a church hymn. The whistling ended abruptly in a series of weak coughs. A line of gelatinous drool rolled from the corner of Heather's lips.

The scent of Christmas trees grew stronger. Laurie's nose wrinkled up as the smell of pine became overbearing. She covered her mouth and nose with one hand, even as she realized the source of the odor: Heather's gaping mouth.

"Hey, hey now, Heather girl." Bruce swooped down and wiped the woman's face with a frayed handkerchief. "You just calm down now and rest. Laurie's here to show me some calendars. Nothing to get excited over. You just relax."

From the edge of Heather's cot, Bruce turned to Laurie, a worried frown carved into his face like graffiti. "She needs her rest. Go on over to the table. You can show me the catalog there. The light's better, and Heather can sleep."

"Okay," Laurie said. But she didn't move.

Bruce forced a smile and pulled himself to his feet. As Bruce passed Laurie, he waved for her to follow him to the small kitchen area, and the table that filled it.

Something snagged Laurie's arm. Heather's hand, wet and weak, fingers flaccid as a tangle of night crawlers, gripped her. Startled, Laurie leaped away. Her head spun. Heather's arm retreated beneath the blanket.

Laurie ran her hand over where she'd been touched. It was slathered in a clear, sticky fluid. She rubbed the area to try and wipe it off, and the viscous substance absorbed into her skin like a lotion. Heat radiated from the spot, tickling up and out of Laurie's arms like sparks of static electricity.

A dark figure emerged from the corner, a man with a head surrounded by a halo of burning light. His bearded face danced in and out of that light, as the intensity of his aura spiked and waned. Shadows and flashes of white-heat distorted his features into unfixed form that didn't much resemble human. Then, in an intense swirl of color and glare, he disappeared into the flash.

Laurie's universe spun violently. A wave of nausea rushed through her, and her vision blurred. The floor seemed to shift beneath her feet. It swayed to and fro like a ship caught upon rough seas. Laurie stumbled towards the kitchen and her feet went out from under her.

She instinctively threw her arms out to break the fall, but they'd gone numb and failed her. Laurie collided with the floor full force, chin and shoulder cracking. The uneven floor sent her small body sliding across the trailer. She crashed into a wicker chest and it overturned. Dolls spilled out. They surrounded Laurie in a flood of plastic arms and legs and molded faces haloed with stringy hair. She screamed and pushed herself along the floor, knees and elbows barely responsive.

"Help me, please, help me—"

Bruce locked the trailer door in response.

Laurie managed to crawl to the far wall, legs mostly useless and dragging behind. Panic set in and the child let loose a miserable wail. Tears cascaded down her face. Bruce retrieved a pair of scissors from a wooden drawer in the kitchen.

"I'm so sorry, I didn't mean for this to happen. But then there you were, a knock at the door. Just when Heather needed you." Bruce snipped the scissor blades in the air. "Maybe *you're* the angel, come to buy her a little more time."

Without warning, Bruce snatched up a handful of Laurie's hair. She wanted to fight but her arms just wiggled uselessly at her sides. Laurie felt like a fish on a stringer. Spreading his fingers, Bruce slid the scissors across a lock of Laurie's curly hair, snipped, and pocketed the clipping.

As he withdrew the scissors, a silver trail followed, as if the blades left some of their essence lingering in the air. This shimmering line of chrome hovered for a moment then dissipated, curling away at the edges like wisps of smoke. Fascination nearly drowned out Laurie's fear. That was short-lived. She saw for the first time that Bruce's right ear was gone. Where an ear should've been only a tangle of ragged scar tissue remained. The old wound bulged outward, purple scar tissue curling, revealing a glimpse of blue, cerulean membrane. The head of an eyeless blue eel pushed through the exposed muscle. Lubricated by a sheen of translucent mucus, it slithered out from between the pulsing flesh.

Laurie screamed again.

Buried far beneath the rising terror, some small, desperate part of her hoped that she was dreaming. Then the eel broke free from the side of Bruce's face and, tethered by its tail, dangled from the bulging hole in the side of Bruce's head. The eel rose like an elephant's trunk, twisted around, and swam in the air towards Laurie. As it swam, the tip of its snout tore open, flesh peeling back to reveal a circular, puckering mouth.

Concentrating her energy, Laurie pushed off the floor. She clawed wildly at the air, desperate to keep the slowly advancing blue eel away.

Bruce recoiled from her clawing hands. Laurie's knees buckled under her and she hit the floor. The impact cut through her paralysis and nausea. In that moment, the pain returned her body to her. Her hands twitched and her legs kicked. Then numbness returned and surged through her.

The eel fell to the floor beside her, squirming and flopping, its bulbous head thumping against the floor as it convulsed.

Bruce stumbled back, legs crossing, as his hands rose up to the spot on his head where the eel exited. With two stiff fingers, he tried to press bulging membrane back into his ear canal. He danced in a tight, flailing circle and whimpered, then crashed against the wall over the cot and collapsed on top of Heather. Her mouth jarred open as if to scream, but only a dry and static cackle emerged. Crying, Bruce wrapped his arms around Heather, pulling her tight, her head cradled in his hands. She shuddered violently, then her body went still.

Laurie willed herself to stand but her legs refused. Fighting the paralysis, she bit down hard on her arm, breaking skin. Pain flared and a semblance of control returned. Her elbows bent, knees curled. She managed somehow to whip herself around, and slammed into a wall, which dispersed the invisible layers of callus that had imprisoned her. Laurie's hands curled into fists, and she beat at her legs until she felt command over them return, too. Then she stood, wobbling, and kicked the eel out of her path. She bolted for the door.

Eyes wide, Bruce spun, and dropped Heather on the cot.

Laurie fumbled with the lock, her hands heavy, fingers not yet nimble enough to work the mechanism. The nausea returned, and her legs threatened again to collapse under her.

"Where you going?" Bruce pulled the scissors from his pocket. The lock of Laurie's hair came out with it and spread like feathers to the floor. He strode forward, kicking through plastic dolls, and pointed at Laurie with the scissors.

Laurie pounded her hands against the door. The spark of pain awoke her thumbs and forefingers. She turned the lock and threw her weight against the door, crashing hard. Fresh pain helped her push, and the door broke open. She tumbled out, tripped over the guide rails of the ladder, and plummeted into the mud. Landing hard, half painted in soggy soil, she kicked off the ground, and ran. Laurie's footwork was sloppy and wild but she was fast, making it halfway to the abandoned refrigerator before Bruce burst through the front door in pursuit.

Cold rain pelted down, hitting her face like pebbles. That helped, too. She picked up speed with Bruce right behind her, the sound of his footfalls in the sucking mud gaining on her. Laurie knew she couldn't outrace him, but had no choice except to run. She drew her bottom lip into her mouth and bit down. Fresh pain and the taste of blood made her legs stronger, more responsive. She sprinted down the center of the road, and passed the now empty porch where the couple had fought.

The policeman and the angry man in the t-shirt were at the front gate. The policeman was escorting Bobby, in handcuffs, to his cruiser. Laurie screamed and both men turned, confusion on their faces.

A hand grasped the back of Laurie's shirt. She shrieked. Both of Laurie's shoes remained planted in the mud as she was yanked up from behind. She caught a blurred glimpse of Bruce's face as she was whipped around to face him. The policeman yelled, "Hey—"

Laurie caught the glint of scissor blades in Bruce's hand. What happened next happened fast.

ONE

With gloved hands, Branson Turaco unfolded the newspaper, careful not to tug or pull. A fine layer of powder insured against accidental smudging of the ink. In Branson's hands was a copy of *The Los Angeles Telegraph*, printed in 1932. The paper had all the telltale aspects of its age: deep wrinkled creases, yellowed edges, faded gray carbon and heavy oil ink. The columns ran straight, not justified, and were repetitive. From a distance the paper could have passed for a bar code. He carefully spread the newspaper on the scanning table.

Closing the scanner's lid with a gentle touch, Branson turned to the computer at his side, clicked the icon marked SCAN, and thought that his job must surely be a high tech step along the evolutionary ladder of carpal tunnel syndrome-inducing repetitive labor. In four years, he'd only made it up to January, 1932. It might well take until retirement to archive the paper's entire history. The scanner processed both sides of the news sheet at once, converting its contents into high definition files, ensuring no one would ever again need to do this work. At least not until more advanced technology rendered the files obsolete, and then it'd be someone else's concern. Each sheet of newsprint took six full minutes to scan, transmit, archive, and index. Then Branson could go on to the next page.

In high school he'd wanted to be a journalist. Not Woodward or Bernstein or any kind of investigative Murrow-award chaser; he'd no taste for politics or activism. Branson's ambitions had followed more along the lines of Hunter S. Thompson.

He wondered what Thompson might think of his current job in journalism, placing old newsprint on a glass, closing a lid, then watching as an intense blue light crawled across one edge of the machine. He was sure it'd make for a brilliant Thompson essay. A satirical literary sleight-of-hand that'd reveal the mundane through irreverence. The exact sort of thing Branson had never managed to pull off. In fact, he was unpublished. This late in the game, especially after all the trouble and his divorce, he was pretty certain it'd stay that way. The scanner light trolled on.

The Mortician. That's what the reporters and office staffers called him. In charge of the newspaper's morgue, Branson had liked that in the beginning. Even signed responses to research requests with the nickname. That was before Madeline went missing, after which he never used it again. Some of the reporters still did. Some few had other nicknames for him as well. Branson pretended not to hear those, which wasn't all that hard to do. He spent most of the workday with a pair of headphones on his ears listening to music, mostly '60's jazz but sometimes *Sgt. Pepper's* or *Electric Ladyland*. Today though, there was no free bandwidth in his head for the chaos of rock and roll. Charles Mingus' *The Black Saint and the Sinner Lady* grooved and groaned as Branson lifted the scanner lid, gathered up the old newspaper, crumpled it into a ball, and tossed it into the trash. Each day he filled the basket and each night the cleaning crew emptied it. It was a true symbiotic relationship, each organism creating purpose for the other: a garbage basket filled meant a garbage basket to empty.

There came a knock on the door, barely audible over the arguing horns and snapping cymbal crashes in his headphones. It was too calm to be a reporter on the run, which would've been followed immediately by a barking order, *I need this*, or *track down that*, and *I need it ASAP*. Glancing up, Branson slid the earphones down to his neck. His eyes didn't follow Mick Grayson as the editor stepped into the room. Instead, they stayed fixed on a second figure that remained shielded in the doorway as if awaiting an invitation.

"Branson, Detective Woost is here to see you," Grayson said.

Frowning, he nodded.

Detective Susan Woost stepped into the newspaper morgue. Branson saw she'd changed precious little since last he'd seen her. In her early forties, Woost still had a youthful face with bright eyes and creamy, unwrinkled skin. As she came closer, it became plain that something *had* changed after all. The Detective's hair, tied back in a tight business-like ponytail, was a lush brown where once it'd been *blonde*. Branson wondered which was the real Detective Woost, the *blonde* or the brunette.

"Where's Detective Faune?"

"You work for a newspaper, Mr. Turaco." Woost's voice remained a carefully strummed instrument, every syllable equal, never wavering. "You really should stay better informed. As it happens, Detective Faune passed away from cancer four months ago."

The voice may have been smooth and detached, but her eyes told a different story. Her partner's death was an open wound. Branson nodded. "I'm only up to the '39 New York World's Fair, so I'm a little behind on the news. I'll get to his obituary in another decade or two."

Detective Woost pressed closer, as if warning Branson not to spar with her. "The purpose of my visit with this man is private, Mr. Grayson—" She never took her eyes off Branson.

"Of course. That's fine," the editor replied as he raised both his hands in a gesture of compliance. He checked his watch, then turned to Branson. "I'll clock you out at three."

It was ten after three. "That's fine."

"Okay then." Grayson headed for the open door. "I have a very sincere retraction to write that's a half hour overdue. Detective, should you need anything further from me, I'll be in my office."

Grayson hurried out. Their guard up, neither Branson nor Detective Woost averted their eyes from each other to watch him go. Then Woost's chest rose, and out spilled a great exhalation. She motioned for Branson to return to his seat.

"I'm not here for the reasons you think."

Snagging his office chair with his foot, Branson rolled it behind him and sat. As circus tricks went, it might not have kept a chimpanzee employed, but it was one of many that passed the workday.

"No? The inquisition is done with? After the first year, I kind of gave up on you ever quitting. Figured you'd come around every so often for the rest of my life, just to kick me around some." He leaned back in the chair. "You get bored and decide to come kick me around before your three hour, taxpayer funded lunch?"

She shook her head. "Cutbacks. Taxpayers only pay for jelly donuts and coffee. Some days I get to have some fun before lunch, though. Slap some jewelry on men who've killed their wives or business partners with monogrammed letter openers, then plead they're innocent. It must've been someone else out there with my initials and fingerprints, they'd say. But those men all lied, Mr. Turaco. Every single one of them now rots in jail, where they belong. Thing is, I always think of you when I hear protestations of innocence. You're the one that got away."

Branson picked up a blue editing pencil from the desk and twirled it between his fingers, a nervous habit. "That must be frustrating."

"It was," Woost said. "But that doesn't compare with how I feel right now. I spent so long hating you, the one man I couldn't dress for the prom."

Since his daughter Madeline's disappearance, Branson had heard enough police talk to know that detectives called handcuffs "jewelry" and why sometimes they referred to prison as the "the prom." It was all about unwanted sexual attention. Cops favored dark humor. Branson figured that came with the job, but under the circumstances, it'd been wasted on him.

He waited for more. At first, he thought she had nothing more to say. Detective Woost stood there, the expression on her face buried behind professional training and personal pride, impossible to read. Her lips quivered when she whispered, "I've come to say I'm sorry."

Branson was utterly unprepared for that. The words hit him harder than any of the accusations she'd leveled against him since the beginning. The idea that life could change so quickly yet again was difficult to comprehend. He'd grown complacent in his awful life. Known as the *Guy Who Killed His Kid* to some of his coworkers, that was a badge that'd become as comfortable in its own perverse way as *The Mortician*. He almost wished he'd never heard what Woost said.

"Two weeks ago, local PD in Santa Flora arrested a man

attempting to abduct a schoolgirl," she continued. Branson strained to hear her. His head was all in a muddle. "Among his possessions they found evidence suggesting that this man may have been responsible for your daughter's disappearance as well."

Tears trickled down his cheek. "Evidence?"

Woost nodded. "A lock of Madeline's hair. DNA tests matched it conclusively to your daughter. It's an old sample, not recent. Maybe five years old. They found it glued to a doll."

"Glued to a doll?"

"Badly. Like it was done with a hot glue gun."

Detective Woost moved over to Branson's side and out of his direct line of sight. He let her go, instead choosing to stare at the empty doorway. Her words barely penetrated the heavy migraine buzz that was building at the center of his skull.

"I'm sorry. I really am. I know you must be holding out some hope that she's alive. We don't have any indication of that. In most abduction cases, the chances of recovering a child diminish rapidly after twenty-four hours and are all but nil after two weeks. It's been five years since Madeline went away."

Branson hit her with a hard stare. *Sorry* wasn't enough. Not near enough to excuse the years of verbal abuse and intimidation she and her partner had heaped on him.

"You don't have to tell me how long it's been. I know exactly, down to the day. You can't know how long five years can be."

"No, I guess I can't. I don't pretend to." Woost stepped in front of him and placed a hand on his shoulder, not warm and consoling, but not cold and insincere, either. "I didn't have to come here today. Your daughter's disappearance isn't even my case anymore, it was designated a cold case last June. I'm just consulting on the arrest and came here because we owe you that much."

Detective Woost headed for the door.

"We?"

Without turning, she answered, "Me and Roy. Detective Faune."

Woost was almost out the door when Branson said, "I want to see him."

Woost stopped in her tracks. Her heels came to a rest on the tile floor, as if she were frozen in place.

"The suspect? That's impossible. That sort of thing could compromise the entire case."

Branson stood. "What's his name?"

He could hear her breathe, as if the decision whether or not to tell him was a labored process. Finally, Detective Woost half-turned to Branson, steadied her eyes on his, and said, "Bruce Donne."

"Thank you, Detective."

As she drifted out into the hall she mumbled, "You work for a newspaper. It wouldn't take you six seconds to find out a suspect's name." She paused. Sighed. "Don't do anything stupid, Mr. Turaco."

TWO

Not for the first time, as Branson dialed, he thought how much of a disaster his life had become. Any man who needed to first dial an area code just to speak with his wife was damaged beyond repair. *Wife*. The word felt like a lie, even though it wasn't, not in the strict, legal sense. Candice never bothered to divorce him, not even after she moved to Arizona with her boyfriend. A call from a pre-paid cell phone was all the notice she'd given him; she'd started her new life.

She told him she'd stopped wearing their wedding ring the day her home pregnancy test came up positive. As Branson waited for Candice to pick up, he imagined the pale band of skin on her finger steadily darkening. He wondered how long it'd take for it to disappear completely. And whether she'd ever bother answering his calls after it did.

"I already know." There was no *How are you Bran*? Not even a hello.

"She called?" he asked.

"Who, the chick cop?" Candice sounded mildly annoyed, as if he'd interrupted something. "No, it was a guy. Sounded like an old beat cop."

Branson lost track of what he'd meant to say, his rehearsed speech vanishing, leaving behind only jagged fragments of ideas that he couldn't puzzle-piece back into coherent shape. "I just wanted to make sure you knew."

"And I do." Her sharp voice cut him off. "Is that it?"

No, that wasn't it. He wanted to inform the mother of his child that he'd not let Madeline's fate go unresolved, that he intended to get answers. Branson would never give up, especially not now there was the chance, however slight, that their daughter might still be alive somewhere. At the very least, he'd bring home a body to bury. Telling Candice all this had seemed important to Branson. More important than anything had ever been in his life, but the words just weren't there.

"Yeah. I guess that's it."

"Okay then."

He closed the phone.

THREE

Branson had two stops to make on the first floor, one at each end of the building. The first, Mick Grayson's office, was located in the honeycomb of offices circling above the presses. Those offices were soundproofed, a startling contrast to the cacophony of noise in the hallways outside. Branson knocked too hard on Grayson's door because he couldn't hear the sound of his own knuckles. The clitter-clack and rumble of machinery drowned out any possible response. After waiting a moment, he opened the door. The editor sat on the edge of his desk, phone in hand, and pointed to an empty seat.

Branson chose not to sit and instead rested his hands on the back of the chair. Grayson raised a single finger to ask him to wait a minute, then their eyes met. Without saying a word, he hung up the phone. "You okay, Bran?"

"They found a lock of her hair." Telling Grayson the news forced Branson to hear it again, and the result was the same. His legs felt weak and the muscles in his neck seized up. "They found the guy who took her."

"Jesus," Grayson mumbled. "Did they say—"

Branson shook his head. "They don't know. But it's a start. I'm going to need some time off. I haven't taken any vacation for damn near five years, not a single day."

Four years and ten months ago he'd taken Candice to Vegas in a last-ditch effort to rekindle their marriage. Only one memory of the trip stuck: feeding a slot machine quarters, and glancing down a stretch of empty seats to Candice working the last machine in the row. Other couples sat together, laughing while they played. They were no longer a couple by then, not in any meaningful way, and that was when Branson knew it for sure.

"Take whatever time you need."

"And there's another thing."

Grayson nodded.

"I'll need press credentials." The editor's face dropped.

"I can't just issue out a press badge, you *know* that. I need to have a damn good reason—"

"Mick..."

"I mean, you're angry and confused, I get that. It'd be better for you just to go home. Call your doctor for a scrip, something illegal to possess within two miles of a public school, and take it easy for a while."

"Mick, I'm not looking to gun anyone down." Grayson's eyes rose to meet his.

"This asshole took my daughter. He's taken other children, maybe a lot of them. The cops have a mountain of dots to connect. I can't wait for that. I need to know *now* what happened to Maddy. If I just go home and wait I'll go crazy." Branson tapped a finger on the desk. "What would you do if it was you?"

"I know exactly what I'd do if someone took either of my kids. I know what I'd want to do, that's why I shouldn't give you the credentials. But..."

"But you will?"

The editor closed his eyes. "Give me an hour. There'll be an envelope in your mailbox."

The phone on the desk rang. Branson was already headed for the door as Grayson said, "Sorry about that Bob. Dropped the damned phone and got disconnected. Then something came up, you know how it is. Where were—"

The noise of the press stole the rest away.

Branson shot across the break room, through the cafeteria, and followed the lockers that lined the building's rear service corridor. He emerged through a set of access doors into the reporter's mall. The mall was divided in half. A long, open loft filled with workstations where new writers worked elbow-to-elbow, against a maze of cubicles where veteran newsmen were ensconced. Elbowing past a huddle of sports reporters holding court in the hallway—Branson couldn't tell whether they were engaged in a serious argument or harmless office bickering—he made his way to one of the back cubicles.

There, clippings covered the partition wall. Stories about citywide corruption and horse-trading deals. Michael Ponds sat behind his desk, head resting in his hands, staring at his phone.

"Does it help, staring like that?" Branson asked.

"Can't hurt, right?" Ponds asked.

"Who're you waiting on?"

"Some suit over at the mayor's office. Gotta get a non-committal, scripted comment before I can finish off the article." Ponds pointed to his computer terminal. "Soon as I get my share of government doublespeak, I can slap it together, press send, and go away for a well-earned four day weekend."

"How long you been waiting?"

"For the weekend?"

"For the call."

Ponds glanced at his watch then answered, "Three hours."

"The respect you command is awe-inspiring."

Ponds smirked.

"Goes with the territory. Starts off everyone likes you, even thinks you're brave to work this beat. Then you write the truth about someone they know, someone they like, or someone they need, and wouldn't y'know it, they all kind of drift away. Occupational hazard." Ponds shrugged. "Fair-weather friend syndrome."

"So why do I still talk to you?"

"Because you need something. And no one else here is going to help you, so it's me or nothing. You've got no choice. Friendship by process of elimination."

"It's true." Branson said.

"Okay, Mortician. What is it you want?"

"Your intern. Greg." Branson glanced over to the far end of the mall, to the long tables where interns usually assembled with their busy work. Greg wasn't there. "I need him to run down some information for me."

"Run down some information? You're not a reporter, Bran. Aren't we supposed to come to *you* for this sort of thing? Isn't that your job?" Without waiting for an answer, Ponds let out a wide, devilish grin and said, "Look, doesn't matter. You can't have Greg. He quit last week, shuffled back to Asstrauma, Iowa or wherever the hell he was from."

"Shit," Branson mumbled and turned away. Ponds whistled him back.

"Wait. You look like I just ran over your dog with a cement roller. You know I'm far too goddamned Catholic to let you walk out of here like that. I've got an intern for you, barely out of high school, just started working a few hours in the afternoons. You can have Abriella."

Ponds rose to his feet and joined Branson. He pointed across the mall to a young African-American girl hunched over a copy machine. The girl's light brown dreadlocks appeared almost *blonde* against her extremely dark skin.

Ponds whistled again, louder this time, and called, "ABRY—"

The girl's head shot up, and her eyes went wide behind a pair of thick, magnifying glasses. Ponds waved her over. She dropped a stack of copies onto the nearest table, and hurried to them, an ankle-length denim skirt swishing behind her like a jellyfish caught in strong current. "Mr. Ponds?"

"This is Branson Turaco. He's from the archiving department." Ponds spoke slowly, as if in doubt she understood all of his words. "You'll be working for him while I'm away."

The phone rang in Ponds' office.

"Starting right now, as a matter of fact."

Ponds leaped for his phone and Abriella turned to Branson with a sour expression on her face, as if through some gift of precognition she'd already divined the rest of the day and disapproved. "Regular or decaf?"

"Excuse me?" he asked.

"Coffee and copies." Abriella's words came so quick they nearly overlapped. "That's what they have me do around here, make copies and pour coffee. Everyone seems to need a lot of both."

Branson shook his head. "You won't be doing either for me." He pointed beyond the maze of cubicles toward a second service corridor. "You mind walking with me while we talk? I've a busy day in front of me."

"Lead on."

"Good." They passed the cubicles without glancing inside. Branson could feel the eyes of old-school reporters on him, their minds full of disdain, convinced he was a murderer. He wondered how fast word would get around that someone else had been arrested for the crime, and whether they'd still cling to the comfort of outrage and disdain. He was certain that an office pool somewhere would come to an end. Someone would lose money; he'd still have enemies. Branson glanced back at Abriella, who followed him a step behind. "Why does Ponds talk to you that way?"

"You mean as if I'm a retarded lowland gorilla?" The words came out of her like automatic weapons fire.

"Yeah, like that."

"I figure it's two things, really. You've seen the photos on his desk of his wife and kids? No, of course not. Those don't exist. Not the pictures, not the family. They'd get in the way of his lifelong pursuit of meaningful ten-minute relationships with women who twirl on poles. And my suspicion is that he only slides folding money into the panties of *white* strippers."

"How long have you been here?"

"A week and a day."

Entering the service corridor, Branson held the door for her and said, "You got all that in eight days? You'll do fine as a reporter. Just for clarification, though, Ponds specifically favors Asian dancers."

"You seem okay." Abriella followed him in.

Branson shrugged. "That surprises you?"

"Here? Yeah." She stepped up beside him and easily kept stride.

"Have you overheard anything about me?" he asked.

"Yeah," she admitted in a voice free from guilt. Almost everyone at the paper would deny up and down that they ever spoke about him behind his back, but Abriella didn't hesitate. "They say you murdered your daughter and got away with it. Did you?"

That made Branson smile.

"You know, my wife spent years trying to find a way to get me to answer that question without ever actually asking it. No, I didn't kill my daughter. The police just arrested a man they think did. That's why I need you. You know how to use the reference systems?"

"No, but I'll be damned good at it."

"I don't doubt you will." The smile on Branson's face grew. "I need you to find out everything you can about a man named Bruce Donne. Everything. Keep detailed notes. I'll call you from the road."

He led her to a pair of metal double doors at the end of the corridor, an emergency exit to the employee parking lot. Branson stopped and turned to Abriella. She curled a sliver of paper into his hand. "Here's my number. Do me a favor, don't let Ponds or anyone here have it, okay? I don't need them drunk dialing me at three in the morning after last call at the Pillowtalk Lounge."

He pocketed the paper. "Thank you."

"That's the first time I've heard *that* here."

"Abriella?"

"Yeah?"

"You seem okay, too."

She shook her head. "No, you just wait. I'm *awesome*."

FOUR

On the car radio an advertisement for weatherproof windows ended, and the DJ's voice mumbled the station's call letters into the beginning of the next song, but was drowned out by it. Branson turned the radio off. It wasn't a song that came on much, but each time it did his mind returned to his wedding day. Such a strange song for a wedding, and he wondered again whether it was he or Candice who added it to the set list. "With some songs," Branson remembered her saying years later, "you hear the music and it sounds like a love song, then you listen to the words and you realize that it's anything but."

Branson supposed that was about as good a description of their entire marriage as any. So many wonderful memories. Pristine, perfect and worthy of a suburban sit-com, just so long as he didn't dig deep into things. With scrutiny, the good memories fell away, and all the bitter arguments and steely glances and awkward silences emerged in their place. Even before Madeline's disappearance, Branson and Candice were unable to hold a decent conversation of any length without it turning into a fight. After Madeline, they stopped communicating entirely.

Silence was worse than the radio, so as Branson turned off the highway, he clicked the radio back on. The music brought back the fire hall's chatter of voices at their wedding reception, the tickle of champagne toasts under his nose, the motion on a half-filled dance floor. Branson parked the car in his driveway and killed the engine, along with the radio and its undesirable wash of memory. He darted out of the car and into his house. Maxine, the stray cat that'd come to stay after Candice left, met him at the door and swished her body against his legs in greeting.

Branson ignored the cat, headed into the living room, snatched his address book off the coffee table, and went upstairs. He paused outside Madeline's bedroom but dared not open the door to peek inside. He knew what lurked in there, the same memory that always flashed back into his head—a clear snapshot of her in bed, sound asleep, face full of innocence and wonder. He'd come home late the night Madeline disappeared, and Candice had met him at the door with an argument. First Branson tried to brush her off, then pleaded not to fight. It'd been a long day and what he really needed was just to catch a quick glimpse of his daughter before hitting the sheets. That was the last time he saw Madeline. Branson regretted that he'd not crept into her room and kissed her on the cheek. But Candice was waiting in the hall to continue her complaint, so Branson settled for the briefest glance and that was that, because come morning, Madeline's bed was empty. Behind the closed door, it still was, a vacant centerpiece in a room still decorated with posters of kittens and unicorns, watched over by a herd of wide-eyed stuffed animals waiting on an antique toy chest for his daughter's return. Dashing the thought from his mind, Branson continued down the hall into the master bedroom and swung open the closet door. He dug through the mess inside, burrowing through clothes Candice had left behind until he came to a large duffel bag buried beneath them. Pulling it free, Branson proceeded to fill the duffel with a week's worth of socks and underwear, shirts, and jeans. Setting the bag aside, he wrestled the stubborn bottom drawer open and reached inside.

The day Madeline was born, he'd put a twenty dollar bill in an envelope and hid that away. Each paycheck contributed another twenty. Pulling out the envelope, Branson felt a stab of guilt. This was Madeline's college fund, unknown even to Candice, and sacred. It was hers, not his. He had no right.

The envelope bulged. After Candice left, weekly twenties were replaced by hundreds. Branson never ate out. Never went to the movies or bought anything except work clothes, sundries and food. Last time he'd bothered to count it, the stash totaled nineteen thousand and change. It'd only grown since then. He stuffed Madeline's college fund into the bag, next to the underwear.

Branson exited the bedroom and made his way back down the hall, with one hand swiping a photo frame off the wall and dropping it into the bag at his hip. Madeline's class photo from kindergarten, a smiling family portrait from Sears, a collage of snapshots. These captured moments were too important to be left behind, entrusted only to fragile memory. Nothing else in the house was as important and Branson left all else behind.

The door open, he scooped Maxine up in his free hand and held the cat tight against his shoulder while they crossed the yard. Branson pushed through a gap in the Oregon Grape Holly that lined his lot, and made his way up the neighbor's driveway.

At the neighbor's door, he knocked.

When Hal Norcross answered a moment later, suspicion and surprise fought for control over his squinting eyes. He scratched his bald, pointed head, leaning toward the surprise side of the argument.

"Branson. Been a while."

"Five years, at least." Maxine grew restless and pawed at his neckline. "Hal, I know what you must think of me; I don't hold that against you. You've always been a good neighbor. I know you don't owe me any favors, but I'm here to ask for one."

"What is it?" It sounded like a challenge.

"The cops got him."

"Got who?" By the time the words left Hal's lips, his expression changed as he realized what Branson meant. Suspicion lost the battle and his eyes widened. "They *got* him?"

Branson nodded. "And I'm gonna be away for a while. I'd take Maxine with me but don't know how long I'll be gone and thought maybe—"

"You want me to watch the cat?"

"Would you mind?"

A smile cut across Hal's face. "You kidding? Janie will love it."

"Thanks, Hal." Branson handed Maxine over and turned to leave.

"Bran?" A contrite expression replaced Hal's smile. "I'm sorry. You know, when the cops asked me if I saw anyone that night on the street or outside your house, I said no. And I wasn't lying. But I never liked how it felt, making you look bad like that. I didn't sleep good for a long while."

Branson grimaced. "I still don't."

FIVE

Driving usually brought some semblance of peace. Nothing as sublime as the calmness from Buddhist meditation or even a catnap in the late August sun, but with his hands on a steering wheel and his foot on an accelerator, Branson forged a pleasant distance from his everyday world. As long as the open road rolled away under the wheels, he was able to let go of his stress, his frustration, his wounded pride and constant sense of dejection. In the first few months after Madeline's disappearance, he went for long drives, leaving behind the square yards cut to exactly one and a quarter inches of growth, and the sterile flower gardens with roses mathematically spaced in rows and columns. When he reached the true California countryside, where the road signs were unreadable and thickets of yellow reeds overtook disused train tracks, he'd dream of pressing the pedal all the way to the floor, never stop, and leave all the trouble in his world behind. His distrustful wife, Detectives Faune and Woost's penetrating stares, his neighbors' quick retreats when he stepped out onto his front porch to recover his paper: all abandoned in his rear view mirror. But he never did escape. Branson always turned back and returned home to more of Candice's questioning glances and mechanical kisses. To another round of police questions and accusations. To more curtains drawn across the windows in others' houses whenever he walked his street.

And now everything was different. Branson drove away and didn't stop, but it wasn't the escape he'd daydreamed about for so long. He felt like a storm chaser driving straight into a roaring tornado, and instead of serenity, what most gripped Branson was fear. He was terrified in a way he'd never before experienced. It was a fear cut both ways—fright of what was coming and terror of turning back. Branson pushed harder on the accelerator.

His cell phone rang and the sound cut through him like a long, thin blade. Shuddering, he struggled to slide a hand down his pants pocket, hooked a thumb around the phone's nubby antenna, and fished it out. Flipping it open, he said, "Listening."

"Is that some kind of tough guy way to say *hello*?" He could hear the smirk in Abriella's voice. "Your phone sounds like shit."

"It should. It's older than you. What've you got for me?" The last residential blocks slipped away in the rear view mirror, out of his life maybe forever. Branson didn't think he'd miss them. Abriella's tone assumed an authoritative heft, like a college professor delivering a lecture.

"Bruce Donne, the man they arrested, he's been doing odd jobs for the last few years. Fast food and janitorial work mostly, never more than a few nights a week, and he never stayed anywhere more than a month or so. Quit sometimes, fired more often. I figured him for just some sort of loser, trailer trash. Then I saw he used to be a soundman for the movies. I found his resume online. He worked on two of my top ten favorite movies. I was kind of flabbergasted by that."

A tremor rumbled under his fingers. Snapping the steering wheel back, Branson swerved the car off the rumble strip alongside the road and back to the pavement. He reminded himself to keep a small part of his mind on his driving.

"Is there anyone he worked with often? Maybe another crew member..."

"Marius Spiegler."

"The director?" Spiegler had been newspaper fodder for several months a few years back, and not just the tabloids, either. Two children had died on the set of his final film, and a district attorney had tried him for manslaughter. It wasn't exactly a crime of the century trial, but media coverage hadn't been lacking.

"Donne worked on six of Spiegler's movies, starting in the early '80s and right through the accident." She paused. Branson heard what sounded like papers being rustled. "After Spiegler retired, he did some work on cheap ass direct-to-video titles. Then some porno. Then paper or plastic at the grocery store."

"I need contact info for Spiegler."

"Give me a minute." A keyboard clattered. "Okay, I've sent his address to your cell. Get it?"

Branson stole a quick glance at the phone and saw the envelope icon pulsate in the corner of its screen. "Got it."

"There's something else, too."

"I'm ready."

"When the cops arrested Donne, there was also an unidentified woman in his trailer. She was in pretty bad shape. They called an ambulance and rushed her to Santa Flora Memorial. She died on the way to the emergency room." Abriella's voice wavered. "And then things just get weird. The police report isn't complete. There's a lot of hedging along the lines of *pending medical test results*, but the general sense of it is that everyone who touched this woman either got sick, disoriented, or suffered hallucinations. They all recovered, but..."

"But what?" Branson asked.

"Well, they described the experience like an LSD trip, a religious experience, life changing stuff. These are paramedics and doctors, not high school dropouts searching for the quick buzz they can buy for ten bucks behind a convenience store. I found this last bit not in the police report but in a statement from one of the ambulance techs. It's... difficult to believe." The cell phone's signal waned; Abriella's voice echoed. "This particular EMT never touched the woman. So, it wasn't a hallucination. But it's not... normal."

"Just tell me," Branson insisted in an impatient tone.

"In her statement, the EMT claims the woman was glowing."

SIX

Abriella didn't merely send Marius Spiegler's home address, but also a link to a map and driving directions too. She'd all the makings of a good researcher.

The retired director lived twenty minutes outside the city in a suburb once thought exclusive. Not anymore. Still, it was far nicer than any neighborhood Branson could afford. If his trial for manslaughter substantially diminished Spiegler's wealth, the man's home didn't show it. A stone-faced colonial mansion surrounded by an army of towering palm trees stood behind a pair of tall black gates, open to the road. Admiring the place, Branson drove up the gray brick driveway and parked in front of the wide double doors of the home. Killing the car's engine, he stepped out and stared up, taking in the enormity of the three-story house. Its footprint would fill a residential block. Somewhat disoriented by the grandeur, Branson pressed the doorbell.

And waited.

By the time the small speaker alongside the doorbell crackled to life, Branson's disorientation dissipated. Nearly drowned in static, a voice croaked, "Who're you?"

Branson hadn't thought how to approach Spiegler. He'd rehearsed their conversation. Planned out how to navigate towards a deal. But he'd neglected to consider how to introduce himself. So he just pressed the SEND button and spoke.

"My name is Branson Turaco. We have a lot in common. Most people think I'm a child killer."

There came another burst of electric noise from the speaker and then it fell silent. Branson thought perhaps Spiegler was done. Couldn't blame him, considering the introduction. Maybe Spiegler was even then calling the police to have the intruder removed. Then the speaker crackled back to life.

"Who?"

"My daughter."

"Did you? Kill her, I mean."

"No."

The great doors opened just a bit. A man of indeterminate age peered from between them. His face was long and weathered, with a bushy brow cloaking one blue eye; the left was missing. The dark recess where his eye should've been failed to balance out the man's face.

"That's too bad, in a way. Surely you've thought it—it would be easier to actually be guilty. Then you could hate yourself with good reason and not just because everyone else does."

Branson was at a loss for words.

Spiegler flashed a grim smile. With a single, crooked finger, he pointed to the empty eye socket. "Sorry, didn't bother to put in my eye this morning. I forget sometimes. Remembered to put my contact lens in, but not the eye. That's funny, right?"

"That must save you money in lenses."

"Yeah, I buy them in bulk. Hundred to a box. Lasts me a year." Spiegler opened the door wider. He stood there wearing rumpled pajamas open to the middle of his hairy chest. "So did you come here to swap quips about my twenty/zero vision or are you soliciting for accused child killers? I have to tell you, my schedule's wide open but I don't like listening to people whine. Tell me you're not here to whine."

"No, I need your help."

Spiegler's brow lowered as he squinted through his one good eye. "I'm not much good at helping people. If I'm your last, best resource, I'm afraid you'll be damned disappointed."

"Just hear me out." Branson's voice was urgent, not pleading. Spiegler reminded him of editors he'd had at *The Telegraph*. They didn't tolerate whiners either. Tough guys, who responded to any and all signs of weakness like a starving shark bearing down on a flailing seal pup. "Please give me a few minutes," Branson said.

Spiegler breathed out deeply.

"I was just enjoying a double-decker grilled cheese sandwich. You ever have one? Don't answer, just come on in and have one with me. I used to get them at this little greasy spoon on Ventura. I don't get out much anymore. Not at all, really. So I make do with what the grocery boy delivers. I'll listen to you. If I kick you out, you can tell me that I can't cook worth a shit. It'd be true."

He stepped aside and motioned with a sweep of his arm for Branson to come inside. As he passed by, Branson caught a strong whiff of body odor and stale breath. Spiegler hadn't lied. He hadn't been out of the house, or for that matter the clothes on his back, in days. Maybe weeks. The room that greeted him was a contradiction, both cluttered and empty. The floor was littered with pizza boxes and junk mail, but he saw only two pieces of furniture, a beaten down leather sofa and an entertainment console. A tall stack of mail-order catalogs stood in place of a television set. Following Spiegler's pointing finger, he sat on one end of the sofa. It was uncomfortable.

Spiegler remained standing. "You don't really want the sandwich, d'you?"

"No."

"Your loss." Spiegler reached for a Styrofoam plate resting atop a stack of newspapers. About a third of the double-decker grilled cheese sandwich remained. He stuffed the whole thing into his mouth. The director chewed it over, then swallowed. "Better than any food service cart the studio ever sent over, I'll tell ya."

"Bruce Donne," Branson said. The name changed everything about Spiegler. It backed him right up until he leaned against the wall. "It was Donne, took my little girl."

Spiegler's lips came together with a popping sound. "I haven't seen or heard from Bruce since just after the accident. A few of us were having trouble dealing with all of it. The kids' deaths. The trial. So we got together at the set to talk it out. That was the last I saw of him."

"Did the two of you fall out?"

"*Everything* fell apart, Mr... what was it?"

"Turaco. Branson Turaco."

"Mr. Turaco," Spiegler continued. "Families, careers, everything. I drank my way through that whole time. I was bad to my wife, my kids, my friends. I lost all that. And I wasn't very good to myself, either." Spiegler pointed to his face. "Took a razor to my eye, one night. Would've gotten the other one too, except I passed out from the pain. By the morning it no longer seemed like such a good idea."

Branson settled back. The sofa's wooden frame poked at his back through a too-thin layer of cushion. Shifting his weight, he asked, "Would Donne agree to see you? To talk with you?"

"Maybe he would. Perhaps."

"I *need* to know if Madeline is alive. Only Donne can tell. The police would never let me talk directly to him. But there may be a way to get you in to see him."

Spiegler dropped the Styrofoam plate atop the mail order catalogs. "Sounds like you came with a plan."

"Not really. Not yet. It all depends on what he tells you."

"I meant a plan for *me*." Spiegler stepped over to the sofa, leaned his hands on knees, and with his one eye stared deeply into Branson's two. "And you think that I'll help you why, exactly? Because I'm still carrying around guilt over the kids who died on my set? You think maybe it'll provide some kind of catharsis to me, to help save a child's life?"

"Something like that."

"What if your little girl's dead? How would that help me? Or what if she's still alive, stashed in some hand-dug hole under some inbred motherfucker's basement? What if Bruce refuses to tell me, and she dies out there? Would that alleviate my guilt or only add to it?" Spiegler's lone eye never blinked.

"I can pay you."

"If its money I wanted, I'd sell this albatross of a house and move to Arkansas. The standard of living there isn't really living at all, but it's cheap."

"You wouldn't fit in."

Spiegler shrugged. "You're right. Maybe Oregon. Wouldn't have to give up the medical marijuana."

"If you won't help, at least point me in the direction of someone who might. Someone with a dash of humanity left and the balls to do the right thing."

"In this town?" Spiegler snickered. "You won't have much luck here. Bruce didn't make friends. If he were a Shih Tzu, you'd say he hadn't been socialized. When Bruce was working, he was fine. Friendly, even. But it was an act, a charade. Guy was a better actor than most of the clowns who starred in my pictures. You won't find any old *besties* to lean on. Far as I know, those don't exist."

Branson stood. "There had to be someone."

"You found me—did you find anyone else? No, you didn't. People pass through Hollywood all the time. Real people with friends and families and pets they don't carry in purses. The people who stick, the ones that make a career out of whatever it is they do to help a film get made, those people have nothing else. No *one* else, mostly."

Branson steeled himself. He could feel disappointment approaching fast. There was no Plan B.

"Don't get pouty. I said mostly."

"Who?" Branson asked.

"A girl. Her name—oh Jesus, what was it? Holly? Heather? *Something.* Hippy girl. Maybe fifteen when she showed up on the set. Any time we shot in the canyons, kids would come out of the hills like ants to a picnic. A group of them lived up there in some kind of commune, like the Manson family."

Spiegler squinted his good eye, crow's feet closing like an accordion, as he dug up memories. "Anyway, we were shooting *Farewell, King Caesar* and this girl shows up, all hairy armpits and pigtails, and Bruce took a shine to her like nothing I'd ever seen from him. She was pretty in her way, but there was a whole lot more *rough* than *diamond* if y'see what I'm saying. He used to go out to the canyon and stay with her between shoots. I don't know, maybe that's where he went when he disappeared after the trial. Maybe you can find her."

Branson shook his head. "I think she's dead."

"Only a matter of time. She used to party pretty hard. Heavy drugs, hostile sex, petty crime. With her gone, I guess you really do need me."

"No, Madeline needs you," Branson whispered.

Spiegler's face went blank. He started to speak, stopped, then started again. "You have a picture of your daughter?"

Branson pulled out his wallet, and with an unsteady hand held Madeline's sixth grade class portrait out to the director. Spiegler didn't reach for the photo. Didn't even look at it. The smiling image of young Madeline threatened to shake right out of Branson's hand. Finally, Spiegler bit his lip, closed his eye, lowered his head, and then stole a quick peek. He didn't linger.

"I'll help," he whispered.

"Thank you," Branson said, pulling back the photograph and

sliding it into its home sleeve. He pocketed the wallet.

Spiegler held up one hand. "Don't thank me. I'm probably not doing you any favors."

"Then why?"

The chuckle that came in response was too dark for comfort. Even mean-spirited, around the edges.

"Nothing I can say will make me sound crazier than you, right? Ever since the... *accident* on the set, those kids—after *that*, it's difficult for me to look at pictures or movies of dead people, even when I know they're fake. It's hard to explain. Impossible, I suppose. But when I saw the picture of your daughter, I didn't feel anything like that. I thought *maybe*, just maybe, she's not dead."

Maybe not dead. The words reverberated through Branson. How far must a man fall for *maybe not dead* to qualify as hopeful?

SEVEN

A wholesome aroma greeted Detective Susan Woost as she entered the Felston house, equal parts homemade muffins, brewing coffee, and flowers in bloom. It recalled biennial Christmas mornings spent at her stepmother's house. Mornings that began with waffles sprinkled with confectioner's sugar, followed by the opening of gifts, and then hours of play while Country and Western versions of traditional Christmas carols played on the radio. The memory should have brought a smile to Woost's face, except the utter gloom that emanated from Donna Felston made that impossible. It was as if the woman's pain was infectious, capable of leaping from one wounded soul to the next, erasing not only all thoughts of Christmas, but maybe even the holiday itself.

As Felston lead Woost to the kitchen, there was a slight stumble in her footwork and a twitch in her fingers, which swayed at her sides. Woost recognized the symptoms from any number of cases she'd investigated, a medically unrecognized mutant strain of shock, as persistent as an urban legend. Donna poured coffee but neither of them drank, choosing instead to wrap their fingers around the warm cups as they sat across from each other.

"The doctors say the poison's out of her system. They've done so many tests and they all came back clean. But... but she's still..." Donna's eyes turned to the window, looking for what she couldn't find.

"Laurie's a strong kid. She'll be okay." Not that Woost was a doctor or psychologist, or anyone whose opinion might matter. It was simply part of the ritual. False encouragement that meant nothing except to offer a shoulder to cry on. In this case for Woost, it was an outright lie. She doubted she'd even pick up the phone if Donna Felston called.

Donna exhaled a wet, stuttering sigh. "Before Laurie was born Glen and I talked about what we'd do if she had autism or something. Special needs... you know, that sort of thing. First time parents have conversations like that. And we made a pact that together we'd see our child through anything. That we'd do whatever it took, and that our little girl wouldn't ever..."

"It'll pass. She'll be back to normal." The ritual continued. Donna wasn't convinced.

"She was born okay, of course. No autism, ten fingers, ten toes. But we still failed her, didn't we? We couldn't protect her. Turns out a monster lived right down the road, and we never noticed. We let him get ahold of our little girl. Our Laurie."

Tears large enough to be pearls welled in Donna's eyes. They held tight to her lashes, refusing to trickle down her face.

"But how could we know? Right? We couldn't have known, could we?"

Woost shook her head. "You didn't do anything wrong. The man who tried to take Laurie is deeply disturbed, but was invisible. You wouldn't have picked him out of a crowd as dangerous. From the outside, he'd have seemed completely normal. You might even have liked him, had you met. He read mystery novels. Clipped coupons. Supported charity auctions. You'd have had no reason to think of him as anything but a good neighbor, if you thought of him at all."

Donna wiped her eyes. "Is that supposed to make it easier? How can I ever let her out of my sight again? I don't know how many more are out there like him. I can't let her walk home from school, or run out to the curb for the mail, or even play in the backyard. You say he was invisible. Maybe. But I'll see him everywhere now. I won't be able to see anyone else."

A muscular English Foxhound galloped into the kitchen, its snout snapping from left to right, investigating, searching out the cause for this most recent bout of grief. After a moment, it sank down by Donna's feet and rested its brown and white head against her heels. Woost extended a hand, waited for the dog to sniff, then asked, "What's his name?"

"Doesn't have one yet," Donna wiped the tears away with a paper napkin. "We just got her. Laurie had been asking us for a dog ever since we moved here. After... after what she's been through, Glen thought maybe..." Donna's voice quivered. Her eyes closed as she gulped down a heavy breath. "Anyway, the dog doesn't have a name yet. We're hoping Laurie will..."

Woost scratched at the scruff of the nameless dog's neck, before straightening up and getting down to business.

"Mrs. Felston, would it be okay if I asked Laurie a few questions? I know what I'm asking is difficult. I promise I'll try not to upset her."

The kind of unpleasant, crippled grin that usually accompanies the punchline of the darkest gallows humor twitched at the corners of Donna's frown. "Detective, you couldn't possibly upset my daughter any worse than she already is. Her face, the way she stares... it's like looking at my mother's face on her deathbed."

Woost nodded. "I'll be careful all the same."

"Okay." It was a meaningless word, spoken to fill the void of an unanswered question and nothing more. Donna's tone made it clear she didn't much believe anything would ever be *okay* again.

Woost rose and went to the door. In her peripheral vision she saw Donna reach for the bottle of Jack Daniels on the counter. As the Detective entered the short, narrow hallway leading to Laurie's bedroom, the slurping sound of Jack being added to the morning's coffee rang plain.

A skinny metal lamp in the shape of a sunflower stood just outside Laurie's room. The bulb in the center of the bloom cycled through a colored wheel of red, yellow, and blue filters not clear enough to break the shadows in the hall. Laurie's bedroom door was cracked open, and the light from within drew a sharp triangle that pointed to Woost's feet as she approached. She leaned forward and peeked inside. Laurie crouched on the edge of a yellow beanbag chair, drawing with a crayon on a sheet of construction paper that lay on the floor. Woost knocked.

Laurie dropped the crayon and looked up, face emerging from behind the cover of hair, wide eyes beaming through a cresting wave of chestnut brown curls. Woost had seen many children suffering from shock. Their ghostly stares were permanently burnt into her memory. This was different. This was more like a predator assessing prey, a cold and ageless study. She sat, young and untouched by wrinkle or blemish, but somehow almost ancient. Woost pushed through the door and stepped inside. Laurie's head tilted, then swiveled to follow her—a well-greased, mechanical movement. Unnerved, Woost stopped and forced an uneasy smile.

"Hi, Laurie, I'm Detective Woost. You remember me, don't you honey? I came and spoke at your school last month."

"Honey," Laurie purred.

"I wanted to make sure you were okay."

Laurie's unblinking eyes locked on Woost's, no more expressive than a pair of security cameras. A familiar chill shot through the Detective. The same sort of sensation she felt at crime scenes and traffic accidents, each and every time she laid eyes on a corpse. Unlike those times, the moment didn't pass. Instead, the chill burrowed into Woost like an electrical surge.

"Will you talk with me, Laurie?" Her voice was cleansed of all authoritative edge. The child disarmed her in a way no criminal had, ever. With only a stare.

Laurie whispered, "He said you'd come."

"Who said I'd come?"

The child's lips curved into a tight crescent smile.

"Your father? Did he tell you I'd come to talk to you?"

Her head moved in a slow, robotic movement from side to side.

"Not your father? Then who?"

Laurie picked up her crayon, and pointed to the sheet of paper on the floor. On it she'd scribbled the rough portrait of a man with long, flowing hair, and an open mouth with a serpent-like tongue extended out. Though the man was drawn in black crayon, the tongue was colored solid blue. Woost knelt down, closer to Laurie. The tingling chill, with its pins-and-needles, neared the threshold of pain. She blinked that back.

"Who is this? Who did you draw here?"

Laurie's eyes narrowed. The predator was wide-awake.

"Is this the man who hurt you?"

"Bruce," the predator said.

Woost pointed to the blue tongue. "And who's that?"

Laurie dropped her crayon.

"Is that the woman who touched you? Heather?"

"She's not a woman."

"She's not? Then what is she?"

"She's an angel."

Victims of trauma often made claims of religious epiphany. Woost had heard dozens of variations. From the Holy Virgin appearing in a divine starburst of light just when she was most needed, to dead family members reaching out from their graves to deliver messages from beyond. Those claims were typically delivered while in the throes of traumatic ecstasy. Laurie's calm declaration of simple fact was more unnerving even than her stare.

"How do you know Heather is an angel?"

"Because when she touched me, I saw God."

Woost pointed to the crayon drawing. "Is that Him?"

"No, I told you. That's Bruce."

A fresh thought bloomed in Woost, eclipsing all others. *Could there have been a second man in the trailer? Another perp still at large?* Then another, more unsettling thought: *Branson Turaco?*

"Was God in Bruce's house?" Laurie's smile waned.

"Yes."

"Could you describe God to me, please?"

Confusion pressed upon Laurie, the first truly human expression Woost had seen on the girl that day. Then it cleared.

"Don't need to."

"Why not?"

"Because He's right there behind you."

For a moment Woost froze. All of her training failed. Terror took hold, a fear every bit as physical as psychological. A return to the dark nights of childhood, when Woost still believed in monsters. And in God.

Her hand broke the spell first, sliding down inside her jacket to the sidearm at her hip. Expertly unlatching the leather holster with a thumb, Woost gripped the gun and turned on her heel, slower than her training allowed. She fully expected to see a dark figure looming just over her shoulder.

Of course, the room was empty. Laurie the little girl predator giggled. Woost released both her weapon and a pent up breath then returned her attention to the girl. Laurie reverted back to the blank slate she'd worn earlier. "Did you play a trick on me just then?"

"No."

"Then why did you tell me—"

"He's *God*." The little girl looked at the Detective like she was some kind of idiot. "He decides who can see Him and who can't."

Woost stood. Her legs were uneasy.

"He wants me to tell you something," Laurie said.

"A message? From God?"

"He followed the angels into the ocean."

Woost headed for the door. There was nothing to be learned from the girl, at least not yet. Maybe after the bizarre after-effects of trauma released her.

"So long, Laurie. I'll see you soon."

She'd said that as she left the room. A routine courtesy, nothing more. Woost was halfway down the hall when she heard the little girl's predator voice whispering from all around her, plain as day.

"No, Detective, you won't. *Goodbye.*"

In the kitchen, Donna was still at the table, head down, eyes focused on the coffee cup in front of her. She didn't look up when Detective Woost entered.

"Did she scare you?"

"Yes, she did." There was no point in lying.

"Glen can't even stand to be the same room as her for more than a few minutes at a time." Donna's finger circled the cup's rim. "I force myself, but it's hard y'know, with all those things she says."

"It'll pass." By then, Woost didn't believe it either.

"If you say so, Detective."

Woost's cell phone vibrated. She retrieved it from the breast pocket of her jacket, glanced at the number display, frowned, then put it against her ear.

"Woost."

As she listened, the Detective's eyes roamed the kitchen. A first-day-of-school photo in a colorful frame on the wall above the stove, a box of cereal peeking out of a half-open cabinet, a backpack full of schoolbooks on the counter. And on the refrigerator...

"Could you hold on a second, Mr. Ponds?"

Two uneven rows of plastic magnets in the shape of letters spelled out:

GOD IS DROWNING

"Mrs. Felston, what does that mean?" Woost pointed and asked.

Donna shook her head. "Dunno. We've had GOD IS LOVE on there for years. Laurie changed it this morning at breakfast. Wouldn't explain when we asked. My husband is a religious man. He was... unhappy with it."

"Detective Woost?" Michael Ponds' voice interrupted her thoughts.

She thanked him for the info and hung up.

"Change the magnets before your husband gets home," Woost said, sliding her business card under the D in Drowning. "Call if Laurie remembers anything useful."

"How will I know if it's useful or not?" Donna asked.

Woost stepped out the front door. "You'll know."

On her way out the front door she dialed out.

On the second ring, Branson Turaco answered.

"Listening."

"Mr. Turaco?"

"Good that you called. I was just about to give you a ring. I wa—"

"Where are you?"

"Why do you ask?"

"Call it curiosity."

EIGHT

His phone rang in his pocket, prompting Branson to dance in his seat, shifting his weight until he could retrieve the device. Spiegler watched from the passenger seat with a mixture of confusion and amusement. It took a moment for Branson to understand why, but finally it dawned on him that a television wasn't the only thing missing from the director's life—he'd sealed himself away from the world and wasn't used to cell phones. Or modern human contact of any sort.

"I remember them being larger," Spiegler said, as if reading his mind. He gestured with his hands. *Once caught a fish this big—*

Branson averted his gaze from the director. His prosthetic eye was indistinguishable from his real one. But he *knew*, and that made him uncomfortable.

He pressed the phone to his ear. "Listening."

"Mr. Turaco?" Detective Woost asked.

Branson said, "Good that you called. I was just about to give you a ring. I wa—"

The detective's voice sharpened, its pitch rising as if her vocal chords were constricting, like a guitar string twining around a machine head. "Where are you?"

He paused. "Why do you ask?"

"Call it curiosity," she answered.

"Maybe I'm at home," Branson said into the phone.

"A little bird tells me different."

"You talking to birds now?" he asked. "Am I still under surveillance?

I thought that ended some time back. Haven't seen any white vans on the street for quite a while."

"And you won't." The Detective's voice was sharp. "We use satellites. The vans are for when we want you to know we're watching."

"Then you can probably tell me where I am better than I can. What is it you want, Detective?"

"I spoke to your boss at *The Telegraph*. He says you've taken some time off."

"Had it coming. Thought maybe I'd go get drunk in the bathtub somewhere. Re-evaluate my life. Not being a murderer changes things, you know."

"Then why the intern? Funny sort of research that must be."

That pissed Branson off. He'd had it with cops trying to intimidate him. He kept quiet, just the same.

"Look, Mr. Turaco, I need to know you're not up to anything stupid. There's been enough tragedy in your life without you needlessly ruining the rest of it."

"How far are you from the Santa Flora sheriff's station?" he asked.

"Right now?"

"Yeah. Right now."

"About twenty minutes, I'd guess. Why?"

"Because that's where I'm headed." Branson hit the disconnect button and slid the phone back into his pocket. Spiegler smirked.

"Girlfriend?"

"Seems like you'll meet her soon enough. She's a real sweetheart," Branson said as he spun the driver's wheel, sending the car screeching onto the thin stretch of asphalt between the curb and the white line. He'd driven right past his turn. Throwing the car into reverse, he backed up, cut the wheel, and steered the vehicle into a residential development. The homes here were large but not luxurious, already-outdated relics of the mid-90s push towards McMansions. Every lawn had a For Sale sign.

He parked outside one of the few homes with a car in the driveway.

"This hardly looks like a police station," Spiegler said. Branson killed the engine and cracked open the door. "The man who lives here is named Szymon Kazanjian. He runs a travel agency, the kind that brings over fugitive rebels to avoid prosecution. He ran into some trouble with the authorities a few years back. *The Telegraph* ran a week's worth of it." They approached the front door.

"So we're visiting an international criminal who smuggles terrorists into the United States?"

"Are they terrorists if they're on our side?"

A crest with a golden crown and crossed scepters was hand-painted on the door. Branson recognized it as the standard of the Armenian Apostolic Church. Framed on a wall, the thing would be called art, it'd been so finely accomplished. Branson knocked hard, right on the holy crosshair of scepters.

A frail old man answered the door. He wore a black tuque rolled down to just over his wrinkled, squinty eyes. The T-shirt he wore did nothing to hide an unhealthily thin and angular body. A human praying mantis.

"Ello?"

"I've come to buy a gun," Branson said.

"A *gun*?" Kazanjian said. "Why should I have a gun to sell to you? There, down the street, in the projects. Black kids have a gun to sell to you. You should visit on them."

Branson pulled the envelope from his back pocket, and spread it open in front of Kazanjian. The Armenian's eyes followed as he ran his fingers over the bills as if shuffling a deck of cards.

"I'm not a cop. And I'm not here to bring you any grief." Branson withdrew the envelope and put it away. "I'm here to spend money."

Kazanjian pointed to Spiegler. "And he, he is a cop?"

"I'm currently between jobs," the director said.

Stepping aside, the old man bade them enter. Framed revolutionary handbills covered most of the walls, sometimes overlapping. Unable to read the complex, blurry text, Spiegler asked, "What's all this?" Kazanjian shot Spiegler an annoyed glance then went to a wall, removed a picture frame, and turned it over in his hands. He showed it to the two men. A half dozen yellowing photographs of young men, some only teens, were taped to the flip side.

"These are the battles we lived." The old man waved his hand to encompass the room. "Battles we still fight, against the communists. These are to make sure we will never forget." Tapping the photo with the tip of a long fingernail he added, "We remember for those who are lost." With dozens of handbills, there must have been hundreds of photographs. "The Russia buried them in unmarked pits, in the woods or on the fields, wherever they fell. Used bulldozers to bury them. There are no gravestones where they lie." He rehung the frame crooked as ever on its nail. "*This*. This here, is their monument."

An irrational impulse to turn each of the picture frames and search for his daughter's face seized Branson. How old was Madeline now? To suppress the desire, he slid both hands deep into his back pockets. The envelope stuffed with Madeline's college fund felt large beneath his palm.

"But you are Americans, these things don't concern you. Not now, not ever. So tell me about this gun you think I should sell you."

Shadows stretched over Kazanjian's face as he turned and gestured them toward a short hall. In half-light his features re-formed to resemble the clay countenance of a golem.

Branson and Spiegler followed at an uncomfortably slow gait as the old man hobbled down the hall. At the entrance to a small room, Kazanjian flipped a switch and light from a harsh florescent, hung from a low drop ceiling, filled the space. The Armenian shuffled over to a large trunk set against the far wall, and worked its combination lock.

"I don't need anything fancy," Branson said from just inside the door. "I don't care about caliber or the number of shots it can hold. As long as it'll put a man down when he's standing in front of it, I'm good."

"You're good," Kazanjian echoed. "I don't think so, not you. Not if you've come here to buy a gun from me. You're here because you're setting the table for a cold meal. You understand?"

Branson nodded. "So long as it fires."

Kazanjian threw open the trunk's lid, fished around inside, and pulled out a small black revolver. He flipped opened the cylinder, spun it, and snapped it shut.

"Something simple, I think for you. This is one-of-kind. Made by a Pole I knew from the old times."

"He sold it to you?" Spiegler asked from over Branson's shoulder.

"No, he didn't sell guns. He raised wheat."

"Then how'd you end up with it?" The old man threw Spiegler a grimace. It was like watching a crack form in an ancient statue.

"I took it from his hand after they shot him down in the street. Even after he was dead, he still tried to pull the trigger." Kazanjian demonstrated with one long crooked finger. He turned the gun around, and offered it to Branson. "The solider who killed my Polish friend walked away. He went back to his wife, his normal life. That man never paid for what he did. This gun, he still wants revenge for his master, but that is impossible. The man you mean to kill, he *deserves* to die?" Branson turned over the weight of the pistol in his hand. It felt about right.

"I don't know yet. Maybe."

Kazanjian's smile faded. The rebel Armenian leveled a gaze at him with a ferocity the like of which Branson had never seen. He didn't wither beneath it, not a bit.

"If he does, this gun will know and it will help you."

Branson paid the man.

NINE

"Somewhere, in the back of your mind, you know this is an absolutely awful idea, right?" Spiegler asked as Branson reached across the front seat and stowed the handgun into the glove compartment. "I don't mean talking to Bruce. That I understand, even if I think it'll hurt to hear what he has to say. I mean this entire journey you're on. I just don't see how it ends well."

"It doesn't have to end well. I don't need resolution or absolution. It's not about revenge or closure or any of those other things, either." They had arrived in front of the Santa Flora sheriff's station.

"Then what?"

"I don't need to succeed. I know the chances are a million to one that I'll find Madeline alive. But I have to *try*. Because what would I be if I didn't?"

Stepping from the car, Branson stared at the sheriff's station, a black silhouette against the heat-blurred setting sun. A modest one-story brick building, it could've passed for a public library or a post office. It was a long road from the night Madeline disappeared, and such an ordinary building didn't seem like a proper final destination. He hoped it wouldn't be that. The passenger door slammed shut. He didn't turn.

"So, you gonna tell me the plan here?"

"Better if you just react," Branson said.

"Not super helpful."

They were met at the front desk by a lanky blonde woman in a blue uniform and badge. Any passing resemblance to an actual police officer ended there. To Branson she looked more like a costumed call girl ten years past her prime. Nail polish in hand, she glanced up over her drying nails.

"May I help you?" she said, disinterested.

"We're here to speak with Detective Woost," Branson replied.

"Woost? With a *W*?"

The woman turned to her computer screen. She sighed and typed with a single, unpainted finger. After a moment, she spun back towards them. "You sure you got the right station? There's no Detective Woost here."

"There will be," Branson said.

Puzzled, the blonde cop pointed to a line of red chairs against the far wall—chairs that were stuffed into a little nook surrounded by cheap wall art and pastel wallpaper. The area could've passed for a dentist's waiting room.

Spiegler muttered, "There's no way on the great polluted planet Earth that I'm sitting on one of those."

"We'll stand," Branson said to the cop.

"Suit yourself, honey." She returned to her nails.

Detective Woost marched in the front doors. The lapels of her three-quarter-length coat flapped and her ponytail swished side to side like a hangman's noose. Spotting Branson, she came at them like a lion on a wildebeest, nose preceding the tips of her shoes, eyes flashing to Spiegler then back to Branson. Woost pointed to the cop behind the desk. "Get someone in here to frisk these two. Right *now*."

It wasn't a request.

The *blonde* fumbled for the phone. "Available officers to the front—"

Branson raised both arms and motioned for Spiegler to do the same. He caught Woost's eyes and held them.

"This isn't what you think it is. My friend here, he just wants to talk to Donne. He knows him."

Spiegler squirmed. "Should I be reacting now?"

Two uniformed cops bolted into the reception area, swung around the desk, and frisked the two men. It only took a moment before they straightened up and backed away, satisfied.

"And what makes you think we'd ever let that happen?" Woost demanded. "Do you have any idea what kind of damage you could do to the prosecutor's case?" Her face flushed with anger. Branson shook his head.

"I don't care about the case. I care about finding Madeline."

"I know what you must be feeling. But you have to understand, our best chance at getting answers is to follow the rules. A plea bargain might—"

"I don't want answers," Branson snapped. "I want my daughter back." Woost closed her eyes.

"Please, Mr. Turaco. Go home."

"Not gonna happen." He nodded toward Spiegler. "This might be the only man in the world Bruce Donne will talk to. Maybe he can find out what happened to my little girl. That's all I'm asking, just a couple minutes and the chance to ask a few harmless questions."

"I've already said no."

"You're saying there's no way?"

"Yeah, that's what I'm saying."

"Okay," he said, and turned towards the door. Taking a step, he cocked his head, signaling Spiegler to join him. Under his breath, he muttered, "Just do what I do."

Spiegler cast a doubtful look, but followed Branson's lead and took two sharp steps back towards the cops.

"I just have a question."

The cop who'd frisked him stepped forward, arms crossed, shoulders raised in his best imitation of a secret service agent.

"That's enough with the questions, guys. It's time you listened to the lady and go—"

Branson struck fast with his right fist, catching the cop unawares. His knuckles landed square against the officer's chin, rocking the man's head to the side. The bones in Branson's hand reverberated from the impact. The cop stumbled back more in surprise than pain, and instinctively reached for his weapon. The second cop leaped in, arms extended with one hand flat against Branson's chest.

Spiegler punched the second man hard in the face. Staggering, the cop grabbed Branson's shirt for support. He snorted, then sneezed, which released a torrent of blood from both nostrils, and that painted his chin a bright scarlet red.

The first cop raised his gun and screamed, "Don't move."

Hunched over, the second cop growled and rushed Spiegler, tackling him with a bear hug that forced both of them to the floor. The cop howled at the top of his lungs, an animal's impassioned jungle scream. His arm swung back, fist ready to strike the fallen man.

"No," Woost yelled and tried to force herself between the men. The room filled with cops. Drawn by the commotion, they poured in from hallways and doors like a colony of ants converging on a picnic. One cop, taller than the others by a head, cut through their ranks. He pushed into the center of the room and with a single massive hand grabbed the second cop by the shoulder, in an attempt to pull the cop off of Spiegler, but nearly lifting both men from the ground in the bargain.

"That's *enough*, Billy. Let the man up." Officer Billy released Spiegler, and stepped back.

"Yessir, Sheriff." Fine droplets of blood littered the front of the officer's shirt.

The Sheriff looked hard at Woost and at the same time said to his men, "You two jokers go get yourselves cooled down and cleaned up. The rest of you, take your dinner breaks or go back to your business."

"Sheriff Sakow—"

"Explanations later." He silenced Woost with a raised hand. Then he addressed Branson and Spiegler.

"First things first. These two freaks are gonna get dragged down to a holding cell by their hair and charged with assaulting an officer of the law."

"No," Woost pleaded. "That's exactly what they want."

The Sheriff took both men by their collars, one in each hand. They were like puppets dangling on strings. Sheriff Sakow eyed the two men up and down. He looked askance.

"What can I say? Today's their lucky day."

TEN

The holding cell's door slid shut, not with a jarring metallic slam but a click, and locked with an electronic bleep. The cash register at Branson's local grocery store was louder. It was almost disappointing.

The officer who'd led them to the cell touched his middle finger to the tip of his cap, turned, and snarled, "Have a good night, gentlemen."

Spiegler ran his hand across the bars. "I spent three million dollars on lawyers to avoid ever spending a night behind bars. Sweated it out for eight months, had nightmares every night, but you know what?"

"What?" Branson asked.

"It's not so bad." Spiegler smiled and closed his bruised fist around a bar.

Eight holding cells were arranged down a single hallway, four on either side. A line of harsh florescent tubes ran down the center and cast striped shadows deep into each cell. At first the other seven cells seemed empty, and Branson thought his plan had backfired. Then, against the back wall of the farthest cell on the opposite side, he spied the outline of a man sitting on a cot. Branson tapped Spiegler on the shoulder and gestured toward the figure.

"Is that our man?"

"Hmmm..." The director shrugged. "Might be. I haven't seen him in years, but this guy's mighty thin. Bruce always had a few pounds to spare."

The man in the far cell was as still as a mannequin.

"Hey, Brucey." Spiegler called out.

There was no reaction.

"Bruce. Bruce Donne. That you in there?"

The man's head turned. He spoke softly, almost inaudibly, as if he wasn't certain where Spiegler's voice had come from.

"Who're you?"

"It's Marius, Marius Spiegler."

Bruce leaned into a column of light. This wasn't the monster Branson expected. Donne's haggard face reminded him of tired commuters standing at bus stops, convenience store clerks desperate for their next break, and solemn relatives sitting in hospital waiting rooms. Too damn normal.

"When did *you* die?"

Branson and Spiegler exchanged questioning looks. Somehow the director's prosthetic eye matched the queasiness reflected in his real one, an effect Branson chalked up to the same kind of optical illusion that makes the eyes of a painted portrait seem to follow a viewer.

"I didn't, Bruce. I'm still alive, right here in this police cell."

Donne mumbled, "Sometimes the dead talk so loud that I can't tell the difference." Donne curled his bottom lip into his mouth and sucked on it, a troubled man in deep thought. "Marius, that really you? I haven't seen you since... when was that, man? I remember the trial. Didn't we meet up at the studio later on? When was that?"

"I don't remember, exactly. I drank a lot back then." Donne nodded.

"Yeah, I remember that about you. I think I did, too."

Both men fell silent, but Branson got the impression that they continued to communicate on some other level, a consequence of their shared history. Finally, Donne broke the silence.

"What're you doing here, man?"

"Punched a cop," Spiegler replied. "In the face."

Donne chuckled. "No shit?"

"No shit. Right in the face."

"Right on." Donne's voice was impassive. Silence enveloped the three men in their cells. Aware of his role, Spiegler broke it.

"What they get you for?"

"Yeah... Little girl flagged down a cop. He pulls out his gun, y'know, he's all *Freeze right there*. So I put my hands up and before I know it he's got handcuffs on me way too tight. My hands were turning white, and shit. Anyway, he brings me in here and all the cops start laying this trip on me, saying I'm a child molester and murderer and all that. You know me, man. I ain't got no thing for kids."

Heat rushed to Branson's face. Spiegler pressed on.

"Who was the girl, Bruce?"

"She came selling calendars with dog's pictures on 'em. Or something, I don't remember. They got my head all messed up in here with their questions." For a moment Donne's expression went blank and Branson feared that he'd say nothing more. "But then, ya know…"

"No, I don't. What, man? You tell me."

"You remember Heather, right? Well, she was buying powder from the nutjobs that lived up in the canyon. You remember them, right? The guys that kept raiding the catering tables when we shot the desert scene for *Farewell, King Caesar*? Anyway, they started supplying her with something new, some gel. Heather called it eel's elood. You put it on your skin and it's like acid, but way weirder. I only did it once. You know me, I never dug the hard stuff. But Heather, she was over the moon for that shit. It was no good for her. She got sick. Bad sick."

"What does Heather have to do with the little girl?" Spiegler tried to lead Donne back on track.

"Hell, dude. *Everything*. The only thing ever got Heather straight was more of what got her sick to begin with. It changed her insides, man. Turned her into some kind of a factory for making more of the goop. It oozed right out of her pores. I couldn't even touch her without gloves or else I'd be tripping, too."

Branson recalled the nurse's statement that Abriella had provided.

"So this little girl, she's just gonna sell me some calendars, see? But she's curious and when she goes over to see, Heather grabs her arm. Now the kid's freaking out, she's got that shit on her. So what can I do? I can't let her leave. I mean, how's that gonna play out? Anyway… I could use her."

Use her. The phrase made Branson want to beat Donne to death. He clenched his teeth and somehow kept quiet.

"You're gonna think this is nuts, man." Donne's voice was like the dying echo from a plucked piano wire. "And it *is*. But the dudes up in the canyon, they stopped accepting cash for eel's blood."

"Then how did you pay?" Spiegler was afraid to, but he asked. Donne let out a nervous laugh.

"Shit, man. They'd hook us up with a couple months' supply at a time. But... you can't tell this to the cops. Or anybody, really."

"I won't."

"Swear?"

"I swear." Donne looked suspiciously to Branson. "What about *him*? You trust him?"

"Sure, he's cool. He punched a cop, too."

"Okay..." Donne lowered his head, as if he couldn't bear to look anyone in the face and say what came next. "Thing is, the only payment they'd take was a kid. They didn't care if it was a boy or a girl, but it had to be between five and eight years old, they were real specific about that. So I couldn't let that little calendar girl get away. We needed her to pay for Heather's supply, and..." Donne's voice trailed off and the cellblock fell quiet with terrible portent. When Donne spoke again his voice was weaker, squeaking.

"I'm a horrible man, Marius. A monster. I know that. But Heather would've died without the eel's blood. Didn't have no choice. You understand, don't you?"

"I understand," Spiegler lied.

"Doesn't matter anyway, what you think or what he thinks or anybody. I've already bought myself a ticket straight to hell. God told me so."

ELEVEN

Asleep in a lounge chair on the second floor balcony, Glen Felston drifted between deep, dreaming slumber and half-awake grogginess. Even at the lower levels of sleep, he could feel the pulse of the Pacific Ocean and salty wind flowing with the rhythm of the tide. A paperback rested on his chest, spreading open and closed with each quiet breath. He'd fallen asleep just moments after Donna had come to the sliding doors and asked if he was coming to bed. "Just want to finish this chapter," Glen told her. "Be right in." Donna remained unconvinced, but she left him to it.

Glen didn't enjoy lying to his wife, but he did it all the same. Ever since Bruce Donne attempted to abduct Laurie, life seemed distant and unreal, a fiction no more believable than the western novels sent to him each month by the book club. Glen's work, the house, his marriage—it all seemed like a house of cards wavering in a light breeze, always ready to collapse. He knew he'd spend the night on the balcony, facing out at the curved shoreline and the starry night sky. He'd try reading about cowboys but that wouldn't help, because all the while Glen would search for answers. He wouldn't pray exactly, although there'd been no shortage of prayers. But Glen wondered: what possible role could a man like Bruce Donne have in the plan of a just and benevolent God? And if Bruce Donne was a part of it, what the hell sort of plan had He devised?

A tug on his sleeve woke him, vanquishing his dreaming thoughts and replacing them with a view of Ursa Minor. Another pull and Glen's attention was drawn to the small hand clutching his shirt. Laurie stood beside him in her pajamas with a sleepwalker's lax eyes. Glen had grown accustomed to the distant look in his daughter's eyes and presumed she was fully awake. That was a horrible thing to get used to.

"Daddy, the angels are coming."

Glen rolled onto his side and reached for his daughter. She took two steps back, and retreated to just beyond his reach. Her expression remained unreadable.

"Laurie," Glen sighed. "You were dreaming."

"Nuh-uhh."

Glen heaved himself off the chair. As he rose, a strange sensation overcame him, a kind of optical illusion where he wasn't looking down at a little girl at all, but rather staring *up* at her, proper positions reversed. Steadying himself on the arm of the chair, Glen wiped his eyes with his free hand and tried to will away the illusion.

"Come on. We'll both go inside, how about that?"

Laurie shook her head. "I have to wait for the angels."

"What angels?"

She pointed past him, looking out over the balcony. Two boats rode on the black waves, high-rigged sails fluttering in the night breeze. Less than half a nautical mile off, the sailboats were on a direct route to the beach, coming closer with every second. Glen saw men and women standing motionless as statues on the decks. He tried to assure himself it was only a trick of the sea and the moonlight, but he could swear these people cast a faint glow.

"Are those the angels?"

"Uhh-huh," Laurie nodded.

Closer now and it became plain that several of these angels cradled what sure looked like shotguns.

"Get in the house, honey."

Glen pushed Laurie inside, pulling the sliding glass doors shut and locking them behind. It wasn't much, but it was something. Grabbing Laurie's hand, they ran to his bedroom, his daughter galloping along in an attempt to keep up. Glen pushed the door open, snapped on the lights, and lifted Laurie onto the bed. Startled awake, Donna leaped up, took hold of her daughter and clutched Laurie to her chest.

"What's going on?"

Glen rummaged through the top drawer of their dresser and removed a black box. He motioned toward the nightstand.

"Hand me my keys."

"Glen, tell me—"

"*Give me the goddamned keys*," Glen yelled as he set the box on the edge of the bed.

It was like he'd struck her, and Donna handed her husband the keys. Choosing the smallest, he unlocked the box and pulled out a Springfield 1911 handgun. He'd inherited the weapon from his father and had never even taken it out of the box. Glen didn't believe in guns but had brought it to California anyway, intending to sell it once they were situated. Somewhere along the line, he'd forgotten.

"Barricade the door behind me. Get your phone and call 911. Then get into the closet. And no matter what you hear, don't come out." Glen kissed Donna, a quick, nervous peck, and followed it up with another on Laurie's forehead. Downstairs, the as yet unnamed dog was barking.

With both hands, Glen held the Springfield close to his chest. As a teenager, he went shooting with his father exactly three times, and never enjoyed it. He'd been a bad shot, and understood his best chance was probably to use the gun as a deterrent. Glen checked the chamber. The good news was that Glen's father had never removed the rounds from a gun in his life, except by firing it, and so the weapon was fully loaded. The bad news was that it held only six shots.

As he made his way down the hall, he heard the sounds of Donna's antique dresser skidding across the floor before it thumped against the bedroom door. Heavy footsteps fell on the wooden porch outside the front door. It sounded like a small army. Glen's grip on the gun tightened as he reached the stairs. The Dog With No Name paced back and forth in the anteroom, ears back, eyes focused firmly on the front door. Glen whistled.

"Here, boy. Here." The dog turned its head to its master and whined.

Stepping down the stairs, Glen extended the gun in both hands and aimed for the center of the entrance below. With his hands shaking, he had as good a chance of hitting the damned dog as any intruder. Movement caught his eye and he reflexively turned to it. Off to the side, a pair of figures stood silent, just beyond the bay window in the living room. Still and unblinking, the man and the woman wore plain white shirts and matching slacks. Their skin pulsed with a gentle halo of light, which even at a distance illuminated the subtlest details of their marble-smooth faces.

Glen fairly stumbled down the last of the stairs as he swung the gun towards the window.

"I HAVE A GUN—" and he made sure they saw it.

A shotgun blast drove a wide, ragged channel through the entrance door. Smoke and splinters filled the anteroom, and the blast sprayed debris over everything. Buckshot sent the coat rack toppling to the floor. The dog went silent. Upstairs, Donna screamed.

Glen was disoriented, each heartbeat a painful spasm squeezing his chest. He couldn't feel his hands. With a kick from the other side, the front door of Glen and Donna's house caved in.

The dog, low to the floor, snarled at the three men in white who stepped inside. Each carried a shotgun. The English Foxhound bolted forward, and launched itself off the floor as the intruder pulled the trigger. The shot grazed the dog, cutting a valley down the dog's side, blood and fur flying, but did not deter the animal's attack. It latched onto the intruder's wrist and clamped down.

The man made no sound even as the dog, dangling by its jaws from his arm, thrashed from side to side, tearing through skin and muscle with its teeth, deepening its hold. The man's shotgun fell to the blood-spattered living room rug. The other intruders went for the stairs. Desperate to stay between the intruders and his family, Glen stumbled back, missed the first step, and dropped to one knee. "I SWEAR, I'LL—"

The man in the lead gave him a quizzical look.

"You'll shoot us?"

Glen attempted to level the shaking Springfield at the man's glowing head. The intruders kept coming like in a military march, and without any regard for the handgun.

He pulled the trigger.

In that moment, Glen wished he'd learned more about firearms from his father. That he'd dutifully gone target and skeet shooting every time the old man asked. Or at the least, that he'd remembered to disengage the trigger lock that he installed the day he inherited it.

TWELVE

A night spent on a cell cot left Branson's back a tangle of knotted muscle and sinew. He woke to the surly tapping of a deputy's baton against the cell bars. The man's voice was like a diesel engine idling.

"Wakey wakey."

Face buried in a thin pillow, without stirring, Spiegler moaned and asked, "If that's room service, have them come back in four hours with breakfast. White, no crust, eggs over easy. Real coffee, not decaf."

"Son, you two got no idea how many folks in this building would just love to scramble your eggs," the cop said as he slid his baton back into its sheath. He swiped a key card through the mechanism of the electronic lock and opened the gate. "Looks like we won't get that chance, though."

Branson rose, straightened out his rumpled clothes, and passed a hand through his hair. Spiegler didn't bother with either, but looked no different than when Branson first knocked on his door. They followed the cop upstairs and down a long, beige hall to an interrogation room.

Detective Woost sat at the far end of a long wooden table, eyes closed, hands folded over a thick manila folder. It took a second glance for Branson to notice the tiny headphones in her ears and the thin black cord trailing down to her breast pocket. Opening her eyes, the Detective motioned the men to two empty seats opposite her. She plucked a smartphone from her pocket, turned it off, and removed the headphones.

"Anything good?" Branson asked.

"Ohio Players."

"I wouldn't have taken you for a funk fan," Branson said as he sat.

"I'm not." Woost curled her lips and wrinkled her nose in a way that suggested a kind of facial shrug. "I read an article on the net last night about urban legends. They say you can hear a girl screaming in the middle of Love Rollercoaster and that she died in the studio during the recording."

Spiegler wiped off the plastic chair before sitting.

"That's not true. Just a story someone told someone else and it took off. Like that whole *Paul is dead* nonsense from the 60's."

"Of course it's not true," Woost said. Her eyes were fixed on Branson. "But people believe it just the same. Like some folks believe the moon landing was faked, or that Elvis is living on an island somewhere in the Pacific, sipping peanut butter and banana margaritas. It doesn't matter how preposterous the idea. If people want to believe it, they will. They cling to their notions, do crazy things to reinforce their beliefs. Anything not to have to face the truth."

Branson expected she'd be angry. If their roles were reversed, he'd have been. But he'd heard this tone of accusation before. Even with evidence in hand she remained unconvinced of his innocence. He let a moment of silence pass before he responded. Branson felt that was only fair, since she'd obviously put some work into the speech.

"Did you practice that all night? Maybe even write it down a few times, edit it, work it until you thought it was just the right metaphor to make me slap my head and say, *Eureka, she's right. I've been such a fool, I should confess to everything at once*?"

Woost seemed resigned. "I didn't want to do this. But I suspected I'd have to."

Woost opened the folder, lifted a photograph from under a paper clip, and slid the print across the table. The image depicted a little girl smiling through a mouthful of braces and colored rubber bands.

"Her name is Kathy Spence. Her mother reported her missing three and a half years ago. Kathy was playing with friends in one of their yards. No one saw what happened, but she never made it home. We found a lock of her hair in Bruce Donne's trailer, glued to a doll's head, just like your daughter's." Woost pulled out a second photo, this one a department store holiday shot, complete with Santa cap. "Tommy

BLUE EEL

Harris. Snatched from a supermarket parking lot while his grandparents loaded groceries into the car. Until Laurie Felston, no solid leads. Then we found a lock of Tommy's hair, too. It had dried blood on it."

Image after image followed, one right after the other. A girl with thick glasses and an innocent smile. Woost slapped down photos of missing children as if dealing cards. Pigtails. Freckles. A baseball bat slung over a shoulder. A stuffed bunny clutched tight.

"Tammy Jenson. Mark Clausen. Teresa Combs. Susie Kolan. Bethany LeGrau. Winnie Cohen—" Branson put up both hands.

"Stop, I get it."

"No, you really don't." Woost slapped her hand down on the photos with a sharp pop like a firecracker going off. "*All* these parents want answers, every bit as badly as you. All of them deserve to know what happened to their children. Yet only you try to pull this kind of stunt? You put all of these cases at risk. Yesterday you said that you didn't care about justice. Well, *these* parents do. Who are you to deny that to them?"

Branson had no reply.

"Look at their faces. Take a good, long look."

Woost reclined back in the chair. She had the expression of a poker player holding a straight flush. If she was bluffing it was good one, because her eyes remained steely and clear, no tremble, no telltale sign of any uncertainty.

"You read the newspaper, Detective Woost?" Branson picked up the photo of Kathy Spence, and turned it over. "Ever read about a tenement apartment complex burning down? I grew up in Philadelphia. Lots of old row houses, some at least a century old, and every day it seemed one of them went up like kindling.

"You know who runs into those burning buildings? *Parents.* Not friends, not husbands, not wives. *Parents.* You can pile a thousand photos on this table, or a million, or a billion, or a billion billion, but you'll never change the essential equation. It's basic nature. And you'd know that if you'd ever had kids."

A fleeting glimpse of vulnerability came over Woost, but she recovered so fast it was like it never happened. The woman was good. The Detective gathered her collection of photographs and slid them back into the folder.

"It took two hours of my own time, off the clock, to convince Sheriff

Sakow to drop the assault charges against the two of you. I'm wondering now if that was a mistake."

"Why'd you do that?" Branson handed her the final loose photo. "It's not like you."

Woost tucked the image away, then leaned forward and locked eyes hard onto Branson's. The intensity of the Detective's stare made the room beyond her seem to quaver and fade.

"You think I feel guilty for the five years I've spent busting your balls? You couldn't be more wrong. That's my job. It's my job to squeeze 'til you burst or until I no longer have to. I'd do it again. *Gladly*, if that's what I thought it'd take to get at the truth."

Branson felt lightheaded.

"You're right about one thing though," she continued. "There're aspects of this case I can't possibly understand, because I'm not a parent."

Branson smirked. Spiegler hunkered down in his chair for the payoff sure to come.

"I can't imagine the pain of having lost a child. But I have lost a soulmate. Don't you dare act like you're the only one who knows something about loss."

"Detective Faune..." Branson guessed. In dozens of interviews with the detectives, he'd never suspected the two shared anything more than coffee-run duties on stakeouts.

"I'm sorry."

"Yeah, so am I. I visited him as often I could. Every day he looked worse and every day I just wanted to hold him. But I couldn't. All he had left was his reputation. So, his wife sat by his side and held his hand. I stood at the foot of his bed and watched him fade away. Right up until the end, he'd sneak me a smile and I'd know he still loved me, that hadn't changed—and that was the worst thing of all.

"So, *Mr.* Turaco, I don't know all you've been through. But I'm no stranger to pain, and I know what it can do to a person. I was so tempted to break down and admit our affair just so I might be able to have some time alone with Roy, to hold him one last time while there was still a moment or two. But if I had, it would have brought even more pain to his final days. It was so hard to stand aside. And that's exactly what I'm asking you to do. The right thing, the painful thing."

Branson looked at Spiegler, whose eyes were moist. With a pinch of his shirt collar, the director cleared them and shrugged.

"There's nothing Sheriff Sakow would like better than to keep you two morons here. So, if I let you walk out that door, can I trust you to behave?"

Neither man answered.

THIRTEEN

"Where've you been?" Abriella asked, her voice tinged with curiosity and annoyance. "I called you, like, six times last night and you never picked up."

Branson wished he could see her face. Through his cellphone it was impossible to accurately gauge her level of irritation. It might all have been stagecraft, or all genuine. More likely some mixture of the two. The last thing Branson needed was for Abriella to abandon him. He already considered her a lifeline.

"I didn't have my phone on me last night."

"You didn't have your phone? Why not?"

"They don't allow phones in holding cells."

Abriella's tone lightened. "Sadly, this isn't the first time I've had a guy give me that excuse. Did you listen to your messages?"

"No," Branson lied. In fact, he'd listened to all six messages from her. Each featured a longer sigh at the beginning, then a request for him to call her back. None gave him any information.

"Well, just delete those," she said with another dramatic sigh. "Here's the deal. I was researching the little girl who escaped from Donne's trailer and found a police dispatch. At first I thought it was something I missed earlier, but this was fresh, only a couple minutes old. Last night, neighbors called police and reported gunshots at her house. When the cops arrived, the parents were dead. Shotgunned."

"The girl?"

"Missing. Which doesn't make a whole lot of sense, does it?

Donne's in jail, right? So who killed the Felstons and kidnapped the kid? It can't be a coincidence."

"The police are looking for an accomplice?" he asked her, though he already knew the answer. The police cruiser in his rear view mirror had parked on the curb when he'd pulled into the diner's parking lot. They had to know he couldn't have snatched Laurie out of her home last night, that was impossible from inside a jail cell, but perhaps they had bigger ideas, some kind of multilayer conspiracy theory.

"I dunno," Abriella said. "But know what? This case pushes the needle on the strange meter way into the red. When the police got there, the family's dog attacked them and they had to shoot it. It was acting really crazy, like it was super-rabid or something. Really freaked out some of the cops, apparently."

Eel's blood, Branson thought. The dog bit the wrong person. Bruce Donne's crazy story echoed in his mind. A broken watch, twice a day?

He joined Spiegler by the diner's glass doors. As they entered, Branson stole a glimpse of the cop behind the steering wheel of the cruiser. A large, padded bandage covered his nose. *That* wasn't good.

"Thanks, Abriella. You've done great. I'll call you—"

"Don't hang up," she blurted out, quick and defensive.

"Got something more?" he asked.

"No," she said. "But, well, I want to come out there with you."

He didn't think that was a very good idea. "I don't—"

"No, wait, listen to me. I'm not the kind of girl who parties with her airhead friends all weekend; I never do much of anything except go to school, study, work, and read bad romance novels." She paused. He sensed it wasn't because she expected a response, but rather because she wanted to choose her words carefully. "Doing your research has been the most excitement I've seen in a long, long time. It feels like I'm doing something *real*, y'know? Something that actually matters to someone."

"This could get dangerous," he told her.

Spiegler turned his head and fixed him with a chastising stare from his one good eye.

"This *will* get dangerous," Branson corrected himself.

She was silent so long he thought he'd lost her. But then her voice came back, not wounded by his warning but bolder because of it. "I'm cool with that. I'm tired of the safety net. Have you ever noticed that there's a safety warning on everything that's worth doing? I don't even drink."

Branson was unmoved.

"Please, Mr. Turaco, let me come out and meet up with you. I'll bring my laptop. I can do all my research on it, anywhere. I'll be able to give you answers a second after you ask the questions. I'm a better help by your side than over a phone line."

He knew he was about to feel old, that the words his tongue was about to form would make him feel positively Jurassic, but he couldn't think of any other answer. "I'll think about it."

"Does that mean no?" she asked.

"It might, I don't know yet."

"I don't accept no, it doesn't really work for me."

"Is this an ultimatum? Are you saying you won't help unless you can come along?" He felt a smile tug at the edges of his mouth. She had that effect on him often, he realized.

"I didn't say that. But call me later and find out."

"I will." Branson hung up. A handwritten sign read *PLEASE SEAT YOUSELF*.

"That's a good omen," Spiegler said. "A proper diner should have a kitchen run by an old Greek man with two teeth and a twenty-word vocabulary learned from Wheel of Fortune reruns."

Branson and Spiegler sat in a booth by a window that looked out onto the street, where they could see the parked police cruiser. Spiegler pushed aside a pair of plastic salt and pepper shakers, and ran his hand over the selection keys on the old style flip-book jukebox mounted to the wall. Branson couldn't help but notice how animated the man had become, how little he resembled the glum shut-in he'd met only the day before. He wondered if Spiegler and Abriella saw this as some kind of adventure. He hoped not. If so, the best thing would be to cut them loose. Maybe not the best thing for Branson, but the best for them, and the moral thing to do. Spiegler spun through the selections, none more recent than the '80s.

"She wants to come out here, I take it?"

"Yeah."

"Let her come. Never know, maybe Abriella can—"

"*No.*" The word was blunt and left no room for further discussion.

"Okay, okay." Spiegler surrendered. "Didn't mean to shit on your private toilet seat."

"And after breakfast, you should go home, too."

The depression and wear returned to Spiegler's face in an instant. The glum shut-in was back.

"Look, I didn't—"

"You haven't done anything wrong, Marius. I'm not angry with you. In fact, I can't begin to thank you for what you've done for me. But you saw me buy the gun that's in the glove compartment. It's not a conversation piece. One night locked up doesn't seem to have done you any harm, but a decade would. I hope it doesn't come to it, but you need to understand that I'll do anything—*anything*—to find Madeline. I can't ask you to follow me down that road. Like you said last night, it won't lead anywhere good."

Spiegler bowed his head and sat still, a grandfather clock with a broken pendulum. His features darkened as he ran a hand through the hair at the nape of his neck. He started to speak, then held back when a waitress in an overlarge blue apron arrived at their table.

"Get'cha coffee?"

Neither man even glanced up at her.

"Black," Branson ordered.

"No thanks," Spiegler mumbled. "Water. And a double-decker grilled cheese sandwich."

The waitress turned and vanished between two swinging doors into the kitchen. As the creaking quieted, Spiegler's head rose.

"Your next stop is the canyon, right? Find the hippies, shake them down for information. See, I'm not some shell-shocked old man too enfeebled to think for himself. I've been paying attention. And I'm not following you anywhere, I'm walking alongside you." Branson went to protest but Spiegler cut him off. "If you go into the canyon, you'll need me to take the lead. It's miles and miles of *nothing* out there. Sand and stones and the same cactus over and over. You think you're gonna just wander right into their camp guided by instinct? You need me. Send me home now, and you're done."

"Okay. I just had to—"

"Don't. I get it," Spiegler said.

"Thank you." Branson cocked a thumb towards the police

cruiser outside. "Course, neither of us is going anywhere with that third wheel."

"No problem. I've dealt with that sort of thing before. In college, back in my guerrilla film days. I'll take care of that once I get my grilled cheese sandwich and maybe wash up a bit."

FOURTEEN

On his return from the bathroom, Spiegler swiped a newspaper off the diner's counter. He dropped it to the table, slid into the booth, and gobbled down the last corner of his grilled cheese sandwich.

"You ever see the first movie I made? It's called *The Wild Times*. It's an early '70s art film, at least that was my intention. The distributor marketed it as a sex comedy. He was probably right."

Mouth full, Branson shook his head.

"Right, no reason you would have, it's not a good movie," Spiegler continued. "But it turned a bit of a profit and got me more work. Point is, we made that movie on fifty thousand dollars. You couldn't *cater* a film for that kind of money today. So we did it by cutting corners wherever we could. Bought raw stock in short ends from the studios, used the crew as extras. Everyone multitasking like sons of bitches. It was madness, really. But who knew? We were young..." Just as Branson wondered if there was a point, Spiegler snapped back to it. "There was one other thing we did to cut the budget: we never bought a single permit. Ever."

The waitress came and scooped up Spiegler's empty plate, revealing a placemat printed with ads for local businesses, bordering a street map. Branson hadn't yet finished his sandwich, but was back to wishing the director would get to the point.

"If we shot on the public street, a crew member would camp out on a roof of one of the buildings, squatting up there like a pirate in a crow's nest, except he was up there looking out for cop cars instead of the British Navy. When a white-and-black headed our way, he'd call down on a radio and we'd pack up and get gone in a couple seconds. Exhaust fumes and the echo of squealing tires."

"And your point?" Branson finally had to ask.

Spiegler offered a wry smile as an apology. "Sometimes we'd be right in the middle of a critical shot and knew we'd never be able to match it, so we needed to distract the cops."

They both looked out the window at the police cruiser.

"Lemme have your phone."

Branson pulled the phone from his pocket and handed it over. He watched with amusement as Spiegler fumbled to open it, his brow creasing with confusion and wasted effort. The director handed it back. "Dial 911 and *then* give it to me."

"911? You sure?"

Spiegler nodded. "That *is* how you contact the police to report a crime. They don't pull a cop off surveillance unless he's the closest to respond to a life-or-death situation."

Branson dialed.

Spiegler thumbed through the newspaper. He tapped the paper, smiled, then turned to the place mat and took the phone from Branson. Spiegler waited a moment, grinning like a mischievous adolescent. Then it was if the curtain went up and the house lights dimmed; show time.

"Hello? Yes. T-t-this is Giles Puluso." He'd lifted the name from a newspaper article.

"My, ah, my mother-in-law, she just c-c-called and, uhh, she says someone is trying... trying to break into the door. Into her house, I mean, through the front door..."

If *Branson* were a police dispatcher, Spiegler would've fooled him. Spiegler's expression became that of a leering Mephisto mixed with class clown.

"1410 Millstone Avenue," the director fairly leered. Branson was impressed.

"You'll g-g-get someone over there right away? I'm on my way there, but I'm twenty minutes out and—" Spiegler abruptly broke the connection and closed the phone. In unison the two men turned to the cop outside the window, behind the wheel of his cruiser. He just sat there, slack-jawed and inert.

After a moment, the cop grabbed his radio and spoke into the microphone. The cruiser roared to life, light bar flashing and siren wailing. The cop spared one last glance back at the diner. Then the cruiser peeled off.

"Exhaust fumes and the echo of squealing tires." Branson dropped a twenty onto the table as they stood to leave. "You feel like a pirate right now?"

Spiegler grinned. "Shoulda worn my eye patch."

FIFTEEN

The turnoff to the canyon, a meanders of sorts, cut through a thick mesh of cedar and fir. Beyond the forest the land opened up into desert, patches of rock cress breaking up the heat-cracked soil. Branson was in awe of the drowsy silence. He'd always thought he understood deafness, but now knew he'd been horribly mistaken.

Spiegler had told Branson of how the site had been used since the beginnings of movies as a setting for westerns and science fiction cheapies, by filmmakers both legendary and infamous. Branson realized it wasn't the canyon or the movies that held Spiegler in such rapture, but the culture of film. It must've been incredibly difficult for the director to quit the business and retreat into self-imposed exile. The man didn't even own a television. It had to be like a priest exiled not just from the church, but from God.

Spiegler had told Branson to pull over and kill the engine. They weren't equipped for off-road travel. The desert was the middle of nowhere and beyond reach of all roadside assistance. They'd have to hoof it from there. Branson dragged a duffel bag across the backseat and heaved it onto his shoulder. The two plastic water bottles inside sloshed. Spiegler stifled a laugh as he and Branson slid baseball caps onto their heads. "We look like goddamned tourists."

A fine layer of dust covered their shoes the moment they hit the ground. Agoraphobic vertigo rushed through Branson, as he stared at the expanse of desert. An identical view in every direction, he felt disoriented and directionless, as if floating in an endless sea without a compass.

"You've got the look. We all get it the first time. Like moonwalking through outer space. I would say you'll get used to it, but you'd figure out pretty quick that I was lying," Spiegler said.

The weight of the pistol tugged at Branson's waistband, the grip rubbing against his hipbone. His skin would soon be raw, even lubricated by the inevitable sweat. "Animals?"

"Oh, they're here." Spiegler slowed his stride to let him catch up. "And even though you can't see them, they're watching us."

"Anything dangerous?"

Spiegler laughed. "Coyotes and rattlesnakes."

Branson felt better about the gun.

"You ever see a Western Pipistrelle?"

Branson shook his head. "A Western Pipistrelle?"

"It's a bat. White body, black head and wings. Come dark, they flood from nooks and crevices of the rock walls by the thousands. Maybe millions, who can say? They cover the sky, you could mistake them for storm clouds from a distance." Spiegler swept his arms in a wide arc over his head. "Up close, they look like a massive swarm of butterflies."

"Thousands?"

"Millions, maybe." Spiegler chuckled.

"I don't like bats."

"How about snakes? Wanna talk about snakes instead?"

"No."

The desert's heat was deceptive. It soaked gradually into Branson's flesh, burrowing deep inside him. Sweat beaded on his skin and ran down his face and arms in searing rivulets. With that came a thirst so intense the dryness slithered down his throat towards his stomach. Dehydration wouldn't take long, in the baking sun.

After some time, the two men sat together on an outcropping of sedimentary rocks to steal a sip of water and collect their breath. Branson closed his eyes and still saw the desert projected as a negative image seared onto the inside of his eyelids. It would've been easy to fall asleep, basking in the sun. Too easy. After another sip of water, Branson motioned to Spiegler that they should get back underway.

"How far, do you think?"

"Too far. But not all that much longer."

The vast heat and scratchy dryness should've made for a miserable walk, but after a while Branson found it pleasantly numbing. His senses dulled a little more with each step, which freed his mind from its normal preventative regimen of processing sights and sounds and smells and tastes. In this absence, a familiar voice spoke up to fill the silence. He glanced over at Spiegler, but saw nothing in the man's face to suggest he'd heard anything. The voice came from within. He'd heard it before, during his loneliest nights. Branson had even given that angry, recriminating voice a name, borrowed from his co-workers. *The Mortician.*

You're a liar, Branson, a man who lied to his wife on the day your baby was born, she's so beautiful, *only all you saw was a crying white worm still glistening with embryonic fluid and blood, pale skin and a pink mouth yawing open like a baby bird's. You lied to Candice because you thought it was what she wanted you to say, or maybe because you wanted her to see you as profoundly moved as she was by the birth of your daughter. But you weren't. Sickness swelled in your stomach and hot liquid swam up your throat. You felt disoriented and frail, barely able to stay on your feet: this was your repulsion at being forced to witness the birth, the expansion of skin and flesh to accommodate the bulbous head that pushed through the stretched aperture, accompanied by your wife's frenzied screams. The eternity it took for the baby to emerge, even with the doctor's hands guiding it out, his gloved hands slick, fingertips dripping, the wet sounds of suction culminating in a warble something like flatulence; the offering of the umbilical cord to cut and the difficulty of refusal, and then the slithering exit of the deflated amniotic sac, so much like a disembowelment. You felt vomit in your mouth as they removed the viscera and wiped away the blood, two hard swallows before your mouth was empty enough to open it and say,* "She's so beautiful."

You lied. You're still *lying.*

"You okay?" Spiegler asked. His hands were cupped over his eyes like a sun visor and his face was pink. Branson wondered how long he'd been walking along, lost in thought.

"Sure, fine. How far do you think we've come?"

Spiegler shrugged. "Four, four and a half miles. Maybe five."

"Thirsty."

"Desert'll do that to you."

"We could die out here from dehydration." As dry as Branson's mouth felt, he knew this was an exaggeration, at least at this point. He did wonder how long it would take to drain out the last of his moisture and leave him a dry husk. He'd read that water accounted for sixty percent of the weight of a human body. He weighed one hundred and forty pounds. Rounding down, he counted eighty-four pounds available to sweat out before dying a bad death. Branson smiled at the absurdity. His lips and tongue felt like leather.

"Look at that ridge over there," Spiegler said. "You see those black specks? Buzzards. Could mean a water hole."

"That'd be good news."

"Water or carrion. At any rate, it's on our way."

They headed for the ridge. Knowing that water might be there made Branson's thirst more intense. He knew it was his body tormenting his brain. Perhaps some vestige of his reptilian brainstem had come into play, urging his feet to move faster, in order to save its life.

Spiegler again took the lead. His figure was obscured by a kaleidoscopic blur of light as he stepped before the sun. Branson followed the sound of Spiegler's footsteps, keeping his eyes to the ground, where the director's shadow swayed from side to side like a branch in a subtle breeze.

As they peered over the ridge, the glare died down, allowing a better view of the valley below. There *was* a water hole, as Spiegler had suggested, a succulent-ringed crevice in the desert floor half-filled with stagnant water. A black and white bird with long tail feathers and an extended neck drank from water's edge, head tilting up between dips to keep an eye on the birds of prey circling overhead.

"What is *that*?" Branson asked.

"That's a roadrunner, city boy."

"Doesn't look anything like the one in the cartoon."

Alert to the intrusion, the bird jerked its head up, cocked it to one side, and froze, the better to survey its surroundings. Branson held his breath, not wanting to spook the bird any further. Though he was terribly thirsty, the balance and tranquility of the natural scene on display compelled him not to disturb it. Branson raised one finger to his lips to signal Spiegler to remain silent, but knew as he did that it was unnecessary. The sight had cast its spell on Spiegler as well. Despite their own thirst, they'd let the bird finish its drink in peace. It was there first, after all.

The roadrunner dipped its beak back down to the water. Then it exploded in a flurry of loose feathers, flailing wings, and kicking legs. A crude arrow shot through its chest and pinned it to the ground. The bird twitched a bit before it succumbed, talons closed tight into fists.

Sudden shock and outrage flooded Branson. Before he acted on the surge of emotion by screaming for the hunter to step into the clear, Spiegler dropped his hand onto Branson's shoulder and squeezed hard. They watched the water hole in silence.

A stringy tube of a man dressed in rags, with long dark hair and a scraggly, uneven beard, stepped from behind a siltstone mound. Swinging his primitive bow, the man swooped down on the dead bird, brought it up to his nose, sniffed, and then slid the carcass into a canvas bag on his hip. The bag bulged.

Without warning, Spiegler stepped out from beyond the ridge into the opening. The man scrambled and ducked down in a defensive crouch. Spiegler raised both hands. "Hey, it's okay, okay? I'm just—"

The man quickly restrung his bow and aimed a fresh arrow at the director. Spiegler's expression mirrored the surprise and terror of the roadrunner's final moments. Rushing out into the open, Branson drew his pistol and settled his aim on the man's chest.

"Stand down. *Now*."

The archer's eyes shifted from Spiegler, to Branson, to the gun. He released the tension on the bow and lowered his weapon. Branson didn't follow suit.

"Cops?" the archer asked.

"No, we're not cops." Spiegler lowered his hands, but didn't relax. With the bow lowered and a gun aimed at him, the man seemed like a wild animal, cornered. Even city dwellers knew those were dangerous.

"What you want?" the archer asked.

"A drink from the water hole, for starters." Branson shouldered past Spiegler, closing in on the hunter. "Then, I want answers."

"You drink from this oversized puddle, you'll squirt brown water outta your ass for months." The man laughed. "Ain't just a watering hole for birds and shit. It's also a bathtub, a toilet, and a graveyard. Take a look see."

For the first time Branson looked closely at the pool of dark water. The bloated body of what might've been a rodent floated in its center, a ball of wet fur around rotting flesh.

"The animals, they're used to it. They *deal*, you get it, man?" With a deliberate motion the archer pulled a flask off his belt and held it out.

"Evolution takes time, but they adapt."

Branson refused to take the flask. The scrawny man uncapped it, took a deep swig, and offered it to Spiegler. The director took it, wiped the rim, and gulped down a mouthful. He nodded, as if to confirm that the water inside was safe and handed it off to Branson. Drinking, he kept the gun aimed and his eyes open and alert.

Replacing the cap, Branson tossed the flask back to the man. "What's your name?"

"They call me Reppy," the man grinned. "That's short for *Reptile*."

"They?" Branson asked.

"Yeah, they, I mean us. Moonmen."

Spiegler hadn't been able to remember what they called themselves, but his eyes lit up the moment *Moonmen* came out of Reppy's mouth. He nodded to Branson, confirming that the archer was from the same commune that used to raid his catering tables.

"Then you're who we're looking for. Take us back to your camp," Branson ordered. The archer's grin only grew.

SIXTEEN

The doorbell spit out a sound that no English word had been invented to describe—not a ring or a buzz or a chime, but an electronic, grinding cough. Detective Woost was sure that whoever had designed it hadn't meant for it to sound that way; surely there weren't hundreds of mass-produced chime units all bleating out the same atrocious noise from front doors across the nation. No, this one must be in the process of breaking down, maybe one or two presses of a button away from death. The house attached to the doorbell gave the same impression. *In this part of town*, she thought, *they all do*.

The young black girl who answered the door was pretty, even beautiful if she lost the thick glasses. However, the look on her face was anything but attractive; an ugly sneer wrinkled across her face as she stared back at Woost through the screen door.

"You're a cop."

"Yes, I am," Woost said as she drew back her coat and flashed the badge on her hip. "Detective Susan Woost."

The girl didn't bother to look. "I wasn't asking."

"Are you Abriella Nelson?"

"You came to me, so that's not exactly an honest question, is it?" Abriella crossed her arms and pushed out her chest, as defiant as a unionist staring down a strikebreaker. Woost smiled, hoping to disarm the young woman.

"I'm not here to interrogate you, Miss Nelson. You're not under investigation. I just have some information for you, some things I think you should know. May I come in?"

Abriella drew a deep breath, then released it in a disdainful huff and moved to the side. Woost stepped around Abriella and went inside, nearly tripping over a duffel bag set next to the door.

"Are you planning a trip?"

"I thought you weren't here to interrogate me."

Abriella led Woost to a small kitchen. Warbling television speakers blared from the adjacent room. The canned laughter from an old sitcom reverberated through the walls. As she went by, Woost caught a glimpse of a squat, overweight man with an empty bottle of gin cradled in the crook of his interlocked arms, asleep on a broken-down sofa. Abriella invited the cop to sit on one of four folding metal chairs arranged around a well-worn kitchen table. Woost sat, Abriella stood. Too low for the table, the chair made the cheap office furniture at the police station seem downright luxurious.

"You know, I get that people are nervous around cops, around *me*. I'm used to it. I can also tell the difference between garden-variety anxiety and the defensiveness that comes from hiding something. So you can lower your drawbridge." Again, Woost smiled at Abriella to no good effect. The detective cut to the chase. "I know you're doing research for Branson Turaco."

A stone, Abriella didn't flinch.

"And I'm not holding you responsible for anything he's doing, or planning to do. Not just yet, anyway. But you need to hear me out. That bag in the hall scares me, Miss Nelson. It makes me think you're planning on joining him. I doubt you've thought that decision through."

Abriella still offered no reaction.

"Does your father know you're leaving?" Woost pressed. Abriella rolled her eyes.

"You make it sound like he'd even notice I'm gone. He wouldn't, not until the fifteenth, when he needs me to cash his disability."

"It's not easy to live under his roof, is it?" Abriella blinked twice with obvious irritation.

"You need to be careful you don't make things worse for yourself. Running *away* from your father *to* a man like Turaco might only make things worse for you."

"Don't you *dare* talk about my Daddy," Abriella snapped. "You don't know him, and you don't know me, and you sure as hell don't know us."

"But it's okay for *you* to talk shit about him?" Abriella's eyes narrowed to slits.

"He's *my* Daddy."

"Oh, I see," Woost said. "Because you're the only one who's ever had a shitty home life and wanted to escape."

"What would you know about it?" Abriella's eyes burned. "What do you know about anything? You get off hounding Mr. Turaco like this? Like you just didn't find the guy who took his daughter? You got something personal against him, or what?"

The Detective leaned forward like a conspirator. Good cop rising, bad cop sinking. She put on her best mask of maternal concern. "I just don't get why a pretty girl like you, bright, so full of promise, would throw away her future on someone like Turaco."

"Whatever you think you know about me, you're wrong."

"Maybe, but I'm sure I know enough." Woost rose from her seat and leaned close to Abriella. "And I know a lot more about Branson Turaco than you do. My partner and I spent years on his case. We interviewed him dozens of times, listened to his story change. I can't count the number of inconsistencies we documented. His story never added up, but there wasn't any mathematics to it after a while. Even his wife felt it. That's why she left him so soon after Madeline disappeared."

"How would you know why she left?"

"Because she told us, that's how." Woost let that sink in. It wasn't necessary to go into her history with Candice Turaco. Conversations that had begun as criminal investigation interviews, then after Roy Faune's death, had grown personal. Tragedy builds bridges. "Did you know that his wife twice filed domestic abuse charges against him, even *before* the abduction?"

Abriella's stone face softened. "No."

"She filed the second charge from a hospital bed." The girl dropped down into a chair. "But, as with almost all domestic violence cases, she dropped those charges. I'm sure Turaco promised to change, that it'd never happen again, that old song and dance offered by all abusers."

Abriella stole a sideways look through the doorway to the living room, where her father slept.

Woost added, "Thing is, beating your wife isn't the same thing as killing your daughter, right?"

Eyes stretched wide, Abriella nodded in agreement.

"It's true that we found evidence in Bruce Donne's trailer that links him not only to Madeline, but to a host of other child abduction cases as well. You already know that. But what you don't know is that in all of those crimes, the children were abducted from public parks and playgrounds, or off the road from outside their house. Not a single one of them disappeared from her own bedroom in the middle of the night. Except for Madeline Turaco."

Abriella's neck bobbed as she swallowed hard.

"No fingerprints were found in the Turaco home except for the family's. No door or window was picked or forced open. No strange footprints were left on the carpeting. In fact, there were no signs of a struggle at all," Woost's voice fell low and threatening. "You wouldn't know this, but there's a feeling common to all crime scenes, a particular sense of unease in the air. You can almost smell it, or feel it like a vibration on your skin. But it's always there. Except, again, in the case of Madeline Turaco. What I did feel there was... different."

"You think Branson was responsible for his daughter's disappearance? Because of a gut feeling? Really?"

"My late partner did," Woost paused and chose her words carefully. "What I know is that I'm following a dangerous man down a very deep, very dark rabbit hole. He's leading me somewhere. I need to know the destination before we arrive. So I can make sure no one else gets hurt."

"So what is it you're asking me to do?"

SEVENTEEN

Reppy walked with a pronounced limp that forced every stride of his left leg to twist, shuffle forward, and then snap back as he went. None of that slowed him. In fact, Branson and Spiegler had a difficult time keeping up, though Branson managed to keep the handgun trained on Reppy's back and made sure the gimp knew it.

"Slow *down*," Branson ordered for the third time.

"So sorry," the Moonman mumbled. They'd confiscated the archer's bow, along with a six-inch hunting knife they found in a crude burlap sheath beneath his pant leg.

Spiegler carried both weapons and was huffing to keep up. "How much farther?"

Reppy looked at Spiegler with contempt. "Close now."

It wasn't close. The three men walked for twenty minutes before they came to the crest of a long sand trough that descended down into a circular valley. Looking downslope, it struck Branson that he now understood the name Moonmen. The canyon where they lived resembled a crater on the Moon. A dozen plywood structures with cloth walls ringed a center section, which featured an enormous tent in the likeness of a Native American tipi. Caught in blasts of tunneling wind, animal skins flapped in the doorways.

"We call it Tranquility Base," Reppy said.

"Of course you do." Spiegler shifted the bow from one shoulder to the other and whispered to Branson, "*Crazy bastards*."

Branson gestured for Reppy to lead the way down into the canyon. "Get moving."

Despite his limp, Reppy traipsed down the steep slope with feral agility. Branson and Spiegler fared worse. Each step brought sliding shoes and waving arms. Branson surmised that Reppy could easily have turned and overtaken them as they stumbled, wrestled the gun from his hand, and killed them both. By the look on Spiegler's face, he knew they were on roughly the same page.

The gap between them growing, Reppy twisted in place, stared back at them with a glowering, hateful expression. It was clear that he understood how the situation had changed. For a moment, Branson was certain that he'd rush back up the trough and attack. Instead, he cackled like an insane old man, a sound like coarse sandpaper sawing into dry lumber, and continued to descend.

Branson struggled down the decline and flailed his arms like a bird with broken wings until the landscape finally leveled out under his feet. Less graceful, Spiegler came up from behind in free-fall, hands groping at Branson's shoulder, until he fell to the desert floor and stirred up a cloud of sand. The director brushed himself off and stood. Branson kept his eyes on their captive guide. Reppy stopped walking, turned his head to the sky, sniffed like a coyote, and released a penetrating chirp.

The sound flowed through the valley and echoed back from all directions. Each echo distorted the original in its own way. Some rose in tone, others dropped a full octave. The chirp seemed to ricochet across the dunes, and in doing so, multiply. No, Branson realized as the noise grew louder, these were not echoes at all, but new voices joining in and adding. The birdcalls came from every direction. Branson spun in place, trying to place the sources, and saw nothing but the rise and fall of the sandy canyon floor like ocean waves, endless in every direction.

Reppy whipped his head back and responded to the other voices with a piercing, staccato whistle. The other voices evaporated into silence like shadows shrinking before light. Branson leapt forward, head snapping from side to side, and slid the gun under Reppy's throat.

"What was that? What did you do?"

The Moonman shrugged.

The new silence was different than before, more menacing, more droning, and it brought a certainty in Branson's gut that at any moment a volley of arrows would blot out the sky and impale them, or an army of camouflaged assassins would spring up from the sand, or any number of other sudden, catastrophic deaths would rush towards them. As his eyes searched for movement, the gun in his hand began to shake.

A woman emerged from the closest shanty, dipping her head to avoid a crumbling corner of cheap plank roof. She was topless, tall and unnaturally thin like a victim of famine, with well-defined ribs that protruded like metal hoops on a wine barrel, below an uneven pair of shrunken breasts. Her face was a slack, emotionless landscape of weather beaten, parchment-like skin.

They all came out, the Moonmen and women, one at a time or in pairs. Some held hands, most wore clothes no more significant than rags, a tribe gathered in response to Reppy's signature call. None seemed even remotely surprised or even curious at the sight of Branson and Spiegler. Neither did anyone appear frightened by Branson's gun, which he waved around for good measure. Sun-blasted faces stared at them from bored, half-closed eyes.

"I'm guessing *that's* what I did," Reppy said as he joined his people. There was no question of Branson stopping him. Clearly, it wouldn't make any difference even if he could. "Put your little gun down, man. There's a whole lot more of us than there are bullets in that cap gun, right? You gonna shoot a few of us, make it up that rise, across the desert and all the way back to your car before we get you? And what about your friend there? He don't look up for that. What 'cha say?"

Even before Branson could process the long odds against escape, a loud groan bellowed out from the tipi. It was vaguely human, but as loud and complex as whale song and as ferocious as thunder. An enormous man pushed through the tent flaps, supporting himself on metal crutches. He stood naked except for a ragged pair of shorts. A tattoo of Jesus adorned the center of his hairless chest—the savior's arms outstretched, fingers pointing to the man's purple nipples, head crowned with a spectral halo and a pair of deer antlers. The gigantic man came into the sun. The Moonmen tracked his every move with clear adoration.

In his left hand the man held a leather strap. Tied to the end of the strap was a young boy of maybe eleven years old. The boy's head was completely bald, devoid even of eyebrows and lashes.

"Drop the gun," the man demanded of Branson. His voice was surprisingly soft and nuanced, in a way that conveyed both power and wisdom.

Spiegler closed his hand over Branson's, and slid the gun out of his hand. Handle first, the director gave the weapon over to Reppy. The archer took the gun, turned it over in his hand, then stashed it under his belt.

"You should bow the first time you meet St. Abaddon," Reppy whispered, covering his mouth as he spoke. "Out of respect. Or fear. Or both."

St. Abaddon wiped the sweat from his forehead. Threw it to the sand with an absentminded swipe.

"It's too hot out here. Bring them inside, but search them first. Take everything they have."

EIGHTEEN

Uneasy on a wobbly wooden chair and with his hands tightly bound, Branson looked around the tipi and his mouth dropped open at what he saw. The tent's upper cone was covered in bones. Intricate patterns were made of spinal columns woven into rib cages, hipbones and yawning skulls, along with thousands of leg and arm bones fused together. Most appeared to be the skeletal remains of desert animals. Most. Spiegler seemed to accept his surroundings without hesitation. Probably a long-term effect of his time on extravagant film sets, Branson figured. The director sat next to him, staring at the sailor's knots in the frayed rope that bound him to the arms of the chair. To Branson it looked as if the director were trying to unravel the complex knots with his mind.

St. Abaddon sat across from them, smoking a long, straight Acacia pipe. The chair that supported him was buried beneath his massive frame. St. Abaddon blew a smoke ring and watched it drift up through the smoke-hole of the tipi with a relaxed, thoughtful expression on his face.

"Have you considered gravity?" Neither man replied. "Even the soil under our feet, it must obey gravity."

He kicked the dirt floor, which brought up a cloud that quickly settled back to the ground. "And the trees, and cactus and animals. And we too... we must obey gravity." The last of the smoke rose from the tipi. "But not the smoke, or the clouds. They are the only ones who are really free. The rest of us, whether vegetable, animal or mineral, are all prisoners. We're chained by gravity, and imprisoned by fate."

St. Abaddon took another puff on the pipe. The smoke was potent. A rich, organic smell like marijuana or burning wood filled the tipi.

"Fate brought you to us. You had no choice but to come, so I do not hate you for the intrusion. You brought a weapon. I suppose that too is fate, but that I cannot forgive. My people's lives are sacred. With anger or fear or even simple misjudgment, you might have taken one of them. So I must ask what fate demands of me today. What am I expected to do with the two of you?"

"Did fate ask you to kidnap children?" Branson snarled.

St. Abaddon let out a monstrous, roaring laugh. The Moonmen crouched on the ground at his feet tittered.

"No, that business has very little to do with fate."

"Then why?"

"For the simplest of reasons. *Food*."

For a moment, the tipi was painfully silent, like the desert outside. Then there erupted a cataclysmic noise as all the Moonmen burst into laughter. St. Abaddon shushed them with a raised hand and mischievous smile that only made him look wicked.

"I'm kidding. I promise you, Branson Turaco, we're not cannibals."

They'd taken his wallet and everything in it. They also took Madeline's college fund and that was of much greater concern. Even bound to a chair in the middle of a desert, the money mattered to Branson because it was *her* money.

A tall, naked woman ducked inside the tipi. Her hair was cropped close to the skull, sculpted like a fresh army recruit. She struck a sharp contrast to the other Moonmen. They were wild and unkempt, like barnyard animals accustomed to living in their own filth. A sheen of cleanliness seemed to light the air around her. Then Branson realized it was no illusion or trick of the light. The smooth surface of the tall woman's skin gave off a delicate shimmer. A very real, if faint, glow.

And she wasn't Madeline.

She walked like a prized show horse, long legs crossing with clockwork grace until she stood over St. Abaddon, the side of her breast against his cheek. Never far from his master's feet, the leashed boy wrapped his arms around one of the woman's legs.

"Did you kidnap her too?" Branson growled at Abaddon.

St. Abaddon tilted his head back for a kiss and the woman obliged.

Twisted chrome woven through an uneven row of misaligned teeth flashed with the kiss. Branson took that for childhood braces, never adjusted by a dentist or removed when no longer needed. They were tearing her mouth apart.

"Did I steal you, Sticks?" Her answer was drunken and garbled, her tongue unable to navigate inside such a distorted mouth.

"Mmmm herrre cost I'mmm loved herrre."

"That's right," Abaddon said while patting her rear. He turned his attention back to Branson. "She was always meant to be here, can't you see? She had no choice. Just like you had no choice. Or me, or any of us. Love is our gravity, that's the secret. That's the *thing*."

Notwithstanding her full breasts and woman's hips, Branson saw only the little girl that was still inside the woman called Sticks. The way she tilted her head and gazed out with lost, curious eyes reminded him of his daughter, always full of yearning to understand the way the world worked. He'd little doubt that Sticks had been stolen away at an early age and brought to live among men and women who'd rejected the modern world and instead chose to embrace a primitive, mystical life. He imagined the tortures of reprogramming for them to gain control over her thoughts, the inevitable physical and mental abuse, the creeping Stockholm syndrome, and finally her complete immersion into their beliefs. Branson wondered at what point the memory of her parents finally vanished completely, and whether she'd remember them ever again. The compelling voice of St. Abaddon jerked Branson out of his thoughts.

"Tell me, why do you think fate has brought you here?"

"You took my daughter."

St. Abaddon sighed. "And you've come to take her back?"

"Yes."

"No." The leader of the Moonmen gripped the arms of his chair to push himself up, shaking off the effort as he approached the bound men. "You may believe that's why you've come, but you're wrong. Not lying, no; you probably don't know enough about what fate intends for either of you, to be lying."

Sticks came up behind him, dragging the boy by his leash, and knelt down beside Branson. She whispered into his ear.

"You collecttt brrroke soulsss, don'ttt you?" Sticks looked toward Spiegler. The director hadn't moved, eyes still staring down at the knots, but his face was red with anger. Sticks was right—Spiegler was a broken soul, and Branson had collected him.

"Tttthey won'tttt safe you."

St. Abaddon drew so close their noses nearly touched, and locked Branson with his fierce eyes. The huge man exhaled, and sent the overwhelming stench of stale smoke up Branson's nostrils. His sinuses opened but his mind fogged, which caused an intoxicated shift in perception. The light brightened, illuminating the tipi's bone tapestry. The walls of the tent shook, bone rattling against bone, the entire tent serving as a percussive instrument. As the strange effect of the smoke slowly dissipated, stillness returned.

Branson shook his head to clear it. St. Abaddon and Sticks nestled back at his throne in the same position as before.

"You see? You cannot trust yourself. Because all men lie, even to themselves." St. Abaddon again raised the pipe to his lips, inhaled, and blew another smoke ring through pursed lips. Branson watched it climb. "Trust only fate. Only fate does not lie."

St. Abaddon stood, locked his hands behind his head, jutted out his gut, and cracked his backbone. It sounded like a bushel of dried reeds breaking. He motioned to a trio of Moonmen.

"Take them to the pit. We'll show them what fate has written for them at sundown."

The Moonmen scrambled over and untied the two men. Branson flexed his fingers and was relieved to see color return to his hands. An ugly purple bruise circled his wrist where the hemp rope had pressed into his skin. Two Moonmen took hold of his forearms and lifted him out of the chair.

The third Moonman finished untying Spiegler and attempted to wrench him up by an armpit. The director, hands still clamped down on the chair's arms, refused to budge. He fixed the Moonman with eyes full of hate so intense that the skinny hippy released him and jumped away, as if the director had smoldering metal for skin.

In a blur of motion, Spiegler leapt from his chair and dove headfirst into the Moonman, fists flying, elbows and arms pumping like the pistons of a massive diesel engine. The Moonman's face exploded with bright red, nose broken and brow cut. The man fell, cradling his head. Spiegler spun, kicked the prone man in the ribs. Mouth agape and screaming, he rushed towards St. Abaddon, civilized man forgotten, subsumed by the angry, primitive animal that lurks in the shadows of every man's soul.

The cultists rushed off the floor to block his path, shoulders down like linebackers. St. Abaddon tripped over his chair as he retreated, reaching out as he fell. The big man took Sticks down with him. Spiegler was surprisingly quick, feet kicking up soil, hands like claws reaching down for the fat man, the Moonmen unable to reach him in time. Then the boy on the leash thrust up from his crouch and collided head on with the director's chest. The sudden impact knocked both of them to the dirt. Spiegler's scream was drowned in a gushing draw of breath. The boy scrambled away. It was only after the boy was hidden behind St. Abaddon and Sticks that Branson saw the tiny bone knife in his hand.

Spiegler rolled onto his back, his hands slapped hard over the hole in his abdomen, blood pulsing up between his fingers. All the Moonmen rose to their feet. They extracted long femur bones, and wielded them like clubs. They converged over Spiegler like swarming insects, kicking and pummeling him with their makeshift cudgels.

Branson struggled to free himself from the Moonmen's grasp, and might have been able to, but more Moonmen joined the fray and pushed him down to his knees. A hard shot from a stiff bone dislodged his arm from its socket. Branson screamed in pain. The base of his skull got squared up, and the next hit rocked him to the earth, jaw flat to the dirt. Then there rained down on him a constant pounding of bone against flesh, a drumbeat of pain. Warm blood spread across his back as the debris sank into his flesh like tiny knives.

Branson's suffering outlived his consciousness.

NINETEEN

There was a time when Marius Spiegler enjoyed dreaming. He even made a robust living out of translating his various fantasies into popular entertainment. Eventually, that made him rich and he climbed through the tax rates to the top bracket. All that was before the accident, before every one of his dreams became reruns of memories he'd rather forget. Spiegler would've happily given away his accumulated wealth and lived on the street, if only the nightmares would end. Except in his heart, he knew they never would. Concussed and unconscious, Spiegler dreamed and remembered.

***

The Assistant Director stood at the edge of the set nibbling on a pencil. Mallory Plaskett half-raised one hand to get his attention, then waited for Spiegler to wave her over to the circle of chairs around the cameras and recording equipment. Once he did, with the agility of a house cat, Mallory goose-stepped over bundled power cords and navigated between the kamikaze crewmembers who sprinted across Sound Stage Number Four. Spiegler couldn't take his eyes off her legs.

"Marius, they're here," she said as she stepped into the inner sanctum of chairs.

He forced himself to bring his eyes up to look Mallory in the eye, but paused as he went by her breasts. Mallory's eyes were blue. He'd never noticed.

"*Who's* here?"

From the side of her mouth she whispered, "The kids."

"Oh, yeah."

Federal law and union rules placed too many restrictions on the use of child actors for the mine car sequence to be economically feasible. He'd twice cut it from the screenplay. But Spiegler couldn't get the sequence out of his head because it was vital to the narrative. He'd sent Mallory to a local Vietnamese market to try to find a couple of kids to hire for the job. It was unethical, illegal and against union rules. But once the scene was in the can it wouldn't matter, and if anything came of it he'd deal with that later.

"Bring them in through the loading bay. We'll shoot it quick and get them outta here before anyone's the wiser."

Mallory grinned, all dimples and wet lips, only reinforcing the image in his head of her in a short Catholic schoolgirl's uniform. She nodded with enthusiasm, eager to please. He'd have to keep that in mind.

"You got it, Boss."

Spiegler watched her scamper across the set. A member of the art department looked up from painting a stalagmite to smile at her and nod. Mallory returned the gesture then exited behind a plaster-of-Paris cavern wall. Spiegler turned to an associate producer.

"I want that painter fired by the time we wrap for the night."

"For what?" the toady asked.

"Anything you'd like."

Spiegler returned to the business of setting up the complex tracking shot of the runaway mine car as it careened down a rickety track. Victor, the cinematographer, scratched out a list of measurements in a spiral-bound notebook.

"We okay, Vic?"

"Yeah. Yeah, I think so."

The studio had imposed a strict ban on smoking inside. From the scowl on his face, Spiegler could tell the man needed a smoke. He told Vic to sneak behind the sound stage and blaze up. Victor thanked him and made for the exit.

Mallory returned, flanked by a tiny, black haired Vietnamese girl and a lanky white boy. They appeared to be ten, maybe eleven, though that would've made the boy tall for his age.

"This is Nhu and Alex." Nhu bowed, slightly. Alex smirked.

They were nothing like the kids he'd imagined. If a different A.D.

had brought him these kids—or, goddammit, an intern—they would have gotten the verbal ass-whipping of their lives. Instead, glancing down for a glimpse of Mallory's ample, sweater-encased bust, he smiled.

"They're perfect. Can you get them over to makeup? Tell them just powder for glare, nothing more. It's not a close-up, no need to get precious."

"Will do, Boss." Mallory winked. She turned to Nhu and Alex and said, "C'mon, guys, let's go see Miss Evelyn and Mister Todd."

She led the children—and Spiegler's eyes—away to the makeup department tables. The children *were* completely wrong for the scene, but what he'd told her was true: it would be a long shot. It'd work. *They'd* work. Given the unrealistic restrictions on child labor, they'd have to. Spiegler wondered how much Mallory had given the kids from petty cash and hoped that wouldn't cut too much into the wrap party.

In the moments leading up to the take, Spiegler rushed between departments, doling out final approvals for lighting, camera, and sound. The Best Boy brought a note that Spiegler's wife had called. Spiegler waved the kid away. The dressed set was cleared, all personnel moved behind a line of red tape on the floor. Bruce Donne adjusted a concealed microphone, and was the last to leave.

Mallory led the children up the incline. The entire crew watched. Spiegler was sure all of the men, and likely the majority of the women, had their eyes on Mallory's ass. At the top she helped the kids into the mine car, gave them a thumbs up, and headed back down the way she came. Once safely behind the red line, she gave Spiegler a mischievous grin and rushed to stand behind him. She gave his butt a not too discrete squeeze. Spiegler thought it promised to be a very good night.

The practical effects team had the brakes on the mine car rigged for remote control release. A burly man sporting a wild red beard held a single-button controller in his oversized hand. He stood ready for Spiegler to give the order. Victor ran in and positioned himself behind the camera. He was huffing, but not as loud as all that.

"Everyone good-to-go?" Spiegler called out.

The essential players called back. All were ready.

"Then... Action."

The red-bearded man hit the trigger.

The brakes released and the coal car raced down the track, rattling, screeching and picking up speed as it went. The children screamed as instructed, decent actors considering their age and lack of experience. The camera whip-panned to follow the car as it sped past.

It was a great shot, Spiegler thought. Provided Victor kept focus.

It happened so fast, at first no one knew anything had gone wrong. At the end of the stunt, the mine car was supposed to dip sharply beneath a low overhang in the cavern set, like on a roller coaster. The crew had rehearsed the scene without passengers and the stunt had gone off without a hitch. With a loud metallic clap, the cart lifted off the tracks then tumbled over onto its side. The children spilled out, flung through the air before coming to a hard stop on the floor. Where their heads landed, no one could immediately say. For a long moment, everyone just stared.

"Oh, God—" someone muttered.

Spiegler heard the camera still running.

In a low, weak voice, the director said, "*Cut.*"

TWENTY

A thin shaft of sunlight slowly faded through a tiny slit in the metal door. A chill skittered down Branson's back like a spider in pursuit of a fly. The temperature dropped quickly, faster than he'd have imagined possible. Branson curled up, wrapped his arms around his chest, and shivered inside the cold, dark shipping container.

At least he wasn't alone. Bruised and bloody, Spiegler lay unconscious on the floor. His open mouth revealed wide gaps in his smile where only recently there'd been teeth. When Branson first woke, he'd feared the director was dead. Then the slow, steady rise and fall of Spiegler's chest proved otherwise. He'd taken a hell of a beating, and bled from the stab wound in his gut, but he was still breathing.

Something crawled along Branson's leg, and that sent a different chill through him that had nothing to do with evening's bloom. An inch and a half long scorpion threaded its way through his torn pants leg. Branson yelped and kicked out, which shook the creature off him and into the dark.

"—sting you?" Spiegler's voice was weak, and sloppy. He remained on the sand-littered floor, but his eyes were open and he was awake. "—hurt maybe, but won't kill you."

"You sure?" Branson asked.

"No." Spiegler spit a wad of dirt and blood to the sand.

The director pulled himself up and Branson settled in beside him. Spiegler's real eye was nearly closed, the skin around it wrinkled and purple. His lip was split in two places. He looked over at Branson.

"You look like shit," Spiegler offered.

Neither man laughed, but the joke wasn't wasted. Spiegler looked around.

"I think it's some sort of shipping container," Branson said.

"It's like being locked in an abandoned refrigerator." Spiegler visibly shivered and spit up more blood. His voice was stronger with his esophagus cleared. "I'm not claustrophobic, or afraid of the dark. But you know, all of this together, it's kind of freaking me out."

"I've lost track of the scorpion," was all Branson could think to say. He took a good look at the grisly, bulbous bruise on the top of Spiegler's head. "I've bought ground beef that looks better than that. How're ya feeling?"

Spiegler didn't quite shrug. Moonlight crept in through the crack in the door that recently was filled by the setting sun.

"I've partied a lot in my day. Always woke up with my head feeling like a nuclear blast had gone off inside it. I gotta say, this is worse."

"What were you thinking, taking them on like that? You might've noticed we were outnumbered and outgunned."

Spiegler snorted a blood-red bubble from his nose. He wiped it away.

"Worked out pretty well for us back at the police station..."

The two men talked deep into the night. Branson wondered how badly the man was injured. They were exhausted, but anxiety and fear didn't allow for sleep. They discussed the Oakland Raiders, traffic on the 405, the marijuana farms in the valley, and many other subjects. Spiegler shared stories about Hollywood in the '70s and early '80s, poking fun at white producers with Afros and screenwriters on amphetamines. Branson told him about the early days of his marriage to Candice, their first apartment, and his early attempts at journalism. They didn't discuss their current situation. At all.

Spiegler was ruminating about chaos and fate when Branson hushed him. Cocking an ear in the air, he whispered, "They're coming."

They held their breath.

The doors of the shipping container creaked open and moonlight flooded in. Three Moonmen stood in the doorway, Reppy in the center, brandishing Branson's handgun. He drew down square on Spiegler.

"It's time. St. Abaddon is waiting."

Two Moonmen lifted Spiegler from the floor and carried him outside. Lowering the gun, Reppy gestured for Branson to join Spiegler with a gesture so casual, it could easily have been mistaken for friendly under different circumstance. Branson was unable to move. Were they being herded out to be executed and buried? Reppy again raised the gun.

"Don't be like that, man. C'mon."

The initial step felt like self-betrayal. He'd no desire to facilitate his own execution. Then after that first hesitant shuffle forward, Branson found his stride. He stepped from the dark into the light of the moon on the desert. He fell in a few paces behind Spiegler and the other Moonmen on the perp walk, Reppy and the gun a half step behind him. Reppy grinned when he saw Branson steal a look back at the rusted metal prison.

"People leave all kinds of shit in the desert, for all sorts of reasons. We use everything. Don't waste nothing out here. We ain't like you."

They walked. It could've been the cold, or maybe just the aftereffects of a solid beating, but the ground felt spongy beneath Branson's feet, as if the earth sucked at his shoes with every step. The procession reached a long, crested dune, beyond which flared yellow tongues of bonfire. Moonmen and their women congregated around the fire. A dozen flares sparked in a wide circle around them. A tall, long-haired Moonman strummed on a guitar that had only two strings. It was a strange tune. Some people danced. Others lay giggling on the ground, passing joints between them. A few people were having sex, though which of those were men, which were women, and who was doing exactly what with whom remained unclear to Branson. Spiegler just stared.

St. Abaddon stood tall in the center of the action. He smiled and chatted with his people. The boy ran free of his leash in tight circles around the fire, hollering to mark each successive orbit.

They dragged Spiegler into the crowd. The Moonmen leered and laughed, pointed and spat. They brought him to the fire and dropped him at its edge. The boy with no leash leaped over him, and ran on.

Branson considered running, but he was in no shape to make it far and he knew it. A failed escape might bring out their bloodlust. Instead, Branson walked straight into the midst of the party with as much a show of confidence as he could muster. His heart raced.

"Our guests have arrived," St. Abaddon called out, head tilted towards the sky, both arms outstretched. "Only two days until the full moon. Fate has provided you to us at a time of celebration. Tomorrow will bring fresh blessings to us. Tonight, we sing and dance and *drink*."

The leader of the Moonmen gripped Spiegler's wrist and helped him to his feet. The director wobbled and nearly fell back, but Abaddon propped him up. The little rose of blood at Spiegler's abdomen shone bright. Abaddon drew his face so close to Spiegler's that Branson wondered if he was about to kiss the injured man on the lips.

"For *you*, don't you see? We're celebrating for *you*. Tonight, fate will reveal its plan for you."

That wasn't promising.

"Bring them water," Abaddon commanded.

Wearing a flowing white dress, Sticks came to them with a flask. She held it to Branson's cracked lips and tipped it back. He'd no reason to trust the cool liquid wasn't poison, but once he tasted it, Branson gulped it down. As much spilled down his chin as in his throat, and Sticks let him drink until the flask was empty. Then it was Spiegler's turn. A Moonman passed Sticks a second flask. Spiegler took only a mouthful before turning his head to refuse the rest.

"You s-s-should really d-d-drink more." He glared at her with distrust. She took a quick swig from the flask and again offered it to him. "Y-y-you'll need-d-d it. W-w-when they rev-v-veal fate's-s-s plan, it'll w-w-weaken you. Th-th-the water-r-r will h-h-help."

They? Branson wondered. Spiegler drank, but did not take his eyes off Sticks.

"Good," St. Abaddon roared. The loose skin of his cheeks curled back to accommodate a wide smile. He plucked a lengthy firebrand from the pit by the cool end and rolled it over in the roaring fire until it made for a proper torch.

"It's time." St. Abaddon waved the torch in the night air and headed off into the open desert. The flicker of firelight cast a demonic glow in his eyes as he addressed his prisoners. "Tonight will change your lives."

Moonmen led Branson and Spiegler beyond the circle of flares. Away from the light, when Branson looked up he saw more stars in the sky than he'd known existed. The rest of the Moonmen and their women followed along in their own time, some walking alone, others in groups. It was like Moses leading a long line of Israelites away from the burning fires of Egypt and into the dark wilderness.

Spiegler gave up trying to move on his own and dragged his feet, which forced the Moonmen to half-carry, half-pull him along. Branson wondered if it was an act, then noticed the abdominal wound was bleeding again, and a fresh circle of bright blood soaked Spiegler's stained shirt.

St. Abaddon led the procession across the dunes to a wide plateau, which overlooked a sharp descent into a shadowed valley below. To Branson it seemed like they'd arrived at the edge of the world. With everyone gathered at the precipice, Abaddon spread his arms.

The Moonmen cheered.

"Open it," Abaddon commanded.

He stepped back and a cadre of Moonmen dropped to their knees. With cupped hands they clawed at the sandy soil, and quickly cleared a large metal rectangle hidden just beneath the ground. It was another shipping container, this one standing on end and buried deep in the earth. Reppy threw open the lock-bar and, with the help of three compatriots, pulled up hard to open the doors.

A pungent odor blasted out, a complex scent that was equal parts seawater, rotten fish, excrement, and city sewage, strong enough to taste it. Branson gagged and attempted to back away, but the Moonmen held him steady. An emaciated old woman with thinning gray hair down to her waist leaned over the edge of the container and held out a flare. The container was filled near to the brim with brackish water. Fine debris floated at the surface, mostly bits of bones and cloth. Branson could clearly make out a shirt button and a tangle of hair.

St. Abaddon brought his hands together and clapped loudly in a straightforward pattern of beats. Except for the two who propped up Spiegler, the rest of the Moonmen joined in, and the noise was deafening. Following their leader, the rhythm tightened and the pace of the clapping quickened.

Branson felt the same sort of anticipation he'd experienced as a child when his grandfather took him to a Southern Baptist Revival prayer meeting. Voices joined in *Fairest Lord Jesus*, the congregation nearly fainting en masse at the crescendo...

Light. Under the water, at first distant and indistinct, faint halos of light flickering in the dark; then rising, forming shapes, long bodies crossing, a graceful dance commencing as they approached. Long, glowing tubes, like snakes—*no*, Branson realized, *eels*—swimming in patterns, the phosphorescent pulse of their bodies casting an eerie blue light against the walls of the container.

Spiegler straightened and stood on his own.

Branson felt a soft breath on his neck. Stick whispered soft and low into his ear, like a lover's murmur just prior to falling asleep.

"They are fate's messengers."

"Show them," St. Abaddon ordered Reppy.

Branson feared they were about to be thrown into the water. Instead, Reppy withdrew from his satchel a short wooden pole fitted with a rusty steel hook, and dipped that into the container. Snaring one of the eels, he pulled and fished it out. It squirmed violently, long tail thrashing.

A Moonman wearing elbow-length rubber gloves grappled with the eel, hands slipping over the length of its body until finally he had a solid, one-handed hold on the thing. The gray-haired woman placed a bucket underneath the eel, and Reppy passed the pole to the gloved man in order to retrieve a hunting knife from his bag. The gloved man released the eel from the noose and stretched the beast taut using both hands. Reppy slid the knife through its center, and in a quick back and forth motion sliced the eel in two.

Both halves twitched furiously in death spasms, spiraling like coil springs in the Moonman's hands. Glowing blue liquid drained into the bucket. The old woman cackled. Once the two halves of the eel were drained, they fell still. The gloved man tossed the carcass back into the water, then bent down and dipped his fingers into the bucket. He stood and approached Spiegler. His slime-covered fingers glistened.

Keeping still, Spiegler only stared deep into the water. He seemed to be hypnotized.

"Welcome your fate," St. Abaddon said as he nodded. The gloved man streaked Spiegler's face with eel juice, painted diagonally from right eye to left jowl. For a moment, Spiegler didn't seem to notice and Branson thought maybe face painting was part of the ceremony.

Then Spiegler blinked. The blinking became incessant. Even the glass eye, as if the director were struggling to see out of both of them. A great shiver ran the length of his body, from head to toe. His arms and legs shook. He collapsed to the sand, rolling and thrashing. His arms slammed flat against his chest as if pulled by powerful magnets, hands curled at the wrists. He screamed out a warbling, roaring wail. The violence of the seizure popped Spiegler's prosthetic eye from its socket, and it rolled onto the sand like he'd laid an egg.

Abaddon laughed. The Moonmen and the old lady laughed. Even Sticks laughed an offbeat, stuttering cackle.

Branson bolted. Head up and shoulders down like a running back, he pushed through the wild-eyed, rhythmically clapping crowd. He came dangerously close to the sparking flares, and those blinded him for a moment, then once his vision returned, it was blurred. Branson collided full on with a naked Moonwoman, and stumbled, all momentum lost. Strong hands latched on to his arms and whipped him around to drag him back through the crowd. Branson screamed an incomprehensible language made up of pure terror. His captors dropped him at Stick's feet. She leaned down over him, and whispered.

"R-r-relax now."

Branson didn't relax. Couldn't. Instead his body went rigid on the sand, jaw screwed tight, fists clenched. He let loose a feral growl.

The gloved Moonman dipped his fingers back into the bucket, then approached Branson with his hands held up like a surgeon. Branson kicked with everything he had left. The heel of his shoe caught the gloved Moonman square in the nose, and he toppled over. His hand reflexively shot to his face, but the moment eel's blood touched his skin, the Moonman yelped in surprise.

Moonmen rushed in and pinned Branson's arms and legs hard to the earth.

"You ass," the gloved Moonman yelled, snatching up the bucket. With a wild swing, he splashed out its contents straight at Branson.

"D-d-don't fight-t-t it. L-l-let it take y-y-you where it-t-t w-w-wants you to g-g-go," Sticks said.

It was as if an electrical charge surged through Branson's body. His mind was aflame with alien thought, his vision exploded with a cosmic tapestry of colors brighter and more vibrant than he'd ever imagined could exist. Branson heard sounds beyond the range a human can hear. Sinister voices, speaking languages no human tongue could hope to form, harangued him. Smells and tastes triggered vivid memories that weren't his own but were somehow more real than real. Branson saw the earth rise up to meet him, though Branson was by then flat on his back, and staring vacantly up at a fathomless night sky.

Only half-heard amidst the chaos of his expanded universe, Stick's voice came to Branson. It was song and prayer and weeping, and the laughter of demons all at once.

"If-f-f you f-f-fight it, y-y-you'll die."

He fought.

TWENTY-ONE

Abriella stepped from the bus, downed the last of her convenience store coffee, and tossed the cup into the trash receptacle outside the motel. She confirmed what she'd written on her left palm: *Stay Inn Tonight, 440 Hunterdon Avenue, Room 212.*

Beneath its canopy, she was surprised by how nice the motel looked, a persimmon London cobblestone driveway curving back to a parking lot lined by a neat hedgerow. Wrought iron fencing separated a wide center courtyard from an Olympic-sized pool. A single white alder tree leaned over a line of cheap lounge chairs. The building itself was three stories high, with fine sand-lime brickwork and fruit wood window ledges.

Her sneakers let out a short peep as she climbed the exterior stairs. Abriella thought of how she'd never heard that squeak over the creaking of the floorboards in her own house. She reached the second-floor balcony. Room numbers started at 200, and all successive numbers were even. She supposed the odd numbered rooms were on the other side of the building.

At room 212, Abriella paused, her hand poised to knock, and she questioned her reasons for being here. She'd sat rooted to the kitchen table for hours, listening to the television and to her father snore, thinking over what Detective Woost had said. She'd told Branson Turaco that she could use a little danger in her life and that she wasn't afraid. The first statement was true. The second wasn't. She *was* scared. But Abriella knocked on the door at room 212 anyway.

Abriella was struck by a strange sensation, a sense of proximity, as if someone were standing immediately behind her. She turned on her heel but of course, there was only the balcony. The sensation that she was being watched remained. She looked over the balcony and down at the courtyard. It had been empty when she'd come through, but now a man dressed in white stood by the alder, and seemed to stare up at her. She could swear his pale skin shimmered in the strong moonlight.

The door to room 212 creaked open behind her. Turning away from the strange man below, Abriella focused on the man who stood in the doorway with his mouth not quite closed. He wore a yellow boxing robe.

"What are *you* doing here?"

Abriella fixed him with a glare that could've wilted an orchid.

"Sorry to interrupt you, Mr. Ponds."

"Unbelievable." Michael Ponds ran one hand through his thinning hair. "How the hell did you even know where to find me?"

"From the post-it note on your desk."

"There's no post-it note," he shot back.

"There *was*. On Monday, while you were at lunch with the receptionist. There was a post-it note then. And I have a photographic memory."

With a condescending nod Abriella cocked her head to one side, never breaking eye contact. She discreetly slipped one hand over the other to hide the handwriting that'd destroy her bluff.

Ponds blocked the door with his hands on either side of the frame. His robe opened at the top, revealing tufts of graying chest hair.

"So, what do you want?"

Looking beyond him, Abriella waved to the Oriental girl in the motel room. She wore a matching yellow robe.

"I need your ride. Don't worry, not the bullshit Lexus. I don't want to be seen around in a symptom of some white guy's mid-life crisis. I want the Jeep parked out back."

"You're serious?"

"Dead."

"Get the hell outta here. Go home. I don't even know you. You're just some kid from work. An intern, no less. Not even smart enough to get paid for the shitwork you do. Why would you ever think I'd lend you my car?"

Reaching into the pocket of her hoodie, Abriella pulled out a sheath of stapled papers folded in half. She handed them to Ponds, who reluctantly took them.

"I can go, if you want. There's another bus in half an hour. But if I have to do that, then your wife gets some juicy reading material. She's home, right? What, you give her the old *working late at the office* bit?"

Ponds examined the printouts. With each successive page, his hands shook more.

"How did--"

"Really? I mean, you ask me to do exactly this sort of thing all the time at work. You know, at that job I'm not even smart enough to earn a paycheck for doing." Abriella stood defiant. "I guess this *is* a little different. I mean, credit card receipts for motel rooms, strip clubs, low rent Asian massage parlors. You'd think this stuff would be difficult to get. But, like I said, I have a photographic memory, while you need to leave notes to yourself on your desk. Your user names and passwords were easy. It took me five minutes to open up your entire financial history."

"That's illegal," Ponds said through clenched teeth.

"Yeah, well, so is hiring prostitutes." Abriella looked past him into the motel room. "But here we are. So. Do I get the keys, or does wifey get the goods?"

It didn't take Ponds long to decide.

As she climbed down the stairs with the keys to Ponds' Jeep in her hand, Abriella looked for the peculiar man in the courtyard by the alder tree. He wasn't there. Even the feeling of being watched was gone. She remembered that she'd also told Branson Turaco she wanted the safety net gone from her life. Now, as she approached the Jeep, Abriella felt uneasy and vulnerable. The net was gone. She was alone.

TWENTY-TWO

Marius Spiegler knew about drugs.

His relationship with pharmaceuticals began when he was twelve years old and bedridden with rheumatic fever. The family doctor prescribed Valium to fight the insomnia that came with the sickness. In high school Spiegler discovered girls, but had little success gaining their affection until older friends first offered him alcohol, then marijuana. Spiegler didn't much enjoy the intoxication itself, but the attention of drunken or high girls was another matter. During his two-and-a-half years of college, Spiegler experimented with acid and cocaine. He discovered that psychedelics weren't his thing. He didn't need complete control, but he needed to keep some. Cocaine, he found, fueled intense creative bursts. And his stabs at painting and photography only led more women to his bed.

As Spiegler released a stream of blue vomit, he swore to himself he'd never touch another drug ever, no matter how attractive the party girl in his sights. Eel's blood was worse than any acid trip ever. It was simply too intense and bewildering to endure.

He'd lived his entire adult life in Hollywood. He knew addicts, some very well. Marius Spiegler knew drugs. This eel's blood was altogether different.

Back in their container, Branson was rolled into a tight fetal curl at Spiegler's side, and when Spiegler touched Branson's forehead it felt like a damp washcloth, loose and wrinkled skin perspiring even in the cool morning air. Branson's unblinking, bloodshot eyes were strained wide open. His breathing was slowed to an infrequent draw, his chest flat and still for what seemed like minutes at a time before he'd convulse, then suck down a quick gulp of air. Twice Spiegler thought his friend had died, but the violent bouts of thrashing and screaming that followed proved differently. During the course of the night, sometimes Branson mumbled random strings of words and numbers, mostly in English, other times in what sounded like gibberish, most often a combination of both.

Though Branson wasn't conscious, he clearly wasn't in any normal state of unconsciousness either. Branson was like a man possessed, all motor control malfunctioning, his personality subsumed by something unknown. He thrashed on the floor, his back arched, extremities flailing.

The Moonmen had left them with a half-filled gallon jug of water. Spiegler drank some, but not much, in spite of his thirst. His stomach hurt with every swallow he managed. He did his best to keep Branson hydrated, pouring water from cupped hands into his dry mouth during those lapses when the stricken man quieted.

Progress was slow, but by the time the sun's heat had built, Branson's fits came with less frequency. He stopped speaking in tongues. Finally, with most of the water gone, Branson fell into what resembled a restless, but otherwise normal sleep.

Spiegler didn't sleep at all. The wound in his side wouldn't allow it. The eel's blood served as an anesthetic while active, but the pain came stronger as the drug's effects faded. Running a finger beneath his shirt, Spiegler felt carefully around the edges of the small, puckered wound. His hand came away slick with blood. The leakage seemed the same, but darker.

That wasn't good.

The morning wore on, and the early coolness inside the container dissipated, replaced by stifling heat. The trapped warmth built, which turned their prison into a crude but effective oven. Spiegler regularly turned Branson to keep him from frying on the sheet metal floor. Spiegler sweated, bled and waited. He gave Branson a last swallow, then finished the water. He wondered how long they'd survive without a refill, as the desert heat rose. Could they make it through an entire day? Given the shape they were in, he was inclined to doubt it.

Branson awoke, sputtering and coughing. It took maybe an hour for him to push himself into a sitting position. He wiped a dab of dried vomit from the corner of his mouth. He parted his lips as if to speak but failed to offer anything comprehensible, so he waited a moment, cleared his throat and tried again.

"—long was it?"

"Don't know exactly, they took my watch. But it's been the rest of the night and at least all morning. By the heat and the direction of the light, I figure it's afternoon."

Branson spit. "Can't get rid of the taste. Assholes leave us any water?"

"Some. I gave you most of it. Anyway, we're tapped. Taste will fade."

"I feel like I died."

The men lapsed into silence. Spiegler didn't know how to broach the subject that was on his mind. He thought from the look on Branson's face that maybe it was on his friend's mind too. Finally, Spiegler asked.

"What did *you* see?"

Branson didn't answer, not for a long time. When he did speak, his voice was stronger but his tone had turned tremulous, as if he was afraid Spiegler wouldn't believe him.

"Most of it was just overload. Too much to process. A lot of stuff that doesn't make any sense."

"Yeah," Spiegler agreed with a knowing nod.

"But some of it..."

"You don't have to tell me if—" Suddenly, Spiegler regretted asking.

"No, it's fine," Branson assured him. "It's just... difficult. A lot of it... wasn't like a dream. It felt real, reliving memories, only they weren't always memories."

Spiegler nodded again. "Dreams."

"No, not dreams." Branson searched for the words. "Too rich for dreams. In a dream, you can eat cherry pie and know it's delicious, but you can't taste *how* it's delicious. This wasn't that. It was more like..."

"Go ahead."

"...like things that haven't happened yet, but will."

That wasn't at all what Spiegler expected to hear. His own trip was a dark ride through the past, a collection of scenes he'd tried for years to drown in a flood of alcohol. Mostly, it was just the accident looping over and over, but slower and more detailed than real life ever could be. Alex and Nhu screaming. Then the low-hung beam flattening their tiny faces and cracking open their skulls before their heads tore off. There was film of it, but Spiegler had only ever looked at that when it played at his trial.

"I saw her, Marius. I saw Madeline." Branson cried. "But it wasn't just seeing her. I was there, with her. We were far out at sea on a boat, and I had a beard, and she called me Daddy. I wanted to hold her but couldn't."

"Why couldn't you?" Branson exhaled.

"They had my hands tied."

"They? The Moonmen?"

"No, someone else." Branson's face paled, as if his dream captors terrified him even in the real world. "I was so close but couldn't get to her. They always stood between us, and I knew that she wanted to escape from them with me, but they held her back. Not with rope. With something invisible, something I couldn't understand."

The heat grew intolerable. They'd need more water and soon, or they'd dehydrate and that would be a bad way to die. An awful stench, equal parts body odor, vomit, and blood, hung in the stale air. Again Spiegler got the impression that Branson held back for fear he wouldn't be believed.

"You think you saw the future?"

"I dunno. Felt like it."

"Was I there?"

Branson thought about that for a moment then answered slowly. "No. But maybe it was just *my* future."

Spiegler reached inside his shirt and with two fingers gently touched his wound. They came away wet.

"Then again, maybe not..."

TWENTY-THREE

No one brought water. Instead, it came from the sky. First, clouds washed the sun from the narrow slit in the shipping container. Then thunder shook the earth, and finally there came the tapping of rain on metal, like a down-tempo snare drum at first, later a steady roll. The rusted container leaked a few irregular drops from overhead. Branson extended one hand beneath the leak and waited. After a few moments, a single raindrop landed in his palm, exploding on impact. Branson drew back his hand and licked off the moisture. It tasted of rust, but it was good. Both men drank, then slept.

After a while, lightning pierced even the gloom of their prison, and the thunderclap that followed shook them from their sleep.

Though the brief respite brought Branson closer to some semblance of normalcy, it'd done no favors for Spiegler. The man looked worse. Less rested, if anything. At his midsection, the director's shirt was colored in a dark crimson stain. Spiegler caught a raindrop on his tongue, smacked his lips, turned to Branson and smiled.

It was the saddest smile Branson had ever seen. It reminded him of his boyhood dog as the vet injected him with pentobarbital. Roughboy yawned once and fell into permanent sleep. From the long lines that etched his face, Branson feared Spiegler wouldn't get off so easy. The thought struck him hard and Branson might've cried, if he weren't dehydrated. He'd known Marius Spiegler for only two days, which under normal circumstances wouldn't be near enough time to form any kind of real friendship, but these were hardly normal circumstances.

Branson couldn't help but feel responsible for the director. As wretched as it might've been, the man had willingly left his life behind in order to help him. He'd given Spiegler every opportunity to decline. Had even asked him to leave. Spiegler stayed anyway, and though he might die for that choice, still he didn't complain. That's the sort of thing friends do.

A volley of shouting voices tore his attention away from thoughts of Spiegler's wellbeing. A fresh roar of thunder and a loud lightning snap swallowed the noise. Many pairs of feet ran in wet soil; storm clouds rumbled. A motorcycle's engine rattled to life; someone barked orders from a higher plateau.

"You hear that?" Branson didn't wait for a reply and half crawled, half pulled himself to the prison's door to peer through the narrow slit, and see what might be seen. It wasn't much.

Branson saw a landscape as fluid as the ocean, mud rolling in windblown waves. Flashes of lightning revealed Moonmen scrambling here and there, long hair and bandanas flowing in the storm. They looked well armed.

"Something's got 'em good and spooked," Branson said.

A second set of voices joined the fray. Unable to see clearly, Branson abandoned the slit, and pressed his ear to the door. The rain on the roof was amplified almost to the point of pain, but the voices outside were made clearer.

"—Stop—"

"—Right there—"

"—Hold—"

"—Lower your weap—"

What sounded like thunder rolling their way grew into the unmistakable sound of a helicopter, moving fast and riding low.

"Police?" Spiegler asked.

Compared to the roar of thunder and the helicopter, the initial gunshots were faint and nonthreatening. Amidst those, voices continued to yell. Some screams trailed off or were cut short. Others wailed on and on. Then a small, round hole was blown through the door. A staccato string of clangs rang through the container.

"Ricochet," Branson yelled. He quickly patted himself down, and called to Spiegler, "You hit?"

"I don't think so."

"We have to get out of here." Outside the container, gunfire continued nonstop. At some point, their luck would run out.

"Can you walk?"

"Not through a metal door, I can't." Spiegler rose on unsteady legs like a newborn fawn taking its first steps. With no small effort he managed to stand, slightly bent, with one hand on his abdomen.

The taste of rust, which still lingered on Branson's tongue from the rainwater, inspired him. How long had the shipping container lain exposed to the brutal desert elements? How many storms had made for how many rust spots, spread throughout the metal like wine stains on a tablecloth? Sliding into position, Branson rolled back on his tailbone, drew in his legs, then kicked at the door with both feet. It rattled. He grimaced, leaned on his elbows for leverage, and struck again. The door shook. Red dust cascaded from the ceiling and threatened to choke him. Spiegler dropped down beside Branson and assumed the position.

"On three?" Branson looked at his friend and nodded.

"One," they said in unison.

A second shot cut through the container. Sparks flew as it careened off the walls.

"Two..." Together, the two men held their breath.

Three was lost in a cacophony of gunfire and thunder, but their kick proved well-coordinated. The door broke free of its lock and swung open to a scene of madness.

Police SUVs tore across the dunes as armed Moonmen ran between the rickety dwellings and rock walls that made for Tranquility Base, firing wildly at anything and nothing. A troop of cops in riot gear chased them through the camp, answering fire.

"There." Branson shouted above the din.

Branson took the lead, and hoping against hope not to get shot in the bargain, both men ran headlong across the sand. Rain sent accumulated sand off Branson's forehead into his eyes and, still dizzy from the encounter with eel's blood, he didn't dare check on Spiegler; the director would just have to take care of himself. But once Branson reached a nook in the rock wall, the first thing he did was look for his friend. A bullet slammed into the rock, kicking up sparks that bit Branson's face like fiery mosquitoes. He dove for what shelter there was in the cleft rock, and huddled there, arms wrapped tight over his head. When someone thumped down hard next to him, it was the wheezing grunt of his friend that identified Spiegler.

The break in the rock wall provided at least some cover. The rain abated, some. Branson peeked out, and from their slightly elevated vantage point, he enjoyed a reasonably clear view of the battle, which seemed to be winding down. Or, if not that, it was definitely one-sided. Police vehicles encircled the camp and the riot squad pressed forward. The Moonmen had no organized strategy so far as Branson could tell. They ran about wildly, individually or in pairs, and fired their weapons into the gathering darkness. Unarmed Moonmen scrambled between shanties, seeking shelter in what was quickly being reduced to piles of rubble. Police headlights illuminated their way.

"Well, would you look at *that*..." Spiegler exclaimed.

The law closed in upon the Moonmen. The police threw a burning spotlight on the camp. Caught like a moth in a beam, a scrawny Moonman took aim with a hunting rifle at the helicopter. A single shot from somewhere shaved off the top of the Moonman's head. He collapsed onto the wet ground, dead before his knees buckled. Branson followed the line of impact to the highest point on the nearest dune. Four police sharpshooters were crouched there.

Another bullet struck the rock wall, perilously close to Spiegler's head. The director curled into the fetal position. As the first cop made the camp's circle, he shouted for the Moonmen to *Stand down, stand down, stand*—when an arrow passed through his neck, and dropped him on the spot.

Perched at the peak of a tall lean-to at the far end of camp, Reppy slid another arrow across his bow. When the police returned fire on his position, he never flinched. Instead, he drew on a second officer and killed him too. The helicopter dipped low over Reppy, a whirlwind of sand and debris rising as if in greeting. The side door slid open. The cops inside aimed their automatic weapons and fired in the general direction of Reppy. The lean-to exploded in splinters and, struggling to keep his footing, Reppy tried to aim a third arrow at his assailants. The pilot spun his craft around and Reppy vanished, a shower of red thrown out by the tail rotor.

Near the center of camp, St. Abaddon fled for his tipi with Sticks close behind. Anger devoured Branson's fear. He needed to act, and act now. If the cops arrested, or worse, killed the leader of the Moonmen, perhaps Branson's best chance to solve the mystery of Madeline's disappearance went with him. Spiegler's hands were clasped over his face. He lay in the sand, breathing heavily.

"You just stay here. I've got to go." Branson chose to take the spasmodic movement of Spiegler's head as agreement.

Branson forced himself to stand, but kept his head hunched down at the shoulders. Hustling as best he could along the rock wall, he cut over behind the shipping container, and from there into the outskirts of camp. His heart pounded in his chest and neck. Bodies of dead Moonmen littered Tranquility Base, with more yet to come. From one of those, Branson lifted a pistol.

He ran fast as he could across the wet sand, ducking in-between huts hung with weathered Indian rugs to avoid getting shot. He came face to face with a trio of armed Moonmen, who raised their shotguns at Branson, but before they could fire were mowed down from the side by automatic weapons fire. Two of the Moonmen dropped dead on the spot. The third was sprawled on the wet ground, holding his neck and gargling blood.

Again the rain pounded down. Lightning lit the valley and Branson caught a snapshot of the camp under siege. In a coordinated attack meant to end things, police were working their way towards the center, hut by hut. There was little time left for Branson to get to the tipi, and to Abaddon. Leading with the gun, Branson made one last, mad dash to Abaddon's lair. He threw back the flap and burst inside.

The floor was aflame with flickering candles. St. Abaddon sat cross-legged at the center. His eyes were closed, elbows at his side, open hands on his knees, palms up. Sticks lay before him, crumpled like a twisted rag. Branson leveled the pistol at St. Abaddon and stepped full into the tipi.

"What have you *done?*"

"Only what fate required." The big man's eyes remained closed and he remained strangely serene, considering the circumstances. "These events have all been foretold to me through the blood of the eels. It was her time."

Stick's head was twisted at an angle no one could survive. Ugly black bruises speckled her neck. Branson imagined St. Abaddon's hands around it, choking and turning until her spine cracked, and bone and cartilage shattered like ceramic. Had this happened to Madeline? Was she taken from him simply to be destroyed by this meditating monster that answered only to his premeditated version of fate?

"Where's my daughter?" Branson yelled.

"Lost," St. Abaddon answered. "Like us all."

Branson stepped past Sticks and pressed the muzzle of the pistol against the huge man's closed right eye. Images of the unthinkable things St. Abaddon might've done to his daughter beset him. Was she beaten? Raped? Even tortured? Was Madeline's death even worse than what St. Abaddon had delivered to poor Sticks? Branson desperately wanted to kill the son of a bitch right then and there, to pull the trigger that'd send metal and fire though his eye socket and explode his barbaric brain. Instead he pressed the gun harder against the man's eye.

"Where. Is. She."

St. Abaddon opened his left eye and gazed at Branson.

"There have been so many children pass through. Do you really think I remember your daughter?"

"What do you do with the children?" Spittle flecked St. Abaddon's face as Branson screamed the question. "What did you do with her?"

St. Abaddon's expression lightened into a cat-like playfulness, as if he were the one holding the gun.

"If I tell you, will you go to her? Like a good father, would you rush to rescue your daughter?"

Branson cocked the pistol.

"And the people who bought her from us? Will you kill them all, if that's what it takes to save her? Would you be able to murder them with a knife, just to feel their warm blood spread across your knuckles? Or with your bare hands? Would you do that? *Could* you?"

Branson looked down at Stick and wondered if he could kill with his bare hands, or a knife. Or even with the gun he now held. He didn't honestly know, and he faltered, searching for an answer.

"Don't have to tell me. *Show* me. Pull that trigger." St. Abaddon leaned into the gun, hard. The front sight of the gun punctured the Moonman's eyeball, which drew yellow fluid that trickled down his cheek. "It's already been shown to me. I've seen you pull the trigger."

The thought of Madeline sprawled out on the tipi's floor, sprawled out like Sticks, with a single thin line of blood leading from the corner of her lips to the soil, made Branson want to. Badly.

"*Do it,*" Abaddon hissed. "Embrace your fate and deliver me to mine."

Branson swiped wet, matted hair from over his eyes with his free hand. He pulled back on the trigger just a little, enough to feel it move. Abaddon was so close. It was so easy. And he was begging for it.

"Tell me."

Abaddon offered a smile of surpassing ugliness. "The Fontainebleau pier, midnight tomorrow. They'll come to trade children for eels. If you truly want your daughter, meet them there."

Branson took one step back, maintaining his aim.

"Now you know what you need. Fate will guide you, if you let it. But fate always demands a sacrifice. Today, it calls for my blood. So you must give fate what it wants. Do it now."

Branson wanted to and decided he would. Bruce Donne had stolen Madeline from her bed to sell to this man, who in turn traded his daughter to others. Perhaps Abaddon really was just a middleman, but if he'd never existed Donne would never have taken her. Branson stared into the hopeful face of the man who'd destroyed his family and his life.

It wasn't even murder, really.

"Put down the gun, Mr. Turaco-"

Branson didn't. He looked over his shoulder and saw two police commandos in body armor standing at the entrance to the tent. They flanked a third figure who removed her helmet. Assault rifles were aimed at his back. Outside, the gunfire died down. It sounded like a last, few kernels of popcorn popping.

Branson returned his attention to St. Abaddon, who remained under the gun.

"Good evening, Detective Woost."

TWENTY-FOUR

Branson eased his throbbing finger off the trigger but kept the gun leveled square at St. Abaddon. He kept the Moonman in his peripheral vision as he tilted his head to address Detective Woost.

"What a coincidence, meeting you here."

"Just put the gun down," Woost shouted.

He had the information he needed, but didn't figure Woost would let him just walk away to put it to use. At the very least there'd be days of interrogation led by men with deep frowns and two-day old stubble. Even in the unlikely event that he wasn't arrested, Branson wouldn't be free in time to pursue Madeline's abductors at the Fontainebleau pier. "I can't do that."

One of the commandos said, "I *will* shoot you."

"Lower your weapon," the other warned. "Last chance."

St. Abaddon whispered low, as if his lips had blown the words directly to Branson's ears.

"Choose. Either sacrifice me, or sacrifice your chance of finding your daughter."

The gun in Branson's hand wavered.

"Time's up—" one of the cops yelled.

"No, wait—" Woost screamed.

Outside, there was a sudden *Whoosh* followed by an ear-splitting explosion, an apocalyptic sound that drowned out all lesser noise in its wake. The bone mosaic on the walls of the tipi rattled in response. A startling, powerful sense of déjà vu overwhelmed Branson; he'd seen those interlocked bones dance once before, after St. Abaddon blew pipe smoke in his face. But there was no time to consider that, no time to pull the trigger of the handgun, much less lower it, no time even to blink.

The police helicopter crashed outside the tipi, sending a huge ball of orange flame into the air. The canvas was pierced by hot shards. One of the cops fell away, apparently struck by shrapnel. The animal bones overhead began to fall, leg and arm bones cascaded down like knives. Skulls shattered against the ground. Woost and the remaining cop ducked and covered their heads. St. Abaddon again closed his eyes.

Branson stood paralyzed in the center of the tipi, still pointing the gun at Abaddon, staring up at the gaping hole where the tipi's peak used to be. Bones, and pieces of bones showered him from all sides. He was staggered by the realization that he'd seen this too, in feverish dreaming induced by eel's blood.

A coyote skull tumbled through the air. It was missing the bottom jaw but grinned nevertheless. The skull hit Branson on the hand with the gun, exploding into a fine, white powder when it did. Branson dropped the gun and staggered back.

St. Abaddon's face went slack. In the center of his brow was a small black hole, like a third eye. A thin trace of blood raced down the slope of his nose, and dripped from its tip. Branson's gun lay on the ground. Had he pulled the trigger, or had fate?

A large rib shaped like a curved arrow plunged into Stick's lifeless body. A wave of heat struck Branson as fire raced up one side of the tipi. The stench of charred animal skins, leather, and hemp filled the air.

Branson saw his opportunity and took it. He leapt through a fresh opening torn in the tipi. The remains of the police chopper, with its main rotor still spinning, reached for the night sky like the crooked, spinning blades of a windmill. The fire spread quickly across Tranquility Base, and by then most of the shanties were involved.

As he made his way, Branson stumbled over both the bodies of Moonmen and the remains of their homes. He leaped over a tangle of wire and lumber, and landed next to a bloody mass of human flesh. Miraculously intact, Reppy's satchel lay near what remained of the Moonman. Branson snagged it off the ground and continued to run. He stumbled and caught himself and stumbled some more, all the way across the camp.

The last of the Moonmen were surrendering. The cops yelled at them to get on their knees and put their hands behind their heads. There were no Miranda warnings issued; this was war. Cast in firelight, the face of the law only darkened. Then the cops opened fire. A volley of shots rang out. After that, the only sounds that remained were the cackle of fire, and the pelting rain. The battle was over. The Moonmen were no more.

Branson clung to the shadows and moved silently along the edge of camp, scurrying past open gaps between structures. He reached the rock wall and followed it. The rain eased. The valley fairly glowed with destruction. The stench of fuel, burning lumber, and gunpowder wafted from Tranquility Base. Branson didn't look back. There was little left to see.

Spiegler was where Branson had left him. Still curled into a fetal ball, the director raised his head from under his arms, mouth open, blood trickling from the corners. Branson dropped down beside him, and caught his breath before speaking.

"We've got to go."

Spiegler attempt to stand but failed.

"Detective Woost is here," Branson said as he spilled the contents of Reppy's satchel onto a flat rock. Dozens of small, carved animal bones fell out, as well as a number of arrowheads, bullets of various calibers, wood screws, and a bundle of wire. Their wallets and wristwatches came last. Branson handed Spiegler his possessions. "And she's seen me. She knows we're here. They'll find us. We have to go."

At the bottom of Reppy's satchel, Branson found an envelope. It was Madeline's college fund. He thumbed through the cash, found it all there, and pocketed it. Pulling himself up, Branson offered a hand to Spiegler. He took it. The director forced himself up, then wobbled. He couldn't stand on his own. Throwing an arm over Branson's shoulder steadied him. Together they headed up a short incline along the rock wall.

They clambered over a jagged lip of rock and began the long climb to safer ground. With every awkward step, the burning Moonmen camp receded. Raging flames sent the men's shadows wavering in front of them, elongated caricatures like stick figures. Spiegler's feet slid out from under him. Branson caught his friend and pulled him closer still. He knew they couldn't continue like that for long. The strain of dehydration, hunger, and fatigue was nearly unbearable, even without Branson carrying the additional load. For his part, Spiegler lolled between consciousness and not so much, lucid for a time, then mumbling like a drunk. Soon, Branson would be forced to make a terrible decision—whether to abandon his friend to the desert, or put his own life at risk.

Branson's heart beat like a timpani pounded by a rubber mallet, each strike reverberating through his body with a simultaneous throb in his lips, fingertips, and toes. His eyesight faltered. The desert blurred and warped as he reached the top of the rise. His ankles twisted, and he yelped in pain as his feet slid out from under him. Falling to the soil, Branson chose to hold on to Spiegler rather than release him and prevent his fall. They hit the ground with a crunch of muscle and bone.

Branson had nothing left; he just lay there on the sand.

Spiegler exhaled, shallow and slow.

"Madeline," Branson whispered, through quivering lips. "I tried, honey. I tried."

He closed his eyes and waited for the pain to drain away into numbness. He waited for his senses to dull and his hearing to fade. Branson waited for his memories to trickle down to nothing, then desert him. Instead, there came the unmistakable sound of an approaching vehicle. He wasn't even sure if it was another hallucination. He kept his eyes shut, not wanting to know if it was. The roar of the engine grew louder until Branson could hear the rattle of sheet metal and the protests of a suspension taking serious punishment from riding the rough desert two-track. The thing skidded to a halt and for a moment, all was quiet. Then a door opened and footsteps approached. A voice sounded very near to his ear.

"No, you don't. I came all the way out here. The two of you best not be dead."

It was Abriella Nelson, and she was no hallucination. To Branson she was as beautiful a creature as ever existed. Unable even to whimper, he mouthed the words *thank you*. In return, she wiped soil from his face with soft, small hands.

"You know, if I'd have listened to you, you'd have been coyote breakfast by morning. So I'll make you a deal. I'll drag your sorry ass out of here, and you don't ever even *think* of telling me what to do ever again. Deal?"

"Deal," he lied. Guilt compounded Branson's pain.

Abriella proved stronger than she looked. Gripping Branson by the armpits, she dragged him over to the Jeep, and heaved him up onto the passenger seat. Then she went back for Spiegler. The smaller of the two men, she had less trouble with him, and dumped the director in the back seat. Branson wanted to ask her if Spiegler was alive or dead, but after having tried twice and failing both times, that'd just have to wait. Abriella jumped into the driver's seat and reached over, tilted Branson's head back and dropped two pills into his mouth.

"They're just chewable aspirin, kid's stuff. I don't know how much good they'll do you, but it's all I got."

Branson gulped the pills dry and didn't have the energy to choke when they got stuck halfway down. He swallowed hard, twice, and cleared his throat.

Abriella hit the accelerator. The tires kicked up a torrent of sand before gaining traction. She headed east, out of the canyon.

Branson relaxed in his seat and let sleep take him. At the very least, *he* wasn't dead.

TWENTY-FIVE

Drumming on the steering wheel with her thumbs, Abriella listened with growing concern to the irregular breathing of her passengers. They were in bad shape. They looked broken and depleted, as if they'd taken an enormous syringe to the heart, extracting the essences of each of them, leaving only empty husks behind.

The road was still slick, but the rain had died down to spittle, and it'd been an hour of open road since Abriella had seen another car, so she kept the speedometer needle on 85. California state highways were infamous speed traps; they'd just have to take their chances. To keep her mind off things, Abriella turned on the radio. Country music blared and she ratcheted it back until the twang was little more than a murmur. It was better than nothing.

"How'd you find us?"

Spiegler's voice drifted up from the back seat, and the sight of him startled her. The man didn't look well. Seated at an odd angle with his back arched, and his head bobbing up and down, he looked like a ventriloquist's dummy. A creature both living and dead, animate yet transparently mechanical, and a mockery of vitality.

For a long moment Abriella found it hard to speak. She stopped drumming her thumbs against the wheel, and clicked off the radio. Tires racing along asphalt hummed loud.

"I've been following the police radio frequencies on the net. And while Detective Woost never came right out and said it, it's Tiffany clear to me that she put a GPS transmitter on Mr. Turaco's car while you two were locked up overnight. They've been on you all along."

"Bitch," Spiegler muttered.

"*Me?*"

"No. Her."

"Uhh-huh," Abriella agreed.

"Got a cigarette? Anything, even a menthol? Beggars can't be choosers."

"Don't smoke."

"Beautiful *and* smart."

Abriella couldn't believe her ears. "You hitting on me?"

"Yes," Spiegler answered. "Never know, an older, dying, alcoholic Cyclops might be just your type."

"Well, older..."

Abriella smiled and Spiegler laughed. That spiraled into a wet coughing fit. He covered his mouth with both hands, and after the hacking stopped, inspected his hands, then frowned. Plainly, Spiegler didn't like what he saw.

"You ever wonder what your death will be like?"

"No," Abriella said.

"Me either. I mean, I don't wonder anymore."

She bit her bottom lip, and glanced over at Branson, still asleep in the passenger seat.

"Will he be okay, you think?"

"They drugged him. Nasty stuff. An overdose. But he did pretty well there, for a while. Yeah, I think he'll be okay." Spiegler's tone left Abriella unconvinced.

"When he came to you, why did you help him?"

"Why did you?" Spiegler countered.

Abriella shrugged. "It was better than what I was doing."

"Me too. How sad is that?"

They rode for a while in silence. Every few minutes she stole a quick look at Spiegler in the rear view mirror. He was barely holding on. Each time he seemed to be hunched over farther.

"There's a small town up here. Norville. Kind of cut off from the rest of the world. They keep to themselves. My Gran lived there. They have a small hospital. Doubt they'll ask many questions."

"Okay." The tone of Spiegler's voice told her he appreciated the sentiment, but had his doubts.

Abriella turned off the highway onto a road named One Mile Lane, which regardless of the name continued on for several miles, then ended at a T. She hooked the Jeep left, passing a weathered sign that welcomed them to Norville, CA, Population 934.

At the center of town was a main street of old houses converted into small shops, complete with porches and hand-painted signs. Everything was closed for the night. The hospital was outside of town, a mile or two farther down the road.

For a hospital, it was tiny. Just a single floor, no larger than most rural grammar schools. The entrance to the emergency room was well lit, while the rest of the hospital was dark. Abriella pulled up to the entrance.

"Can you walk?"

"I've had a little rest back here, so maybe." Spiegler forced himself out of the car. He shook like an old man as he struggled to maintain balance, but somehow remained ambulatory. Abriella killed the engine, and started to get out to assist him, but he put his hand against the door, and shook his head.

"No. Even in the smallest of Lilliputian towns, there will still be questions. You two can't afford those. Go. Get him somewhere safe."

"Okay." She knew he was right. Spiegler winked.

"Take care of your sweet ass."

Though Abriella blushed, sadness overwhelmed her. She had to resist the urge to wake Branson for the chance to say goodbye to his friend. More than anything, what he needed was to sleep. So for both of them, she said simply, "Thank you."

TWENTY-SIX

An Air Tractor AT-802F released a geyser of water from the tanks hidden in its floats. Fire trucks couldn't navigate the canyon, so the airplane was called in to extinguish the flames. Detective Woost wondered why they'd bother. As far as she was concerned, the entire encampment should be left to burn to the ground.

The SWAT team attended to the wounded and fallen. Medevacs were called in to remove police and Moonmen alike. Dead cops were secured in black body bags by their brothers in blue, who with grace and surpassing dignity loaded them into unmarked, all-terrain vehicles.

A figure moved among their ranks in quiet fury. Police Commissioner Warren Gideon had an Old Testament name and the personality to match. Locating Woost, he dropped words on her like boulders from on high.

"You have any idea what this is?" His hands swept through the air. "This is Ruby Ridge. This is Waco. This is Senate hearings and investigative journalists going through your trash at three in the morning—"

"Commissioner, this wasn't—"

"I'm told we've got seven dead troopers in the desert and dozens of civilians likewise. God knows how many injured. And I didn't even know there was a damn operation going on, much less that you played a part in it."

"It wasn't—"

"—Supposed to go down like this?" Gideon cut her off. "Every time someone screws up, that's exactly what I hear. Things didn't go according to plan. Please, at least tell me you had proper authorization to ride along."

"It was my information, and I called in a few favors. ATF, state police, the moment I mentioned this site, these people, everyone wanted in. It got very serious very fast."

Gideon breathed out hard and for so long, she thought he might deflate.

"What are *you* doing out here anyway? Looking to get yourself killed?"

"It's my case."

"*What* case?" The Air Tractor looped around for another pass.

"Branson Turaco."

"You've a suspect in custody," Gideon fumed. "More than a suspect, from what I've been told. Got a full confession, right?"

The plane dove close to the flames and released another stream of water. The white-noise hiss of dying fire drowned out all other sounds. Woost waited for it to fade.

"Thirty-eight pages of confession, yeah. I ask Bruce Donne whether he kidnapped Tyler Davis, he says yes. Lauren Sunnyfield? Yes, ma'am. Tiffany Mason? Certainly. I give him my nephew's name and Donne's eager to say he took him too, which would be a surprise to my brother and his wife. And my nephew."

"Happens. Henry Lee Lucas gave false confessions to every crime the Texas Attorney General threw at him. Doesn't mean Donne's not telling the truth about most of the kids."

"The Turaco case is different. Nothing adds up. There's something else going on here."

"Roy Faune thought it was different, too." With mention of Roy, Gideon's anger seemed to fade, and while the statement wasn't invested with emotion, the insinuation was clear. "Well? Didn't he?"

"Sir, this isn't—"

"Roy was a friend. There was a little Italian dive where we'd meet up after work and talk. Sometimes. Sometimes that's just what he told his wife. And I stood ready to cover for him, though I never had to. It wasn't that I condoned what the two of you were up to, but I respected you both enough to let you make your own judgment and deal with the fallout when the time came." The past tense of respect hit Woost like a slap. Gideon paused, and sighed. "But *this* case. I've known investigators who get fixated on a pet case. This is something different. That's the word you used, right?"

Woost hadn't realized Gideon knew she'd had an affair with her partner and had no response.

"Do you think Roy would've thought catching Branson Turaco worth the lives of all these people?"

Woost blanched.

"A man kills his daughter, that's the worst sort of crime. But how many more bodies are you willing to put six feet under to chase justice? The case is five years old. You know the odds. You wouldn't roll the dice like this in Vegas, and that's only money, not people's lives."

"Five years' worth of casework. I'm supposed to throw that away? All of Roy's work?" Woost turned her head away from the Commissioner and pretended to watch the last standing shanty burn. She didn't want him to see her cry.

"No, of course not. But this is one first class fubar we've got on our hands. The press is going to latch on to this like nobody's business. You just helped turn this cult into a symbol of police violence. There'll be enough consequences to go around, and you shouldn't be surprised if a lot of that falls on you."

"So where does that leave me?" she asked softly.

"I won't file suspension paperwork until the publicity demands it. Stay in your office until then. Catch up on your filing, or something."

Woost dabbed her eyes, cleared her throat and turned to face the Commissioner.

"Thank you, sir."

"And Detective Woost? Hire a lawyer."

TWENTY-SEVEN

Marius Spiegler waited until Abriella pulled away from the curb before releasing a deep, pent-up breath and letting his body slouch forward. He bit his lip to distract from the pain radiating from his abdomen. Spiegler muttered backward from ten, which effort leaked bloody saliva from his mouth to the wet pavement below. A dim red light pulsed in the reflection at his feet. Spiegler lifted his head enough to follow the light across the street to its source: a neon sign mounted atop what resembled a train car. The sign blinked *DINER*.

Spiegler took one last look back at the brightly lit double doors of the emergency room. He wiped his face with one hand, made up his mind, and shambled on across the road.

The diner door felt heavy as solid rock, as if the hinges were rusted in place. Spiegler grew weaker by the minute. The director screwed his face into a mask of determination and will, then threw his shoulder against the glass and pushed. The door opened just enough for him to squeeze through.

The young woman at the hostess station gasped at the sight of him. Having caught a glimpse of himself in the glass as he passed through the door, Spiegler understood why. He was splattered with dirt and debris from head to toe. His skin had an unhealthy pallor and his untucked shirt hung heavy, burdened as it was by a large, wet splotch of blood. Spiegler had seen healthier-looking corpses at funeral viewings.

"Can I get a booth?" The only other customer in the place was an old trucker who sat at the counter, and he was concentrated on reducing the number of fries on his plate.

"Yeah. This... this way."

Spiegler followed the hostess to a booth halfway down the length of the diner, and slid into its red leather-like bench seat.

"My waitress, she called in," the hostess stuttered. "So I'll be your server tonight." The hostess' hands shook as she fumbled a pad from the back pocket of her slacks. She pointed to a pair of tri-fold menus that stood like sentinels at the far end of the table, and tittered nervously. "It says French Melt wrap is our special tonight, but we're out of that. So, no French Melt, okay?"

"Okay." Spiegler's voice was little more than a whisper wearing a rasp for an overcoat. "I just want a grilled cheese sandwich and a large Pepsi."

"Coke okay?"

Spiegler figured a death row prisoner shouldn't have to make any such concession. Instead of protesting, he met the hostess' gaze and said, "That's fine. Provided you make it a *double-decker* grilled cheese sandwich."

She scampered away past the counter and through a swinging door that led into the kitchen. There was a television mounted on the wall above a dusty pie case. On it, a young Marlon Brando and a not-so-young Rod Steiger rode in the back of a cab. The sound was down, but that made no difference to Spiegler; he knew every line. He'd seen the film maybe a hundred times, but not for years. Not since the accident. He'd not watched any movies since then.

The director averted his eyes.

The set's remote control lay on the counter. Had he the strength, Spiegler would've jumped up, sprinted across the diner, snatched the remote in his hand, and turned the damned TV off. He couldn't watch movies anymore without feeling a hole in his gut. And then there were the hallucinations. Over the years, he'd almost been able to convince himself they were the sum total of the massive quantities of drugs and alcohol he'd consumed. He no longer thought so.

It started at the trial when the prosecution ran raw footage of the accident to the judge and jury. The prosecutor ran the footage a total of six times, ostensibly to point out a new detail each time, but really just to drive home the horror of two children being decapitated due to Spiegler's negligence. In truth, the footage wasn't all that graphic. There was no excessive lingering for gory effect and no real money shot to speak of. The footage was short, quick and ultimately, very effective.

The sixth and final time the film was run, Spiegler saw something he hadn't before. Just before Nhu and Alex's heads went away, their already screaming mouths shared a single word in common. Though he wasn't at all a proficient reader of lips, Spiegler knew the word the children screamed just before they died. That word was a name. His. *Spiegler.*

After that, the director couldn't watch any movies. Whenever he tried, he'd spiral into thoughts of suicide. Anytime an actor or actress who'd passed away appeared on screen, he saw them only as dead men and women. Sometimes they were freshly deceased, sometimes long dead and decayed, all still speaking their lines and hitting their marks.

Spiegler stopped going to premieres. He put his television out with the trash. It wasn't long before his third wife packed up and left. His friends stopped visiting.

The hostess returned from the kitchen. Spiegler didn't see her until she sidled up to his table, because he was busy avoiding the television. She kept her head down and spoke into the open pad in her hand.

"Just found out we're out of the special because we're out of cheese. So, no French Melt and no grilled cheese either. Sorry. Is there something else I can get you?"

Inside, the condemned prisoner laughed bitterly. Spiegler folded his hands in a gesture of serenity, and looked up at her. A few years older than he preferred, but if she was to be the last woman he ever laid eyes on, not bad. He tried to smile.

"Just bring the bread then. And my Pepsi."

"Coke," she clarified.

"Right." He sighed. "Coke."

Before she could leave the table, her attention turned to the front door, and whatever she saw made her mouth drop open. Spiegler followed her gaze. Near the hostess station, three men stood dressed all in white. Against the dark windows, their skin pulsed with pure white light, which blurred their features with each cycle. The hostess dropped her pad onto the table.

The glowing man closest to the door thumbed the lock and flipped the sign over from *OPEN* to *CLOSED*.

The trucker at the counter spun on his stool, still chewing a French fry, his eyes narrow. He dipped one hand into his jeans and pulled out a pocket knife. The glowing man nearest to him reached into a side-holster and withdrew a large caliber handgun. The trucker carefully set his knife down on the counter, pushed it away, then held up both hands. The hostess took a quick step towards the kitchen but skidded on her heels, and stopped before she'd really even begun. A young Hispanic man wearing a short-order cook's apron and hairnet came in through the kitchen door, hands behind his head, a look of fear and bewilderment on his face. A fourth glowing man was behind him, gun in hand.

Two of the intruders filed past the windows and drew the blinds. With the grace and confidence of a lion stalking the savanna, the third glowing man moved to the service counter. Passing the trucker, he snagged a fry off the plate, popped it into his mouth, and swallowed it without chewing. Reaching past a line of ketchup bottles, he closed his hand around the remote control for the television, and headed straight for Spiegler.

Blinds closed and the diner secured, the two glowing men pulled out their own weapons. One positioned himself behind the hostess, the other behind the trucker. The apparent leader of the group dropped the remote on the table and sat across from Spiegler. With one finger, he spun the remote in lazy circles. The man's features were obscured by the brightness of his skin; Spiegler couldn't place his ethnicity. He could have been Mediterranean. Or Indian. Or even Egyptian. Each luminescent pulse of his flesh offered a glimpse of a different lineage. Unnerved, the director realized that race was irrelevant to such a creature. Perhaps he was all races from all time, or none.

"There's no escaping this," the glowing man said. "I've seen this moment."

Spiegler nodded. "So have I."

The man stopped spinning the remote so that it faced the television. "Once you've had the eel's blood, you share our eyes and ears. Our lives. Our pasts, our futures. I saw the cop through the little girl's eyes, and then the black girl through her. And from her, to you and your friend in the desert. One path, one fate."

Spiegler shrugged. "But no grilled cheese sandwich."

"Shall we, then?" the glowing man asked.

He pressed a button on the remote. At the same time, a shot rang out and the trucker collapsed to the counter, rebounded briefly, then crumpled to the floor.

The man with Spiegler reached across the table, took hold of Spiegler's head, and forcibly turned it to face the television. On the screen, a shirtless Bruce Lee had replaced Marlon Brando. Leaping in the air, Lee kicked two assailants to the ground, one with each foot, and his mouth was contorted into a wild expression of victory.

The hostess screamed, and a second shot rang out. Her head cracked against the table on her way down. She left a bright red streak on the Formica just about where Spiegler's hoped for double-decker grilled cheese sandwich should've been.

The glowing man released Spiegler and pressed the button on the remote a second time. Bruce Lee vanished from the television, replaced by beautiful Lana Turner in a white head wrap, wearing matching top and shorts, with a long expanse of glorious midriff bared. Lana stood near the end of a decidedly similar counter, minus the bloody dead trucker and the dead waitress on the floor. Spiegler wanted Lana. He'd always wanted Lana, but had come along too late. He couldn't look away from the television, though he tried mightily.

The glowing man who shot the trucker came to the table and slid a glass of water under Spiegler's nose. He tore himself away from Lana to see a glimmering blue eel no larger than a garden worm swimming in the glass. The creature did figure eights and loop-the-loops. Even with Spiegler's one eye and no stereo vision, he could see it was extraordinarily graceful, almost a thing of beauty. The eel's slow dance through the water was as calming as a lullaby.

A gunshot tore Spiegler out of his awe. The water rippled in response. In the drinking glass's reflection, Spiegler saw the short order cook collapse onto the counter. The faux-marble laminate turned red.

Spiegler didn't have the energy left to react.

The glowing man who controlled the TV tipped Spiegler's head back ever so slightly, and with the same finger he'd used on the remote, he opened Spiegler's mouth. Realizing what the man had in mind, he willed his mouth shut, but Spiegler no longer had control to exert. The man raised the glass to Spiegler's lips. Cold water entered his mouth, shocking his system as it trickled down his throat. The eel slipped onto his tongue, and the glowing man forced the director's mouth closed. The eel slithered down Spiegler's throat.

Spiegler slumped back in his seat, eyes again on the television. Lana's face deflated, cheekbones pushing through her skin, eyes sinking into their sockets, fresh jowls pulling back to reveal the bony jawline of a mummy.

"Are you ready?"

Spiegler couldn't answer. He felt a tingling sensation as the eel moved inside him, navigating through his digestive tract. The chemical effects of the creature surged within Spiegler. He became lightheaded and disoriented. The diner's lights shone a rainbow of impossible colors, like an alien prism. Ghosts seemed to shimmer and dance in the air. This was different than at the camp. This time, there was no future in the visions that swirled around him. The glowing man took Spiegler's hand in his own. He was surprisingly gentle when extending one of Spiegler's fingers and pressing it to a button on the remote. Spiegler knew it couldn't be, but it felt as if the button pressed back. The television flickered, and mummified Lana was replaced by static—dark alternating with light, random blips of color and perverse shapes. Then an image surfaced through the visual chaos. It was hazy at first, then instantly recognizable. The diner drifted from his thoughts. In its place was nothing but a television screen.

Mallory Plaskett lowered Nhu, then Alex into the mine cart. She joked with the kids. Mallory had a talent for putting people at ease. Nhu and Alex smiled and laughed, enjoying their adventure. Mallory withdrew.

The mine cart started down the track, rocking back and forth as it gained speed. It rocketed towards the sudden decline and the scenery built too low for safety. The children screamed as they went. First they were acting, then suddenly they weren't. The mine cart's wheels rattled and spat out sparks as they careened down the rails. The front end of the cart lifted. Its wheels left the track. The deed was done and the television went dark.

Something solid struck the diner's kitchen door, flinging it open and drawing Spiegler's attention away from the television. The rusted mine cart, wheels destroyed but still turning, rolled out across the diner floor. Crashing into the end of the counter, the car rocked over the sprawled body of the hostess, then came to a rest against Spiegler's booth.

It was exactly what he'd seen at Tranquility Base. This was what he'd been running from ever since the accident happened.

This was his fate.

Two tiny, headless bodies crawled from the rusted cart and onto Spiegler's table. Nhu and Alex each wrapped their hands around fistfuls of Spiegler's hair, and with inhuman strength yanked him from his seat, dragged him across the table, and pulled him, screaming, into the mining cart.

TWENTY-EIGHT

A violent fit of coughing woke Branson. Heaving, he pulled himself up, threw his hands around his throat, and hacked. When the coughing fit subsided, he opened his eyes and took in his surroundings. He'd not done much traveling in his life outside the occasional family vacation, but he recognized all the telltale signs of a cheap hotel room: garish wallpaper, generic mass-produced art, a vintage television atop a particleboard entertainment cart, and a utilitarian headboard over a pair of twin mattresses.

Branson was still in his damp and bloodied clothes. At any other time in his life, the ambiguity of the situation would've been terrifying. Instead, after the previous night's events, he felt safe. Except, then he noticed light leaking from under the closed bathroom door, and that brought him to a sudden surge of panic.

His memory of the night before was, at best, hazy, especially after the helicopter crash and the rain of bones. Was it he who'd killed St. Abaddon? Branson couldn't say. He'd a vague recollection of Detective Woost and of carrying Spiegler through the desert night, but beyond that, nothing.

The light went dark and the bathroom door opened. Abriella emerged. When she saw Branson was awake, she smiled, but that quickly faded in a flush of self-conscious reflex. Without glasses and makeup, her features were smoother and more feminine. He realized Abriella used her glasses as armor—two thick but transparent shields against the slings and arrows of a prying world. She reached for protection as she sat on the edge of her mattress, but then thought better of it and left her face naked.

"How d'you feel?" she asked.

Whenever people asked how you were doing, they expected a cursory *Fine, and you?*, not the truth. Branson could've told Abriella that every muscle ached, a migraine raged through his head, and that he could feel every one of the hundreds of tiny cuts and scrapes all over his body. Instead, through a wry smile he said, "I'm great. Thanks for asking."

"That's funny, 'cause you sure look horrible."

They both laughed.

"How did you find—"

"I'm brilliant. Let's leave it at that. She leaned forward, hands on her knees, and studied him. "You have *shit* embedded in your face."

"Shit?"

"Metal, rock, *whatever* it is, it's buried in there balls deep." She reached over and picked at his cheek. "I found a first aid kit in Ponds' Jeep. What'ya say we get you cleaned up, soldier boy?"

Michael Ponds' Jeep? Branson didn't want to know. He brought two fingers up to his temple in an awkward military salute then recoiled when his fingers brushed against a patch of raw flesh. Pain resonated through his skull like an electrical shock. He whistled through his teeth as he inhaled with force.

Abriella rose from the bed and led him to the bathroom. The seat of her white sweat pants was decorated with the word *BITCH*, in bold red letters.

Branson sat on the toilet lid while Abriella filled the sink with water, and cracked open the first aid kit. She pulled out a pair of tweezers, a couple of sealed alcohol swabs, and a threaded needle.

"You ready?"

"Sure," he guessed.

With the tweezers she plucked a decent sized bone fragment out of his jaw. It felt like she'd removed one of *his* bones, not a bit of debris from the tipi. He chomped down hard with his teeth each time she removed another piece. After plucking a half dozen or so, Abriella cleaned her work with an alcohol swab. That too, hurt like hell.

"Better?" she asked.

It wasn't. Numb, maybe. Somewhat. Abriella dug around in fresh territory. Branson winced sharply, which made her clumsy and that only made things worse.

"Sorry. Think of it like getting a tattoo. You work yourself up, it's crazy scary the first time, but after that, it's nothing."

She slipped with the tweezers and the seed-sized bone lodged in his temple remained planted. Her second attempt proved more successful.

"You've got a tattoo?"

A line of blood snaked down Branson's face. Abriella wiped it with another swab, then told him to hold that over the wound. She turned and lifted the back of her shirt to her shoulders. Between her shoulder blades was an inked portrait of a provocative black woman surrounded by a halo of roses. The clasp on her thin black bra cut the woman at the throat. Abriella lowered her shirt and turned back to Branson.

"Someone special?" he asked.

She nodded. "Mom."

"Sorry."

"Never knew her. Don't know why my dad only had the one photo, but this is taken from that. Paper's just paper, y'know. This way, she ain't going anywhere."

Branson dabbed at his wounds. "How'd she die?"

Abriella pushed his hand away from where he'd been holding the swab over his wound, and rather brusquely, Branson thought. She took the needle and thread to his temple and closed the hole with a few quick turns of her wrist. Branson's vision blurred with the sensation. She leaned in close and severed the thread with her teeth. Her breath was warm against his cheek.

"She gave birth to me on Tuesday, brought me home in a wicker basket the next day. Was back in the hospital by Friday. Buried a week to the day I was born."

"That's horrible."

She shrugged. It was about the saddest shrug he'd ever seen. "I wonder sometimes what my dad would be like, if she was still here."

"Loss changes people. It changes everything."

Abriella rinsed the needle beneath hot water, wiped it with a swab, dropped it back into the first aid kit, then went for the tweezers again.

"Not for me. How things are, that's all I've ever known, and I don't see a whole lotta different ahead." She plunked a miscellaneous piece of grit into the sink. "I'm done with your face. Get topless."

Branson pulled his shredded shirt over his head, and a fine cloud of sand fell from it as he did. He tossed the shirt to the floor and inspected himself. With all the brown welts and blue bruises, his chest resembled a nautical map of an island chain. Referring to one mark in particular near his right nipple, he looked up at Abriella and said, "I think I've found Bikini Atoll."

"You should be shot in the face for that joke," she said with a straight face, held it for a moment, and then let out a sly smile. She opened a fresh alcohol swab and proceeded to his ribs. Branson yelped. Abriella might've enjoyed it.

She slid a hand over his dislocated shoulder. "Well, this doesn't look right."

"Doesn't feel great, either," he said with a wince.

Pressing her palm against his skin, she pushed until the joint cracked. The pain hit with enough force to vanquish all thoughts from his head. His hand shot up to protect his shoulder, but that contact initiated a second wave of agony. His face flushed with heat. Gritting his teeth, he swore under his breath.

"I've been busy, you know."

"Yeah?" Branson said in a weak mumble.

"Oh yeah. If you two stupid white boys would've called me first, I could have given you the lowdown. But no, you had to go rush in there and nearly get yourselves killed."

With that, Branson remembered his friend. His voice stabilized as the pain began to subside. "Spiegler?"

"Dropped him at the hospital." Abriella pinched him with the tweezers, changing the subject. He was grateful. "I found out where you were headed by eavesdropping on the cops while they eavesdropped on you."

Branson shot her a quizzical look.

"Yeah, Woost, I've no doubt. Bitch. Put a GPS tracker on your car. Probably while you were cooling in jail overnight."

"Okay, then. I promise to keep you in the loop from now on."

"Like hell you do," she snorted. "It doesn't matter, 'cause you're not going anywhere without me from now on. Clearly, you can't be trusted to look out for yourself or anyone else, for that matter."

She'd unintentionally hurt him with that. They both managed to let it pass.

"What'd you find out, Detective?"

Abriella brightened at that, then quickly got back down to business.

"The Moonmen cult started back in the late '60s. Free love and shitty folk songs, you might even remember." Branson winced, and it wasn't because of his wounds. "But they weren't like the rest. They didn't just stage demonstrations and sit-ins. The Moonmen actually declared war on the United States government. Bombs, arson. Real anarchist stuff."

Tossing the bloody swab into the trash, she continued.

"It came to a head in '69. The two brothers who led the cult tried to kidnap the Los Angeles District Attorney. They failed, but in the process they shot a member of his staff. The cops captured one of the brothers, Benedict Kendrick Shallcross, but the other one, Ambrose, escaped. The staff member died a couple weeks later, and they charged Benedict with murder. The press was all over the story, so the judge ordered the trial moved out of town to avoid a tainted jury. Ambrose's people took advantage and ambushed the prisoner transport van, killed the guards, and whisked Benedict off into the night."

She opened a fresh swab and began to clean off his breastbone. "In '82, a homeless man is arrested for weapons possession, for a gun that was used to kill a liquor store clerk. The guy cops a plea, says he's from Ambrose's group, and says they now call themselves the Moonmen."

"Ambrose became St. Abaddon," Branson whispered.

"Yeah," she said. "Apparently the brothers went separate ways. Ambrose disappeared into the desert. Benedict went farther. Wanted to cut all ties with America, so he and his people stole two trawlers. They sailed out past the twelve mile maritime border."

She hit a sensitive spot and he winced.

"They never came back. At least not to stay. The homeless man said they sometimes come back at night to trade with the Moonmen or steal what they need. Benedict named his floating community the Pacificans."

She finished up, crushed the swab into a ball, and threw it away.

"The Pacifican women got too old to give the cult children, so they started coming ashore to... recruit. That's probably not the right word. Shanghai comes a lot closer."

Abriella dropped the tweezers into the sink. She stood up and pulled back the shower curtain. Turning on the water, she tested the temperature with the back of her hand. She ordered, "Get yourself clean."

Branson pulled himself up with one hand on the sink and groaned when he stepped towards the shower. Abriella took his place on the toilet seat. Realizing she didn't intend to leave, he unbuttoned his pants and let them drop. Self-conscious and confused, it took another moment for him to work up the courage to slide his underwear off and enter the shower. Once he did, he pulled the curtain closed.

The water was perfect. Its warmth soothed the irritating wounds as it washed away the dirt and dried blood that Abriella couldn't. Branson saw her through the translucent curtain, her long, thin body distorted by the folds of plastic. She sat with legs crossed, eyes cast down, staring at her hands. She picked at the chipped polish on her fingernail. She was beautiful.

"Detective Woost visited me," Abriella said.

That worked. His erection withered.

"Oh?"

"Yeah. She warned me that you're dangerous to be around." The sound of the water couldn't drown out what she'd said. He wished it had. "She really believes that you killed your daughter, or at least had something to do with it."

"I know."

"She told me you beat your wife but that she dropped the charges."

Abriella didn't ask whether or not it was true. Branson couldn't tell if she believed it. He almost told her it was all a lie and left it at that, but she deserved more.

"Candice and I... We didn't have the perfect marriage. You'd have to know her to understand. She's got an ugly side. A side that's hidden until after you live with her, sleep in the same bed, pay the same bills..."

"You don't have to tell me if you don't want to." For once Abriella's tone was crystal clear. She very much needed an explanation. The water pressure softened.

"She was having an affair. I never met the guy, but I found a... it doesn't matter. She was sneaking around with him and I called her on it. She got angry and started screaming, telling me that it was my fault... that he was a better man and... she said lots of things. Not nice things. I turned to leave. I had to get out of there, but she grabbed onto my arm and spun me around and kept screaming. When I tried to turn away again, she slapped me. I tried to push her away but she latched on and wouldn't let go. Her slaps became punches. I just wanted to get her off of me. That's it. So, I hit her. Harder than I meant to."

"And she pressed charges?" Abriella asked.

"The police questioned me. Candice and Madeline moved out for a while. We got a court date. Then one morning Candice is just there in the kitchen with two cups of coffee like normal, and she tells me she's dropped the charges." The soapy water that swirled down the drain was an ugly shade of pinkish-brown. "That was the first and only time I ever hit her."

"Woost said there was more than once."

"The second time... I don't know what happened. Candice was still sleeping when I left for work. Cops showed up just before lunch and interrogated me in my office. Candice was in the hospital. She claimed I'd beaten her up. But I swear I didn't touch her."

"Two-faced bitch." Branson had no idea if Abriella was referring to his ex-wife or to Detective Woost. Didn't matter. It worked for him either way. Abriella stood. Their eyes met through the plastic.

"After Madeline went miss—after *they* took her, it was just over. Candice stuck around just long enough to figure that out for herself."

Without a word Abriella left the bathroom. As she went, she pulled her shirt over her head and dropped it to the floor.

Branson wondered where she'd gone, and why. Had she not believed him? He turned off the water, stepped from the shower and toweled off. The bathroom door was ajar, but he couldn't see much beyond it, just that the room looked darker than it was when he'd left it. He rejected the idea of sliding back into his filthy boxer briefs. Naked, Branson headed for the unoccupied bed at the far side. Probably, she was every bit as exhausted as he was, and she had every right to be. Branson peeled back the comforter and sheet on his bed.

"Where the hell are you going?" Abriella asked.

He looked into her eyes and wished he'd never have to look away, ever. She pulled back her covers to reveal her long, slender, naked body. Heart-shaped diamond nipple rings sparkled in the dim light, contrasting with her dark skin.

"I'm gonna take serious offense if you get into that bed." Abriella patted the space next to her. "*This* is where you'll be spending the night."

Branson did as he was told.

TWENTY-NINE

The call to Woost didn't come through official channels. Les Franklin, a dissolute desk cop two months from retirement, had spent six months in an unmarked cruiser alongside Roy Faune. It was a short stint as partnerships go, spent mostly on stakeouts and shakedowns. Apparently, that time together was sufficient to convince Les to give his old partner's mistress one last tip-off before he shuffled off to a golf course in Florida.

Susan Woost sat up on the couch, closed her cellphone and wiped her eyes. How long had it been since she'd slept in her bed? After Roy's death, she'd placed a small, framed photo of him on the bedside table. It was just a hasty snapshot, badly lit and a bit out of focus, but it was the best she had. The insomnia started that first night. She simply couldn't sleep next to the photo, and she couldn't bring herself to remove it, either. There was nothing else to do but migrate to the couch. Woost could sleep there... sometimes.

She wiggled into a pair of jeans, and threw a black blazer over her white t-shirt, even though she was braless. She buttoned with one hand and swiped her keys off the top of the television with the other. She didn't bother to look at herself in the mirror as she headed out of the apartment, and neglected to check the lock after she had. The harsh light of dawn hit her in the eyes as Woost swung behind the wheel of her car and keyed the ignition. She slid on a pair of aviator sunglasses, cut the wheel and stomped on the gas. It would've been nice to have a cup of coffee, but there was no time to stop.

The rain of the previous night showed in the sheen of moisture on the asphalt. With the rising sun came fog, at times thick enough to give Woost serious pause. She took her chances and pressed through it.

She imagined Roy in the passenger seat, chewing on the butt of a cigarette, mauling it like he would, rarely bothering to light any of his smokes. It was easy to picture him beside her, every detail still vivid in her mind, his unruly, cowlicked hair spiked up in front, the slightest hint of sideburns framing his face, the way his glasses hung on the tip of his narrow nose. If he were alive, with her now, in this moment, he would have stared out the side window with his head cocked at an uncomfortable angle, licked his top lip, and said, "Last night, bad goddamn night, the kind that kills prom queens and war vets. A night for hungry vultures."

Roy could be like that, a head full of drowsy poetry and morbid thoughts. Then, in the next moment, he might run a finger through one of her curls and ask her why she had to be *so damned beautiful*. But he was always ready to shatter a carjacker's jaw with his steel-toed boot. Roy Faune wasn't an easy man to pin down with simple adjectives.

Dead, there was one that applied. He disappeared from her imagination and the passenger's seat. It would have been too easy to let him stay.

Woost drove the remainder of the way in something of a stupor, both hands gripping the steering wheel tight. She pulled into a parking lot, killed the engine, and stepped out onto broken asphalt. Local police cruisers surrounded a diner in a rough circle. Woost made sure her badge rode clearly visible at the hip, though that meant unbuttoning her jacket so every grunt beat cop would see she'd not bothered to wear a bra. She ducked under a line of police tape and headed into the diner. Most of the cops inside were young, inexperienced, and clearly overwhelmed by the scene. Woost spotted an older man in plain-clothes, bent at the waist over the body of a woman. She pushed through the uniforms to stand beside him.

"Witnesses?" Looking up, he definitely glanced at her tits.

"You mean at ninety-eight point six and still kicking? No." The old cop rose wearily and looked at Woost with awkward, astigmatic eyes. "You're a city cop. City cop means city crime's spilled over onto my backwater doorstep. So, why don'tcha just spill. What's this we're looking at here, some kind of drug activity? Maybe a gang war?"

"No, Sheriff Taylor. Organized criminals are organized, precise. At least they try to avoid collateral damage. This looks more like Aurora without the popcorn." She made her way across the diner to a booth. "Your guys already gone over all this?"

"Photos, fibers, fingerprints, the works. You got here fast, but not *that* fast..."

Woost slid on a pair of latex gloves, sat in the booth, reached across the table, and lifted the victim's head by the hair.

"Marius Spiegler." The Sheriff was interested to hear it.

"You know him?"

"We met. Recently." Woost gently placed Spiegler's head back down on the Formica and ducked down for a view beneath the table. "Flashlight?" she asked of no one in particular. A short cop not as queasy as the rest handed one over. She spoke to herself. "Apparent knife wound, lower abdomen. Small. Almost delicate, but jagged. Maybe he bled out."

The Sheriff knocked sharply on the tabletop, which drew Woost's attention. She sat up.

"That's what my men came up with too, though I'd like to wait for the coroner's report before casting my lot. Don't see much of this kind of thing around here."

"At all," the young cop said as he took back his flashlight.

Woost didn't reply. She exited the booth, again pushed through the crowd of cops and headed for the door. Sheriff Taylor was close on her heels. Out front in the blazing sun, she gestured to the three civilian vehicles in the diner's parking lot.

"The beat up Civic and the ancient Sunbird. Employees, right?"

"Yeah," the Sheriff said. "It's a small town. Everybody knows what everybody drives. The Escalade, I figure that belonged to the guy by the counter. I've a call in—" Detective Woost cut him off.

"Does that dead hillbilly look like he drives a Caddy? Twenty bucks says it's a truck and that it's gone. Stolen by the perps, probably."

Some of the young cops snickered. The Sheriff didn't.

"Then where's the Escalade from?"

"The Felston family."

"The who?"

"Family from up north. Mom and Dad aren't breathing."
"Sounds like you know who did this," Sheriff Taylor said.
"Sounds that way."

THIRTY

In the rear view mirror, Branson saw a wary, fragile man. Overnight, the stubble on his cheeks and chin had thickened into nearly a full beard. There was plenty of gray. He felt *old*. A heavy cloud of guilt hung over his head as he'd watched Abriella get dressed. She slithered into a pair of panties, tight jeans, a patterned bra, and a V-neck T-shirt. It was as much of a turn-on as any striptease.

"We need to talk about last night."

"No, we don't."

"I think it'd be better if—"

Abriella shook her head and put a finger against his lips while keeping one hand on the wheel.

"I'm not in love with you or anything, okay? I ain't that girl. Last night was good, after we got you cleaned up. I just wanted some, is all."

"It's that easy?"

"I have tits."

"Indeed you do," Branson smirked.

"Yeah, it's *that* easy."

They'd filled her backpack with motel room incidentals. Toothpaste, mouthwash, a big wad of tissues and soap. Even coffee packets. Though they lacked the means to use them, one never knew. Branson had loaded up from the breakfast bar while Abriella returned the key card.

"While you were sleeping I researched the Fontainebleau pier."

Branson unlatched his seat belt. It was too snug against his battered and bruised chest.

"You mean after... Don't you sleep?"

"A little." She freed one hand from the steering wheel and held her thumb and index finger an inch apart. "Insomnia is way underrated. Want to know what I learned?"

"Yes."

"Good, 'cause I was going to tell you anyway. The Fontainebleau was a private pier in the '20s, part of an exclusive resort for celebrities and politicians. Basically, it was an upscale speakeasy. Rich folk went to the club, chatted for a while about flappers or Art Deco or whatever, then got into these pleasure yachts docked at the pier and went out into international waters to drink, do drugs, gamble, and screw prostitutes.

"A few weeks before the Twenty-First Amendment becomes law, the Fontainebleau gets raided and the state seizes the property. For the better part of a decade, the resort goes unused. Then, in 1941, the federal government buys it from the state and turns it into an army recruitment center. After the war, it's sold back to California and becomes an orphanage. That stayed open until 1983. Now, it's condemned. The last news story I could find was about former employees suing the state for asbestos exposure."

Branson squinted into the sunlight blasting through the windshield. Some of what she told him seemed familiar. He wondered if he'd run across the Fontainebleau's history in *The Telegraph's* archives. "Was there a scandal?"

"At the orphanage? Yeah," she said. "Turns out an administrator was selling children. Real human trafficking, international black market. They'd burn the kids' paperwork, tell the staff they'd been adopted, and then poof—it was like they'd never been born. The administrator committed suicide in police custody; there never was any trial."

That *did* sound familiar. Anger flared up in his chest, igniting the bruises and punctures throughout his body like a string of firecrackers. "Sounds like someone's re-opened the operation under new management."

"S'what I thought."

The sun hurt Branson's eyes, and when he brought down the visor a small bi-fold wallet fell on his lap. About half a dozen business cards spilled out. The top card read, *DT. SUSAN WOOST, HOMOCIDE & MISSING PERSONS*. He tossed the wallet and remaining cards onto the dash. Handwritten on the reverse of Woost's card was, *Every little detail helps. Call me.*

"Whaddya suppose the chances are that Ponds hasn't called Woost about his Jeep?"

"I'm pretty sure he won't. I might be out of a job, though."

Branson didn't want to know. "Still, we need to be careful. Woost won't stop. She'll never stop. And if she knows you're with me, then you're in her cross-hairs, too."

"I can take her." Abriella's grin gave the impression she'd been kidding, but Branson wasn't so sure. "Besides, I haven't broken any laws, no matter what she might think."

"Impeding an investigation? Withholding evidence? Helping me and Spiegler evade the law?" Even with the visor down, the sun was unbearable. Branson put a hand over his brow and wondered why Abriella didn't seem bothered.

"I was off-roading in a friend's car and came across two men who needed help. And you haven't been charged with anything, have you?"

"Not to my knowledge…"

"Then I ain't abetting shit." She turned left at a fork in the road and the light shifted away from his eyes. "Why do I get the feeling we're headed east?"

"'Cause we *are* headed east."

"The Fontainebleau is west."

"So it is, Captain Geography. We have a stop to make first. Look in the glove compartment. Tell me what you see."

When Branson reached forward, his midsection protested and he had to sit back for a moment to gear up for the effort.

"Are you okay?"

"Beat to hell, is all." In the glove compartment Branson found the usual crap, along with a device the size of a credit card. He turned the thing over in his hand.

"What is it?"

"It's the GPS satellite tracker that Woost put in your car. I jacked it out at the Canyon before I drove in."

"And you brought it with? What the—"

"Relax. It was hardwired to the battery. It ain't talkin' to anybody at the moment. But there's an old-school electronics shop off the 395 that should have what I need to rig it up."

Branson sat back. "You can do that?"

"I can do that."

"And why would you do that?"

"I figure if everything goes wrong tonight and you disappear, with that thing stuck up your ass I can track you from my laptop."

"That's almost sweet. And you said the sex didn't mean anything to you."

"No, I said it was *easy*."

A weak chime sounded as they entered the store. The slack-jawed clerk didn't bother to look up from the magazine on the counter. Abriella approached him with a playful smile and asked for what she needed. Branson heard the word *polarity* and ignored the rest of the conversation; none of the technical words meant anything to him.

Turning, he assessed the store. Dusty boxes cluttered discolored shelves, and sun-bleached board-and-blister packages dangled from mismatched hooks.

Again the door chime sounded. Branson leaned back to see down the aisle. A short, thin customer stood not far inside the door.

Branson came upon a row of video cameras mounted high on the back wall. A sign read, *NEW TO YOU - $AVE*. Below each camera was a vintage television set and each of those displayed a slightly different view of the store. In one of those, Branson watched as the new arrival joined Abriella and the clerk at the service counter.

It was *the Boy*. The boy on the leash.

Branson tried to sprint up the aisle, and collided with a wire spinner rack that overturned and sent dozens of rolled, colored wire coils across the tile floor. Everyone turned towards the commotion. The Boy smiled at Branson and extended a fist.

"GET AWAY FROM—"

The Boy giggled like a broken toy vibraphone. Branson finally reached Abriella, grabbed her wrist and yanked her away. The Boy tossed the contents of his hand on the counter as if throwing dice. The clerk squinted, then took two quick steps back.

Only *one* of the eyeballs was glass, and it wasn't at all hard to tell which one was which.

Again the door chime sounded and three men entered. They wore white. An iridescent glow pulsed from their skin.

Two of the men carried shotguns. The one in the lead held a familiar handgun at his hip. It was the gun Szymon Kazanjian had sold

Branson. The glowing man turned his full attention to the clerk. His voice was soft and soothing, like a pastor or a hospice nurse.

"Is there a panic button under that desk?"

"No," the clerk said as he inched his way even further back from the counter. The man raised his gun.

"Then pick up the phone, please."

"What?"

"These two," the glowing man motioned to Branson and Abriella, "are here to rob you. Pick up the phone and dial the police. Say nothing. Just dial, then put the receiver down by the cash register."

The clerk didn't hesitate, he was no fool. Fumbling with the cordless phone, he dialed 911 then set it aside as directed.

"That's good. Now come out from behind the counter."

As the clerk did, a voice came through the phone, tiny and distant.

"All three of you, get down on your knees," one of the men with the shotgun shouted. Branson whispered to Abriella. "When I say run—"

"I'm already gone," she said as she reached behind and grabbed a tiny rectangular box off the shelf. Abriella slipped behind Branson. Together, they dropped down to the floor on their knees.

"Hello? Hello?" The police dispatcher called out through the telephone's tinny speaker. *"Do you need assistance? Hello?"*

The Boy drew out a folding hunting knife from a back pocket and snapped it open. He wagged it in the air, gesturing wildly from Branson to Abriella.

"Put that away," hissed the glowing man. The Boy sneered at him, eyes wide.

"I said put it away. There's no place for it in the narrative." Reluctantly, the Boy returned the knife to his pocket.

"Do you need assistance? Hello? Hello..."

"Wait in the truck," the man said.

The Boy huffed and cast a harsh look back over his shoulder as he shuffled towards the exit. He was cowed, but unrepentant. The Boy hit the door hard with his palms, and disappeared into the bright sunlight.

"Do you need assistance? Hello?"

From her knees Abriella hurled the square hockey puck at the glowing man's head, which made for only a glancing blow, but it was enough. She sprang to her feet, yanking Branson up by his arm in the process. Shocked by her strength, he was on his feet and running with her towards the back of the store, where the red-lighted sign over the door read, *Employees Only*. Branson hoped the door wasn't locked. A shotgun blast rocked the store, sending shattered plastic, metal, and wood in a cloud of dust and debris throughout the place.

"You don't..."

A second shot came and blew out a wall of pegged CB accessories close behind Branson.

"...listen very well."

The clerk's scream was silenced by a third thunderous crack. At such close range, his body ricocheted off the closest wall. In the interim, Abriella led Branson to the employee door.

"Sure hope it's not a bathroom," Abriella said. As they pushed through the door, Branson noticed she carried a bag in her hand.

"What's that?"

"Been shopping." Then they were through, and the door closed behind.

Beyond a flimsy manager's desk was a metal door marked *EMERGENGY EXIT ONLY – ALARM WILL SOUND*. As they reached it, a shotgun blast obliterated the door they'd come through. They stumbled together out into the back parking lot, and an alarm did indeed sound. They ran past a rusted dumpster and stacks of flattened cardboard. Their feet slid on loose gravel as they rounded the corner to the front of the building.

Abriella beat him to Sand's Jeep but Branson yelled "I'll drive." She leaped into the passenger seat. Out of breath and fighting back the pain, Branson slid behind the wheel. Abriella handed him the keys, he fired the ignition, and threw the thing into reverse.

The glowing men were at the front doors of the shop, shotguns on the upswing.

"Get down," Branson shouted.

Abriella slipped from the seat onto the floor. Branson stomped on the gas. The Jeep lurched backward over the concrete curb. He hit the brakes and the wheels locked, which sent the vehicle skidding into the front entrance of the shop with a tremendous crack. Glass panes shattered, wood splintered. A lone brick from the roof toppled down onto the Jeep's hood. The glowing men beat a hasty retreat from the blocked exit.

"I'll be right back."

"Don't you dare," Abriella yelled, but he was already out the door. He snatched the brick off the hood and sprinted to the red truck. The Boy stared out at him from the passenger side window with cold, emotionless eyes. Branson yanked on the door handle. Locked. Branson smashed the brick against the window. Inside the truck, the Boy slid to the far side of the seat.

The window spider-webbed but remained secure. Arm aching from the wrist to the elbow, Branson struck again. This time the blow did its job and the inside of the cab was sprayed with beads of shattered safety glass. Branson unlocked the door and forced it open. Crouched on the bucket beat, the Boy brandished his knife.

The glowing men rushed back to the door.

"Will you *come on*," Abriella yelled as she ducked under the dash.

Branson reached for the Boy, who lunged at him with his bone knife, but missed. The knife lodged in the backrest. Branson punched the Boy as hard as he could, twice in the face. The Boy screamed, curled up, covered his head with his hands and whimpered.

Breaking down the remainder of the door frame with the butts of their shotguns, the glowing men cleared their line of sight.

Abriella screamed, "NOW-"

Branson grabbed the Boy by the scruff of his neck and pulled him from the truck. The Boy collapsed to the asphalt.

A double-barreled blast rang out and sent shot across the back of the Jeep. Abriella slid over to the driver's side. Another gunshot removed the driver's side-view mirror. Flinching, Branson threw the Boy into the backseat and hopped in the front. A tail-light exploded. Abriella gunned the engine, and they got the hell out of there.

THIRTY-ONE

Every time Branson looked back to check if they were being followed, he saw the Boy, who whimpered an intense melody of miserable sounds. Every time he looked down at the Boy, he saw the blood-soaked seat where Spiegler had been. Finally, he couldn't stand it.

"You said Marius was safe and—"

"I left him at the emergency room."

"Dammit." Branson hit the dashboard with his fist. It wasn't worth the effort, as pain shot through his midsection in response.

"Maybe your little *friend* there can tell us what happened." A velvety purple bruise had bloomed across the Boy's face, its tendrils growing redder as they stretched across his cheeks, then faded into thin pink tributaries at the ears and below the mouth. The Boy sat in the center of the back seat, knees drawn up to his chest, arms wrapped tight around himself, mourning his broken nose.

Branson found it hard to find in this boy the vicious animal that with surpassing glee had stabbed Spiegler. Still, considering the eyeballs the kid had carried in his fist, Branson's friend was most certainly dead, and the little monster sitting behind him had something to do with that. As a parent, Branson was half surprised to feel no empathy for the child. But if it weren't for that tiny bone knife...

A rest area came up quickly on the right, not much more than a dirt clearing surrounded by trees and shrubs, off by the side of the road.

"Pull over."

Abriella did just that, and parked the Jeep beneath a top-heavy white cedar. The bristled branches swept downward like a stage curtain, and blocked the view from the highway.

"Abry, looks like there's a little stream down there beyond that break in the trees. Y'see it?" Branson kept his eyes on the Boy in the rear view mirror. "You should take a walk down there and see if you can see any fish."

"Fish?" she said in an incredulous voice.

"Yeah, fish. Go see if there're any fish in the creek. Abriella stole a look at the Boy, who was crying. Then she nervously gathered up the things she'd taken from the store, along with the tracer from the glove compartment.

"I... have to put... all this together... anyway—"

They both got out of the Jeep and met at the rear bumper. Branson reached for the hatch, and Abriella slid her free hand over his before he could open it. She looked Branson straight in the eye.

"Don't—"

"I won't." But Branson couldn't look at her when he said it. After a long moment, she headed down a slight decline towards the creek.

Branson opened the hatch and straight away found what he'd sought. Cracking open the small red toolbox, he rummaged through its contents. Beneath the Phillips-head screwdrivers and loose sockets, he found a half-full roll of duct tape. He retrieved it, closed the box and the hatch, and made his way around to the passenger side door. He pushed the front seat forward until it rested against the dashboard, and climbed inside. The Boy hadn't moved, but he was hardly still. His entire body shook as if an electrical current were passing through.

"You're scared of me." Branson dropped the tape and used his hands to push the Boy's legs aside to reveal his downturned face. "You should be. Your people took my little girl, snatched her right out of her bedroom while I slept just down the hall. You helped kill a man who tried to help me get her back. He was my friend, and in spite of himself, a very good man."

Branson wrapped his hands around the Boy's throat, making his eyes bulge in raw panic. The kid's tiny hands snapped closed around Branson's wrists, and dug in with overgrown fingernails. The pain of that was negligible.

"I could snap your neck. It would feel good to do. And later, we could call it justice."

The Boy kicked with his legs and flapped his arms like wild wings, but Branson held on and squeezed tighter. A quickening pulse surged under his hands. It wouldn't take much more pressure to crush the larynx with his thumbs. It would all be over so quickly. Branson had learned that murdering a child could be an easy thing.

"...no..." the Boy croaked. Branson eased off a little, but pushed the Boy tight against the seat, still holding his throat.

"Why? Why shouldn't I, after what you did to Spiegler? Why the hell not?"

The Boy wept. Branson gave him a disgusted shove, and released him. The Boy coughed, rubbed his throat, and spat. Then, in a voice that could have belonged to any kid, he whimpered, "Because they took *me* too."

A chill swept through Branson. He felt lightheaded, and after almost falling forward, managed to scuttle out of the Jeep and slam the door behind him. Unable to draw a full breath, he leaned against the hood and vomited on the pavement. Once he regained his composure, Branson went back around to the rear passenger door and opened it again.

The Boy sat upright in his back seat, in Spiegler's blood. The Boy smiled at Branson. Then he giggled.

A ferocious anger consumed Branson. He dove into the Jeep, wrestled the Boy flat, and shouldered all of his weight upon him. There was no struggle, no squirming, no attempt at escape. But the giggling turned into wild, crazed laughter.

Branson reached for the duct tape.

THIRTY-TWO

Standing at the edge of the tiny creek, Abriella wrinkled her nose. The place stank and wasn't far enough away so that she couldn't hear the sounds of struggle that drifted from the Jeep. She split the difference between sound and smell, then sat down beside the path and got to work.

One night when she was twelve, Abriella's father brought home a woman from the factory where he worked third shift. She was a decade younger than her father, recently homeless, and she wore her clothes in a manner that suggested she didn't often stay in them. Abriella had been at the dinner table, puzzling over math homework, when they'd come through the door, drunk and shouting, holding each other up, until they fell, together, onto the kitchen floor.

The woman's name was Cleo, short for Cleotilde, but her father couldn't quite pronounce the syllables—so the woman pulled herself up to the table, wrestled the pencil out of Abriella's hand, and scrawled her name diagonally across the worksheet in uneven, child-like letters.

Her father sent Abriella to bed soon after. She spent the night with her pillow over her head, praying for sleep, thinking of her mother, and trying not to hear the sounds coming from her father's bedroom.

The Boy's distant laughter stopped.

There was another shriek from the roll of duct tape.

Cleo, short for Cleotilde, stayed the rest of the week, sleeping and smoking pot and locking doors as she moved around the house. She never seemed to eat, regarding the refrigerator as a piece of furniture no different than an end table or ottoman, but the alcohol and joints seemed to fuel her just as well as any Thanksgiving dinner. She and her father argued, swore, broke ashtrays, then kissed and retreated to the bedroom. Sometimes they argued even then, the sounds of sloppy passion mixing with vicious insults.

After the first few nights, Abriella discovered the secret to ignoring the noisy lovemaking and bickering. She'd tunnel under her bed with her comforter and wrap herself up as tight as an Egyptian mummy, leaving only a breathing hole over her mouth, and slide her index fingers into her ears. Then she'd hum a song, and her voice box would resonate through her entire body, blocking out all other sounds. With her eyes closed, Abriella's world drifted away, and she could imagine herself not yet born, her fetal ears listening to her mother's voice singing a lullaby.

The Boy's muffled voice cried out.

Abriella slid her index fingers up to her ears.

It was a Thursday, a detail she had no rational reason to remember, when she found Cleo in the living room, tearing up the sofa cushions.

Throwing down her schoolbag, Abriella asked, "What are you doing?"

Cleo brushed some white fiber out of her kinky hair, put her hands on her hips, and sneered. "Looking for the money yer daddy hid on me."

It wasn't difficult to see through the lie.

"Where's my father?"

Cleo sniffed at the air like an animal in the wild. Abriella never considered the woman attractive, not in the least, but now she'd become something else entirely—a frazzled, witchy stick figure. "He went out to get us... some stuff."

"What'd he go for?"

Cleo shook her head. "Don't you worry about it."

"I am worried about it," she answered.

Although it wasn't the hardest punch she would endure from the woman, that first time Cleo hit her, it hurt the most. Her father never seemed to notice the bruises.

The sound of duct tape tearing ended. The silence was worse. For a horrible moment she wondered if Branson had stopped because the Boy had died. *No*, she told herself, *he promised. He wouldn't. Would he?*

In time, Abriella sewed the sofa cushions back together, but not everything was so easily mended. Eventually Cleo and her father stopped drinking, fighting, and fucking. Instead, they did nothing at all. They sat in the living room in a semi-catatonic daze, staring at the television, but not watching. There were no more family meals. Abriella learned to cook frozen dinners. She continued to sleep in her cocoon under the bed, no longer to block out sound, but to escape. From everything. Just *everything*.

It wasn't stealing when Abriella took money from her father's wallet and bought groceries. There wasn't much money to take. It was theft, however, when she began to swipe rolls of toilet paper from the stalls at school.

The Jeep door slammed.

It went on like that for six months.

She woke in her cocoon in the middle of the night. Her stomach was cramping. Squinting with pain, she stumbled down the hallway to the bathroom. Opening the door, she hurried to the toilet, not bothering to flip on the light switch. She sat, then rolled forward as a knot tightened in her bowels. Gritting her teeth, she reached out for support toward the edge of the tub and—

Later a paramedic asked Abriella when she'd last been in the bathroom, and she said she couldn't remember, not exactly. The man went back to his business. After a while they wheeled Cleo, short for Cleotilde, out of the bathroom, out of the house, on a gurney under a damp white sheet. Her father was inconsolable.

Branson came down to join Abriella, grimacing with each step. He sat on the grass beside her.

She saw Branson was crying.

"You shouldn't be here with me. I'm not sure... I'm not sure I'm a good man. You're not safe with me."

She ran a hand through his hair.

He turned to face her. "You should leave—"

Abriella took Branson by the arm, and helped him to his feet.

"And go where? I haven't had a home for years. You still don't get it, do you? I hope we find your daughter, I really do, but don't think I'm here for her. I'm not here for you, either." Branson wiped his face with his hand, then wiped his hand on his shirt.

"Then why?"

"You ever really hate someone, for really good reasons? Nursing that hate, no matter the cost?" Abriella took Branson by the hand and walked him back towards the car. "All that hate, all that evil... it turns you into what you hate."

Branson sniffled.

"I won't die curled up in a bathtub with meth in my bloodstream and no one in the world knowing my middle name." She squeezed his hand. "That make sense to you?"

"Too much sense."

THIRTY-THREE

"Detective Woost, ya look like ya kin use some sleep."

Woost signed the document, returned the clipboard to the uniformed officer, and sighed. Beside her at the motel desk, Sheriff Nevarez slouched with his flabby arms crossed. Another town, another crime scene, and yet another local police department that didn't take kindly to outsiders. Besides the provincial pride that came with an elected badge, they were often unreconstructed sexist pigs, too.

"I'm fine, thanks."

"You sure? 'Cause that's one helluva set of bags under those pretty brown eyes," Nevarez said. "Maybe you should book a room for the night while you're here." Woost couldn't believe it. The corrupt old man actually winked at her. In response, Woost coolly turned to the motel manager.

"You say the bodies were found by room service?"

"Yes, Ma'am. They called down for a bottle of wine. Done that every time they've been here. We don't really have room service, but he always tipped well, so the girls, they'd bring up a bottle and a couple of clean glasses."

"They were regulars?"

"Oh no, you don't get it." The manager shook his head. "Mr. Ponds, he comes in all the time. Every week, I'd say. But he's always with someone different, if you see what I'm saying."

"Prostitutes?"

"I didn't say that. I mean, I don't know." He raised both hands in a defensive gesture. "Our guests' business is their business. We don't get involved."

"Uh huh." Woost lifted a photocopied pamphlet off the counter. It advertised a local escort service. Pulling her cell phone out, she dialed the number at the bottom of the sheet. The motel's phone rang.

Woost smirked. "We're not here for that. Wouldn't be my business anyway. But don't play games with me, okay? The dead girl, did she work for the motel?"

"Not in a—"

Woost cleared her throat.

"Yes Ma'am, she did."

"So, save yourself a lot of grief and provide the Sheriff here with everything you've got on her. Start with name, address, and phone. Then go from there. I find you've held anything back, then you and I are gonna get real well acquainted."

Woost left the locals to sort things. She didn't much believe that the dead Chinatown prostitute would prove pertinent to her case, but it'd keep the blue starch boys out of her hair. She climbed the stairs to the second floor balcony.

"Detective Woost," a voice called.

A uniformed cop chased after her, taking the stairs two at a time. As he came to the top, she peered over his shoulder at the view of the courtyard below. She imagined the cop had retraced the steps of Branson Turaco, machete in hand, prepared to kill his colleague.

"Detective Woost, there's a call for you inside. Came in right after you left." The cop was young and in shape, but out of breath. A pack of cigarettes bulged in his shirt pocket. "It's a police commissioner. Someone named Pigeon."

"Gideon," she corrected. "Tell you what. Take your time going back. Stop for a smoke along the way. Then when you get down there, tell Commissioner Gideon that you just missed me. Tell him you don't know where I'm off to, I didn't say."

"You want me to lie to a police commissioner?"

"To a police commissioner who the Governor has on speed dial? Yes, that's exactly what I want you to do." The young cop was bewildered. "What's your first name, Officer Hales?"

"Justin."

Woost gave him a womanly smile. She could do that when she had to. "Justin, the Commissioner has some bad news for me. I already know what it is. He doesn't really want to deliver it, and I definitely don't want to receive it. So, I'm just playing phone tag for the weekend. You understand?"

Officer Hales considered it.

"Not really. But I'm due for a smoke break anyway."

"Thank you, Justin. Now tag, he's it, okay?"

As Woost approached room 212, her mind raced. There were five messages from Gideon on her cell phone already. She'd just have to ignore them until she could catch up to Branson Turaco. Whatever came after that, she'd deal with it then. Woost opened the door to room 212 and stepped inside.

Michael Ponds and the Asian girl were stripped, not just of their clothes, but their skin, too. It was as if they wore dripping red body suits. So much for the carpet. Maybe the ceiling of the room below as well. The initial police report proved deficient even at a glance. It reported multiple lacerations made by a long, straight blade, maybe a machete. But the detail didn't precisely map to the extreme nature of the injuries. The cause of death for the victims read *loss of blood*. As regarding Ponds, it might as well have read, *loss of head*.

Two uniformed cops stood in the room by the dresser. They scrambled as she entered, hands ducking into pockets. A leather wallet dropped to the floor. Woost reached down, picked it up, and held it open.

"How much did we get? You *were* going to cut me in, right? You look like team players."

The officers looked at each other but said nothing.

"Get out of here. *Now*." They scampered out of the room and closed the door behind them. Woost brought out her cell phone, ran through the stored numbers, found the one she needed, and hit *SEND*. She balanced the phone in the crook of her neck while she snapped on a pair of latex gloves and began to examine the scene. Woost gave the room a cursory search, opening dresser drawers, and taking a peek inside the empty closet. She didn't expect to find anything. No one packed heavily for a tryst.

"Hello?"

"Candice."

"Susan? I can barely hear you. The—" Taking hold of the phone, Woost brought it closer to her mouth.

"Yeah, it's me. I'm standing in a motel room over two very dead bodies. One of the victims is one of your husband's co-workers. He'd been reporting Branson's activities to me."

"Jesus."

Since Roy's death, Woost had spent hours on the phone with Candice, and over time they'd grown close. They shared the story of their lives, gave and received encouragement as needed, and even occasionally gossiped. But Woost never directly revealed her conviction that Branson was responsible for Madeline's disappearance. And it felt like a betrayal of their friendship to do it this late in the game. Woost hardly knew where to start.

"A few days ago, we found—"

"I know," Candice interrupted. "He called me."

That was a relief. Not that it made the next bit any easier.

"This isn't the first crime scene since then. I believe he's had a serious psychotic break. He could be striking out against everyone he thinks has done him wrong. I believe that puts you in danger." The next sentence was the hardest. "I don't see how this doesn't end with him on your doorstep with a gun." The phone was silent. "Candice? Are you—"

The call ended.

THIRTY-FOUR

Once they got back on the highway, Branson took the wheel. He couldn't stop checking the rear view mirror for a red pickup truck that he expected would race up behind them, ram the Jeep and force them off the road. In a way, he almost welcomed the paranoia. It helped distract him from mulling over the choices he'd made. Branson looked to Abriella and swallowed hard. She fidgeted with the GPS tracker, using her thumbnail as a screwdriver, then squealed when the nail broke. She slammed the unit down on the dash and turned her attention to her phone. A moving map filled its screen.

"Just keep to the speed limit and we'll hit the Fontainebleau by dusk, give or take."

Branson gripped the wheel tighter. "No, *we* won't," he said. "I'm dropping you off at the first bus terminal we come across. You're going home."

Abriella glared at him. "Says who?"

In the backseat the Boy grunted through his duct-tape gag. His arms were bound at his sides, with yet more tape tightly wrapped around his midsection.

"Says the—" Branson searched for the right word for a moment. He didn't like the one he settled on, but he realized it was accurate. "—*kidnap victim* in the backseat. Maybe you weren't a criminal before, but you are now. That is unless I leave you off, and you call Lt. Woost straightaway. Tell her I forced you. Or that you came along under false pretenses. Tell her that you're a silly young girl and didn't know what you were doing, she'll like that."

"I won't do it. You know I won't."

Only empty road showed in the rearview mirror.

"You *will*. You've no choice. I've broken all sorts of laws. There's no going back, not for me. But you can still walk away. And that's what you'll do."

"You're not worried about the law. You're thinking about Spiegler. That's not gonna happen to me." She sought solace in the cell phone on her lap.

"Damn straight it won't." Branson jerked the wheel and steered to the curb. The GPS tracker slid across the dash and fell in a clatter to the floor. The Jeep came to a lurching halt.

"Get out."

Abriella shook her head. "No."

"I said *get out*, now."

"And I said *no*."

Branson reached across her and forced the door open. Abriella didn't budge, not even when he unlatched her seatbelt and shoved her shoulder hard with the palm of his hand. His face reddened.

"Just fucking go."

She shook her head again, this time with less conviction.

Anger flared up inside Branson. For five years he'd heard nothing but accusations and insinuations from police officers, and co-workers who used to be friends, that he'd been responsible for Madeline's disappearance. All Branson wanted was for Abriella to get out of the Jeep and go as far away from him as she could. He desperately wanted to do the right thing. He *needed* Abriella to be safe. Because the reporters at *The Telegraph* called him The Mortician, and he couldn't stand another death on his conscience. Marius Spiegler's demise was about all he could take.

Branson struck Abriella with an open hand, a quick slap across her face. Her hands rose too late to block the blow. A bright purple bruise bloomed across her ebony face. Pearly tears built up in her eyes. Branson checked the rear view mirror for red pickup trucks and whispered softly, with as much gentleness as he could muster.

"Please... go."

Abriella placed her cell phone in the cup holder between the seats. She spoke quietly, with a voice that should've belonged to someone else, someone weaker, anyone but her.

"Don't touch it and it'll take you all the way to the Fontainebleau. The volume's on the side if you prefer audible instructions. I don't like the voice, so I don't use it. But maybe it'll give you some company."

Branson closed his eyes. "Thank you."

Abriella climbed out. Before closing the door, she retrieved the GPS tracker from the floor and put it on the empty passenger seat. Then she stepped away from the Jeep.

The door swung shut. A pang of regret struck Branson hard. It was difficult to leave behind the young woman who, in all probability, saved his life, then tended his wounds, and finally nourished him with her kindness and her body. He was leaving her at the side of the road like trash. Abriella deserved better, but that meant she deserved to live.

Branson pulled away and resisted the urge to watch as Abriella's image grew smaller and smaller in the mirror. He focused on the road ahead.

THIRTY-FIVE

In daylight Fontainebleau Pier looked like any of the other abandoned beachfront properties perched along the rim of the Pacific Ocean. Branson parked at a discrete distance, and studied the deserted resort through a pair of binoculars he'd found stashed in the compartment between the seats. The grounds of the pier were overgrown, but Branson could see enough of the wooden boardwalk, gazebo, and main Tyrolean lodge to imagine what the property had been like in its heyday. A line of imperial California Bay Laurels rimmed the estate, reinforced by a row of sickly woodrose shrubs and a high, wrought-iron fence that in places was rusted through. Once it'd been a palace for the rich; now it was derelict.

As night fell the Fontainebleau took on a more sinister appearance. Shadows across the stucco and red clay shingles cast wild figures with spidery legs and grinning faces onto the lodge. Each leaning tree trunk, roots exposed like tentacles, conspired with the cowering shrubs to infuse the property with a fresh sense of anxiety. There was simply too much hidden.

A dim light flickered in a few of the yellowed windows. Someone was most definitely home.

Branson eased the Jeep down the block. Abandoned houses stood at the shore's edge, victims of a boom and bust economy. Pulling into the cracked driveway of a presumably empty house, he killed the engine. Then Branson leaned over into the back seat and shook the Boy.

He awoke with a feverish spasm, head tucking into his chest for protection, every muscle tensed. Branson grabbed him by the shoulders, forced him up so they'd see eye to eye.

"I'll take the tape off your mouth. Not gonna have any trouble, am I?" The Boy shook his head.

Branson gripped a frayed edge of duct tape and without mercy, tore it from the child's face. A thin layer of skin remained on the adhesive. The Boy gasped for air in big mouthfuls and blew that out between pursed lips. Branson let him go on for a while, puffing like a fish, until his breathing became more regular.

"You know where we are?"

The Boy turned and peeked over his shoulder. A look of recognition passed over his face. He nodded.

"Do you know why I brought you here?"

With obvious concentration and effort, he whispered, "Daughter."

"Madeline," Branson said.

"Mad-a-line," the Boy echoed faintly.

Without taking his eyes off his captive, Branson thrust his hand into his sock. He pulled the Boy's folded hunting knife free. Swinging it open, he turned to the Boy and cut through the tape that bound his wrists. The Boy brought both hands to his chest and curled them against his breastbone.

"They took her, just like they took you." Branson moved the blade lower and freed the Boy's legs. "Do you remember that? Do you remember your parents?"

A confused grin crossed over the Boy's features as he stretched out his legs. When he spoke, the words came out slow and tortured, some syllables elongated and others rushed, like a halting attempt at some foreign language.

"My- Mom- mie?"

"Do you remember her?"

The Boy eyed the knife. Branson had unknowingly raised it in the excitement of the question. He retracted the blade, and set the knife on the dash behind him. The Boy's defenses came down a notch.

"No- but- she—"

"Go ahead..."

"Pwitty," the boy said. He seemed proud of himself, perhaps as much for dredging up the memory as the word. "She- was- pwitty."

"Madeline was pretty, too. Like her mother. Only, without the evil that gets into you as you get old." Plainly, the Boy understood nothing of what he'd just said. It didn't matter. Branson didn't really expect the conversation to be two-sided. "I'm sorry for what I did to you, I really am. But, I think some of that evil got in you too, put there by those people in the desert. I hope that you can get all of it out and have a good life after all this is over."

"Over?" The Boy asked, as if the idea was completely foreign. Perhaps from his point of view, it was. The Boy's past was stolen from him and his future was uncertain. If he couldn't remember when it all began, how could he guess that it would ever end?

Branson hadn't noticed the raft of tiny, scribbled scars on the Boys face, arms and hands. He slid the Boy's shirt up, and found even more striking wounds. Time had closed the lacerations, but Branson doubted they'd ever really heal, at least not in the ways that mattered most. He couldn't imagine what the Boy had gone through, living with the Moonmen at Tranquility Base. Branson looked away, not wanting to see Madeline in the Boy's condition. He stared at his own hands, hands that not long before had pummeled a child he now couldn't face.

"Can't- be- over," the Boy said.

"Why not?"

"Cause- you- still- alive." The Boy burst into gibberish sprinkled with spare words, as if Branson's newfound concern was being mocked. "She- was- pwitty- pwittypwittypwitty—"

Branson fell back in the front seat. His hunched shoulder blades slammed against the steering wheel, and the horn sounded briefly. He swiped the knife off the dash, flipped it open, pointed at the child and screamed.

"Shut up."

"Pwitty- pwitty Mommy—"

"Shut up. Shut up—"

"So pwitty- like- daughter."

"Shut UP."

Branson lunged forward with the blade and stopped at the Boy's throat. He pressed the knife against a tough white scar, and didn't want to stop there. It would've been an easy thing to end the mocking. It only required a flick of his wrist. The laughter quickly dwindled and again the Boy shook with fear.

Branson reached for more duct tape.

He taped off the Boy's mouth and bound the child's hands anew, behind his back. They sat in silence, waiting for the cover of night. The Boy's body odor was overwhelming in the closed car, a smell more like a wet animal than a human. Branson opened the windows.

The sky darkened and a chill wind rolled in off the Pacific. No crickets chirped, no cicadas sang. Besides the dry tree branches brushing against each other, there was no sound at all, not even from the ocean. Then the wind died, the trees quieted, and the din of profound silence became too much for Branson to bear.

"If you were my son, I'd do this for you too, every bit of it. Please remember that."

The Boy didn't so much as twitch, and gave no indication he'd even heard him. Branson believed there was still a spark of humanity in the Boy, buried somewhere beneath the scar tissue and brainwashing. Branson *had to* believe that. But just then, the Boy might as well have been carved from granite, more like a statue of a child, no longer a part of the human world.

In the silent night, with only a mannequin as a companion, Branson felt as if he'd slipped out of time altogether. He tried to imagine Abriella arriving back at her home, ready to resume whatever she could make out of her regular routine after everything that had happened, but he couldn't. Nothing existed outside the Jeep. Only black night, and then the void.

The sound of outboard motors cutting through water echoed up from the ocean. Grabbing Abriella's backpack, Branson jumped from the car and pulled the Boy roughly from the rear seat. He slammed the child against the Jeep while he slipped the pack over his shoulder, then put the point of the knife under the Boy's chin.

"Stay quiet, keep up, and do everything I tell you, if you don't want to die."

The Boy remained vacant, but when pushed towards the driveway he obeyed, and led Branson forward, towards the pier. The odd pair kept close to the curb. With one hand tight on the collar of the child's shirt, and the knife still clearly a threat, Branson prodded the Boy to move quicker, and he responded like a well-trained dog. Most of the streetlights were out. Moonlight drifted down through the trees, which made for weird shadows that danced as clouds crossed the sky. The crackle of the gravel and crumbled asphalt beneath their feet seemed unusually loud. Branson worried about that, but he'd come too far to turn back for fear of detection. He was too close to the answers he needed, and with every step forward, his resolve to confront those who'd taken his daughter grew.

The rusted wrought-iron gates of the Fontainebleau pitched crookedly towards the road, like a mouth full of misshapen teeth. Branson was forced to release the Boy to duck under a padlocked length of chain that loosely bound the gates together. He feared the Boy would bolt, but instead he stayed within reach, and even waited for Branson to grab hold of his collar and reposition the knife.

The cobblestone driveway of the Fontainebleau was in complete disrepair. Moss grew between the upturned stones, reducing what must've once been a purposefully geometric pattern to a random assembly of more or less flat rocks. From that distance, a ridgeline of empty flagpoles atop the Tyrolean lodge looked like nothing more than a row of spikes marking a medieval encampment's defensive perimeter.

Branson moved off into the overgrown lawn. There, grass rose to their knees and scraped across their pant legs as they went. Something snapped beneath Branson's foot. It was like a gunshot tore through the silence. He instinctively dropped to his haunches, and dragged the Boy down with him. After a minute Branson rose just enough to have a cautious look, like a wary animal loose on night-shrouded grasslands. As far as he could see, nothing moved, save grass in answer to the breeze.

Branson kneeled low to catch his breath and collect his thoughts. The Boy remained beside him. Branson's hand came across a smooth, curved surface on the ground, rougher than glass but slicker than rock, then with his fingers found two holes in it. The initial impression was of a bowling ball, but the object was too small and the idea too incongruous to stick. Branson's second impression wasn't near so benign. He had to rock the thing a bit, to remove it from its place in the ground. Lifted to the moonlight, the child's skull in Branson's hand fairly gleamed. A good portion of its eggshell-crisp crown was crushed when Branson had stepped on it.

"*Madeline?*" His daughter's name was carried on a whispered exhalation of breath, which hung there for a moment before lifting into the night. Branson dropped the skull. *It isn't her. It can't be. Madeline's not dead.*

He tried to remember the names of missing children Detective Woost had read off in the sheriff's station. *Kathy Spence, Tammy Jenson, Mark Forter. Teresa Combs...* It was one of *those* children, not Madeline. A tragedy of the highest order, sure. But not Madeline.

A malicious gleam shone from the Boy's squinting eyes. Branson raised the knife hard against his neck, and the tender skin there tightened under the blade. Again, the Boy's face fell slack.

The rear door of the lodge was just a short distance away, and the utilitarian entryway with the cracked and faded *Deliveries Only* sign above it beckoned to Branson. Still crouched low and on high alert, he led the Boy by the collar through the tall grass. Just as Branson was about to break cover to make a mad dash for the door across the clearing, it swung open. Branson yanked the Boy close. They both watched, wide-eyed and silent, from their hiding place in the grass. A glowing man in a spotless white gown exited the lodge, trod down the short stack of concrete stairs below the door, stood on the uneven pavement, and lit a cigarette. He took a long drag and exhaled. The smoke rose over his head like a released spirit. The man looked much the same as any factory worker out for a quick smoke—except for the flowing robe and iridescent skin. As far as Branson could tell, the man was unarmed.

From within the Fontainebleau, an indistinct voice called. The glowing man smirked, flicked away the cigarette, and turned to re-enter the building. At the top of the stairs, he stopped, turned, and tilted his head at an odd angle. A full minute passed. The voice called more urgently, and the glowing man returned inside. He left the door open, but the interior of the lodge was too dark to see anything in it.

Branson considered finding another way in, but the only other door visible was the main entrance, which was in the open, where the moon was bright, and that was far too dangerous. After a while, he nudged the Boy, and together they headed for the concrete steps.

As they skittered forward, Branson kept his eyes focused on the dark doorway. At the top of the stairs, he pushed the Boy on. They moved inside in jerky bursts of motion, a few footsteps at a time, until they came to another open doorway. The door was not on its hinges; it lay on the floor just before the threshold. It see-sawed on the uneven floor as they stepped over it, and Branson couldn't help but wonder if anyone else heard the death rattle. They stepped into a banquet hall.

A row of stained-glass windows lined the high walls, each depicting a scene of children at play. The window closest to Branson showed a young girl and boy sitting on a blanket with an open picnic basket between them. A small hole in the girl's face radiated a spider web of cracks that spiraled out chaotically. Moonlight poured through the hole, making the girl's head shine with a sinister halo.

An enormous dining table stood in the center of the room, a relic of long-forgotten banquets. It was festooned with ornate wooden inlays that were separating after decades of wear. Upon their approach, cockroaches scurried across the table, traipsing between discolored ceramic soup bowls. Branson dipped his finger into one. What soup remained felt warm. Branson led the Boy quickly beyond the banquet hall and into a smaller, darker room. Branson stumbled over something on the floor. He inadvertently drew back on the knife, and the Boy yelped right through the duct tape. A tiny drop of blood raced from a superficial slice on his cheek.

Scanning the carpet, Branson saw a dozen or so small sleeping bags, empty, each encircled by a length of old, brittle hemp rope.

And loose tangles of children's hair.

And dark stains.

A final sleeping bag sat bunched up in a corner like a giant caterpillar. That one was occupied, and a swarm of flies buzzed around it. Branson threw the Boy to the floor and motioned for him to stay put. The Boy offered no resistance. Branson didn't particularly want to know what was inside the bag, but at the same time it pulled him with an irresistible gravity. Swatting through the cloud of flies, he leaned down and pried back a flap on the bag with the point of his knife. Branson thought he'd found Madeline.

The girl in the sleeping bag was dead, open eyes cloudy, cheeks as pale as white marble. Some kind of infestation beneath the skin of her face caused tidal ripples, from across her cheeks to her distended ears. A single white maggot hung from the girl's right nostril and wriggled as if waving.

Branson's heart broke.

He fell to the floor beside his daughter.

He couldn't breathe.

Branson shut his eyes tight, dropped the knife, and brought his fists up to his face. The warmth fled from him, leaving behind a cold, empty shell. What he'd been told for the last five years but refused to believe was true. His daughter, his baby, his Madeline was dead.

And nothing else mattered.

Except...

When Branson again opened his eyes he realized that the dead girl on the floor was only a child. Madeline would be a teenager. And the cheekbones were too high, the brows too bushy. It couldn't be her. Couldn't be. This dead girl looked nothing like his Madeline. Branson retrieved the knife off the floor.

"Get up," he whispered to the Boy.

As he rose, a bluish halo grew around the Boy's head and his features darkened with the contrast. Branson took hold of him by the sleeve and tossed him to one side. Behind the Boy, the same glowing man they'd seen taking a smoke break outside stood in the doorway. His luminescent skin pulsed as he entered, throwing uneven shadows over the walls. The man moved with a dreamy, aquatic grace as he reached with a long, glowing arm under his robe.

Branson rushed at him with the knife. He collided hard with the larger man. The knife struck the man in the breastbone and collapsed flat to his chest, a glancing blow. A jagged red blotch streaked across the robe. The glowing man didn't flinch. Instead, he grabbed hold of Branson, clutched one hand across his face, seized Branson's wrist with the other, and squeezed. The knife slid from Branson's hand. The glowing man forced Branson to his knees, then forcefully jutted a knee to his chin. Branson's jaw exploded in agony, and he fell on his back, the crown of his head cracking against the floor. He kicked against the glowing man's legs, trying to topple him, but only succeeded in pushing himself a few inches away. The man released Branson's wrist in order to reach back into his robe. Branson never hesitated. He scrambled for the knife before his adversary could properly respond. Branson rolled, righted himself, and launched at the glowing man. This time he held the knife with both hands and aimed for the neck.

The glowing man slid the narrow mouth of a metal whistle between his lips. Before he could blow a note, Branson jammed the knife into the man's esophagus. As Branson cranked down on the hilt, the blade tore upward under the man's jaw, through his tongue, and lodged in the soft palate beyond. Blood gurgled from the whistle. Branson fell away.

The glowing man reached for the knife, now stuck deep in his chin, but he couldn't close his fingers around it. A look of profound frustration passed over his face, followed by a flash of panic. Then the man fell forward on the knife.

The glowing man's luminescence failed, and his skin darkened, until only a pale, nearly featureless corpse remained.

Branson stared at the body, unable to look away. If someone else rushed him right then, he'd not have been able to respond. This wasn't like St. Abaddon, who'd died in a moment of chaos and confusion. No, Branson meant to kill this Pacifican.

Crouched among the sleeping bags, the Boy grinned.

Murder, Branson thought. The word stung.

The idea meant less to him than he'd imagined it would.

THIRTY-SIX

Branson led the Boy quickly through the remaining three rooms in the lodge, which were dimly lit, decayed, and empty. When they arrived at the double-door front entrance, it was wide open, each side propped with broken planks from the boardwalk. They exited and walked side by side, Branson's hand on the Boy's shoulder, down the edge of the walkway. Branson kept his eyes in motion, watching for figures hiding in the shadows. The boardwalk moaned and creaked with every step. The breeze freshened as their path forward narrowed, with the trees on both sides forming a canopy of rustling leaves. The moon disappeared. Together they walked on.

The canopy ended at the end of the boardwalk. Sand on the beach reminded Branson of Tranquility Base. Moonlight reflected on the ocean around a monolithic pier. They passed through a pair of huge barn-like doors into a covered wooden bridge. Past that, the platform divided off into three separate fingers, each docking bay progressively larger. Light beamed from the far end of the center bay.

Branson pressed the knife tight to the Boy's ribs.

Each step drew them closer to the light. As they exited the bridge, Branson squinted at the group of Pacificans gathered at the end of the pier. Some of the white-hot silhouettes simply stood and waited, while others crouched and worked ropes and winches. It wasn't that they were bathed in light. The light emanated *from* them, intense enough to blur his vision. Like a flock of birds, they turned as a group to face Branson and the Boy. They all looked alike, as if race and gender and all traits of heritage were in the process of being scoured away. Even their expressions matched. As Branson and the Boy came forward, the Pacificans on the pier remained still.

Below them, six boats bobbed in the water. Five small dories and a larger lugger, all tethered to the dock by thick mooring lines. Children stood aboard each boat, still and expressionless. Branson recalled how his own dazedness lingered on, well after his exposure to eel's blood.

A glowing woman emerged from among the others. She moved toward Branson and the Boy with a sense of authority and purpose.

"Who are you?"

Branson pulled the Boy close and slid the knife under his chin. Even the woman's eyelids glowed.

"I'm here for my daughter."

"You believe she's with us?"

"I know she is."

"I assure you, she's not."

Branson had come too far to be denied so easily.

"She may not be on this pier tonight, but your people took Madeline, and I'm here to bring her home." The quizzical tilt to the woman's head made the declaration seem foolish.

"And how would that work, exactly?"

"You'll take me to my daughter, right now." Spittle sprayed from Branson's mouth with each syllable. He yanked back hard on the Boy's hair and when he pressed the knife tighter to the child's throat, a trickle of blood ensued. The Boy yelped. "Or I'll open his goddamn neck all over the pier."

In response, the glowing woman merely arched a single eyebrow, which under the circumstances amounted to a wildly emotional response.

"You will?"

"I *will*."

"I suspect perhaps you would. A father's love is an awesome thing. We understand that here and we know just how far a man might go for his children. Sadly, I'm in no position to make any arrangement with you."

"Then you'll take me to Benedict Shallcross."

The name caused a stir in the group, but the woman remained unperturbed. She took a step towards Branson and the Boy. Branson jerked back and the woman stopped.

"You assume the life of your young hostage has value to us. Have you considered that it might not?"

Branson suddenly felt very exposed. His hand shook and his voice crackled with uncertainty even as he tried to regain control of himself.

"You get those kids off those boats. Then take me to my daughter."

"No."

It wasn't the glowing woman who spoke. Both masculine and feminine, the voice drifted up from behind Branson and the Boy like the melody of a song echoing through a hallway. Branson whirled around, bringing the Boy with him. The glowing man from the electronics store approached, dragging a large canvas bag behind him.

"You stop right there," Branson hissed.

The man swung the bag to the pier in front of him, then stopped. Branson snapped his head back and forth between the man and the woman. He was lightheaded. Every better instinct screamed for him to run. But he didn't.

"Both of you, just freeze."

The glowing man overturned the canvas bag. A body spilled out onto the pier.

"Now *that*," the woman said, "is a proper hostage."

At first, it didn't appear to Branson that Abriella was breathing. Panic surged within. Then Abriella's chest rose and fell slightly, and his panic receded a bit. The glowing man removed a familiar handgun from a pocket and aimed it at the back of Abriella's head. The woman spoke in the same cool tone as before, as if the entire situation hadn't changed.

"So now, I'll make the demands and you'll follow them. Understand?" Heart and mind racing, Branson couldn't respond. "I want you to slice this child's throat, just as you said you would."

The Boy tried to bolt, but Branson held him tight with the knife still against his throat. The child's eyes went wild with fright, and he looked younger than ever. Not *innocent* exactly, but sympathetic and crying for simple human compassion, as is the plight of all lost children everywhere and for all time. Branson knew then that he'd never be able to kill his hostage; in the end, it was all a bluff.

"Back and forth, saw right down to his spine," the woman demanded.

That wasn't possible. He was unable. The woman motioned to the man who stood over Abriella.

"Do it, or I'll have Lennon here put a bullet in your girlfriend's brain." Her tone remained frighteningly impassive, which convinced Branson she'd follow through. "Or maybe a two-shot to her skinny belly. One in the pancreas, one in the liver. That would be painful and it'd wake her up just long enough for you to say goodbye." The Boy stared up at him. "Could you stand the agony of watching her bleed out?"

In the Boy's pleading gaze, Branson tried to find the monster who'd stabbed Spiegler. He could not. Instead, he saw a vulnerable child molded by evil—lost but not yet *lost*.

"Mad-a-line," the Boy mumbled through the duct tape.

Lennon pulled Abriella up by the armpits and draped her face over the metal rail that ran along the dock at water's edge. Then he placed the muzzle of the pistol against Abriella's stomach.

"Stop," Branson whimpered. "Leave her be. *Please*." With that, the woman's glow intensified.

"Then do what I've told you."

"I... can't." Branson dropping both hands to his sides, and the knife clattered to the pier. "I won't."

The Boy stood. The woman removed the duct tape from his mouth. He spit. Then his eyes narrowed and a faint glow pulsed from his face and hands. As the woman assisted, the Boy tossed off all restraint like a dog shaking off rainwater. Then he removed his shirt. As his scars came into fresh sight, Branson saw that they weren't, in fact, simple evidence of child abuse. The lines that marred the Boy's flesh formed a nearly perfect, almost natural pattern, the sort of thing found in nature, if one only looked closely enough.

A sudden blow struck Branson. The pier spun, and he collapsed head-first onto the dock. The wooden plank met his forehead with a loud crack. Lennon towered over him, and his glow left trails of light like vapor in the air when he moved.

"Didn't work out quite like you'd planned, did it? What did you think? That you're the first to come looking for their precious lost child? That's what *I'm* for, to tie up loose ends. Like you."

Lennon's boot connected with Branson's hip. A shockwave of pain exploded from the point of impact. The force of the blow rolled Branson to the edge of the pier. Loose planks clanked under his weight like the keys of a wooden vibraphone. A swift kick to the ribs folded him over, as the breath fled his lungs.

The woman wrenched Abriella off the railing by a fistful of hair and shoved her into the closest boat. The Boy snatched the knife off the dock, and thrust it against Branson's abdomen, cutting into him at about the same spot where he'd stabbed Spiegler, but much more shallow. Blood burst from the wound. Branson screamed, expecting the blade to sink in again, this time deeper. Instead, the boy whispered into Branson's ear, "Mad-a-line."

Scooping up the pack, the Boy swung it over his shoulder as he backed away, and winked.

"I'll take care of this," Lennon said to the glowing woman. "You go. Leave me the last dory, and I'll catch up to you. This piece of shit killed Leaf." The glowing woman gave Lennon a casual wave of the hand. "Make him squirm for a long time before he dies."

"I intend to." Lennon glared at Branson, the words slurred out through lips curled in a bestial snarl. "I'm going to draw this out as long as I can. Don't worry, I'll be there."

One by one, the gathered Pacificans filed aboard the boats, an assembly line of glowing automatons. The Boy glanced back at Branson before joining them.

The last dory, children on deck, remained docked as the outboard motors around it roared to life. Sails turned to catch the wind. None of the children reacted either to the noise or the sudden motion, but from his vantage point at the edge the pier, through watery eyes, Branson thought he saw the girl closest to the bow of the moored dory blink.

Lennon thrust the heel of his boot into Branson's gut. Branson tried to scream, but the air had been driven from his lungs, and the sound he uttered was desperate and puny. Lennon aimed, and planted a kick square in Branson's ribs. The force of it flipped him over onto his side. The rotten deck planks clattered and creaked under his weight as he landed. He clutched at the dock, and tried to pull himself away. Lennon grabbed Branson's hair, yanked back, and slammed his head flat to the planking. When Branson felt the muzzle of the gun at the back of his neck, he wondered if he'd hear the shot, or if death would outrace sound. Instead, Lennon unleashed a series of quick, violent blows on Branson. Inflamed flesh bubbled with hot blood. Breathing hard, Lennon took a step or two away.

Branson pulled in his knees, righted himself, and pushed off. He struggled to his feet, vision wobbling as if the dock moved in a mad to-and-fro. He bent at the knees, balled up his fists, and figured he must've have looked pathetic, assuming the stance of a bare-fisted fighter. He swayed, and was unable to properly focus, but the man *glowed*, and that was enough.

Lennon laughed as he pocketed the gun. The throaty hum of outboard motors grew distant.

Branson's arms fell to his side and his fists unfurled. He hadn't the strength left to fight. It would be futile. He was exhausted. Then Branson thought of his daughter and fresh anger fueled him.

"Stay out of my way," Branson commanded as he went for the remaining dory.

"Even if you got past me, look at how small those lights are out there, on the great sea. Soon, they'll vanish in blackness. You really think you could find them out there?" Lennon snickered. "You've *lost*. You'll never see your daughter again. And now you're going to die."

Branson made as if to head towards the dory regardless. But then he lifted one leg and rammed it back down, his heel cracking through a discolored wooden plank. It broke in two. As the shorter half teeter-tottered up, he caught it his hands. Three rusted nails protruded from the end. Drawing it back, he rushed forward as Lennon retreated a step, and swung with every ounce of strength he could muster. The board landed flat across the side of Lennon's face, nails disappearing into his temple.

Lennon howled in pain, stumbled, and fell. Flat on the deck, he wrapped his hands around the plank and pulled, but the nails were too deeply embedded in his skull. He screamed and thrashed, muscles flexing, trying to tear himself free.

The handgun dropped out of his pocket.

Branson reached down, took hold of Lennon's ankles, and pulled him to the edge of the dock. Still screaming, he left a thick trail of blood behind him. Straightening up, Branson kicked the board attached to the Pacifican's face. Lennon's frantic movements became convulsions. The blood seeping out of his head darkened. A urine stain spread across his white trousers.

A second kick sent the dying man over the edge. He splashed face down into the shallow water. It didn't take long for the air bubbles to cease.

Branson bent to retrieve the gun, but fell to his knees instead, then onto his back. He closed his eyes. He yawned once, and the world tasted of blood, so he let it go.

THIRTY-SEVEN

Branson awoke dazed and flat on the pier, surrounded by the children from the final dory. They stared down at him with curious expressions, as if they too had just awakened. The only exception was the young girl he'd seen at the bow. She held Szymon Kazanjian's gun in her hands and seemed groggy, but more alert than the others.

With a heave, Branson sat up. The children all took a step back, and gave him room. Branson held out his palm.

"Give that to me, sweetie?"

She didn't hesitate, and handed the weapon over.

"Are you God?"

Branson stowed the gun in his belt.

"No, I'm not God."

The girl pointed over the side of the dock. Lennon's body floated, caught up on one of the dock's supports.

"Only God can kill an angel."

Branson looked past the dead Lennon, who no longer glowed, to the single empty boat still tethered to the dock.

"How long was I... asleep?"

She shrugged.

He tried again. "What's your name?"

She squinted her eyes and puffed out her cheeks. Branson was afraid she couldn't remember, but then she answered. "Laurie. Laurie Felston."

"Okay, Laurie." He dug out Abriella's cell phone, and a well-creased, folded envelope from his back pocket. The phone was scuffed and the screen cracked, but he checked it, and it worked. "The girl that was here. Do you know where she is?"

"They took her," Laurie nodded.

"And the Boy? The one who..." Branson's hand went reflexively to his abdomen. The wound was superficial. "...stabbed me?"

"He went with them."

"Laurie, I'm gonna need you to be very brave. You need to lead these other children out of here. Just follow the boardwalk off the pier and keep going. There's a convenience store down the road that should still be open. You go in there, and tell them to call the police."

"*Call the police*," Laurie said like she was memorizing.

"And, when the police come, ask for Detective Woost. *Woost*, got it? Tell her everything you can remember about what's happened. Tell them about the people who took you."

"The angels."

He pointed out to the sea. "Tell Detective Woost that I followed the angels into the ocean."

There wasn't much money left in the envelope. That didn't matter, as he'd nothing more to buy. Rifling past the remaining bills, Branson selected a laminated badge. He clipped onto Laurie's collar the press credentials that Mick Grayson had prepared.

"Give them this. They'll know what to do with it."

Branson turned his attention to the phone, and to the best of his memory followed the directions Abriella had given him. He was half surprised when a nautical map came up. A red dot in the center of the screen represented the GPS device still in the backpack taken by the Boy.

The children milled around, with Laurie at the center. There was nothing to be done about that. Branson started with a shuffle, then limped towards the last boat. Suddenly, he realized Laurie was at his side.

"Your face was hairier when I saw you in his trailer."

He ran a hand over his chin. The fast hair growth had to be an aftereffect of the drug. "How much longer was it?"

She indicated an inch between her forefinger and thumb. At the current rate, that meant a couple days more, at most. He stepped down into the boat, untied the mooring rope, and the dory lifted on the tide.

"What're you gonna do?" Laurie asked.

Branson saw no reason to lie to her.

"I'm going to kill all the angels."

THIRTY-EIGHT

Branson's stomach growled. He hadn't eaten since... he didn't remember when. There was certainly nothing to eat on the boat, so he listened to his stomach while counting his blessings that at least the pain in his gut had subsided. He steered the boat towards the open sea.

The red dot sat motionless on the blue cell phone screen. As an experiment, he backed off the throttle and let the boat slow. Only then did the red dot move from the center of the screen. Not wanting to fall behind, he tightened his grip on the accelerator. The boat was incapable of catching up to the Pacificans, but he knew that they had to be headed somewhere, and that they would stop once they arrived. He only needed to keep the red dot on the screen long enough for that to happen. To lose them would be disastrous; Lennon had been right, it *was* a big ocean and, with their lead, he'd never be able to find them otherwise.

You should really stop lying to yourself, The Mortician said, echoing in his head the same way it had in the desert. *That feeling in your gut, that twisting knife? It's not worry or regret. You knew you were putting these people in danger. And you didn't care. What you're feeling is guilt, pure and uncut. You've called yourself innocent for so long, but do you really believe it? You didn't beat your wife, or did you? Do you know? Your wife left you because she couldn't deal with the stress of losing a child, right? It wasn't that she fell in love with another man? You were in your bed asleep the night that Madeline—*

A shape bobbed on the surface of the water, almost invisible in the darkness. As the point of the bow approached it, the outline of the floating object became obvious. It was a dead child floating facedown upon the sea. Branson looked only long enough to know it was dead, then he closed his eyes. He didn't open them again until he was sure the child was behind him, in the boat's wake.

He let the cellphone map lead him. Though he'd only traveled a few miles out into the ocean, it already felt like an incalculable distance. If there were a point of no return, he'd passed it and sailed into an endless alien world, beset in a darkness so profound that even moonlight couldn't dispel it. Abriella's phone was Branson's only umbilicus to a world he recognized. On that phone, the *LOW BATTERY* icon started to blink.

He was helpless, a prisoner of the battery in a cheap electronic device small enough to hold in his hand. If the cell phone failed, Madeline was lost. Forever.

The battery icon blinked faster. With each flash, the icon only grew weaker while doubt gnawed ever harder at Branson.

Stop pretending. There was never any real hope of finding Madeline. You know that because—

"No," Branson said aloud. "No," he screamed to the indifferent sea and sky. He smacked the phone twice with his palm, the universal last ditch effort to keep all small electronics going.

The screen went blank.

He let the phone drop to the boat's floor and brought his hands up to his eyes. Tears came, large and plentiful, careening down his face and neck. He stammered, lips trembling, and felt the last bit of hope inside him die. Branson's chest sank. His head pounded. Every wound on his body, every deep laceration and surface scuff alike, flared up in outcry. His body went flaccid and weak, and he slumped back against the idling outboard motor.

He wanted to scream out at the night sky and demand an apology from any god who might be listening, but his throat had gone dry and words were impossible.

Branson gave up. Not only on recovering Madeline from the Pacificans, but on life itself—on goodness in the world, on hope, on any chance for salvation. There was no light in the universe, only endless darkness, endless black waves against a matching horizon.

The outboard motor on the dory cut out, and the boat went adrift upon a silent sea.

After a time, Branson stopped sobbing. He wrenched the pistol free from his belt and held it in a surprisingly steady hand. He gazed at the night sky. As a child he'd sit with his grandfather at night on a backyard swing set. Grandfather would point out a constellation and he'd name it. Together they ate apples from Grandmother's tiny orchard and talked about the universe, and distant stars, or whether there was any life out there.

While Branson watched, clouds scudded across the sky. They ate the stars and his universe first imploded, then collapsed. There is no life, Grandfather. Not in the cosmos, and not here adrift on the terrible indifference of existence, either. Branson didn't know what it was, but it could hardly be called life. Branson raised the handgun and pressed the muzzle against his temple. His head dropped and he found himself staring into the water, which was black like the heavens, except for a bit of rippling reflection on its surface. In it he saw himself, a piece of broken human machinery. A broken and despairing body, nothing more. The boy he'd been, the man, the husband, all those were gone. The figure that stared back at Branson from the inky sea was empty, meaningless and pathetic.

Branson slid his finger over the trigger.

Maybe Madeline was dead after all. Had he known it all along but simply refused to believe? Had the police, his co-workers, and neighbors all been right? Maybe Branson had been wrong to enlist Spiegler and Abriella on his maniacal quest. Maybe he could find his daughter with just a quick pull of the trigger. He meant to find out.

Upon the sea, his reflected face began to glow. Branson lifted his eyes back to the sky, expecting to see a break in the clouds and the bright face of the moon beaming through the opening. But the heavens remained dark. Pivoting back, Branson stood agape as his reflection was consumed by a pulsing glow, until that was replaced by a shimmering ball of energy that crackled and sparked across the surface of the sea.

Branson lowered the pistol.

A tangle of phosphorescent eels rose from the depths of the ocean as one, bodies interwoven and twisted together in a slippery knot. In their union Branson found a pattern he recognized. It was the same as the scars that covered the Boy's body. Then like a flock of startled birds in flight, the eels scattered, and darted off through the ocean like little electric bolts of lightning, heading northwest.

Branson secured the gun back in his belt and went to work. The outboard motor was stubborn, but with a cough it fell to Branson's will.

He hit the throttle, and the boat roared to life. Following the streaks of guiding light that swam just beneath the water's surface, he remembered that St. Abaddon and the Moonmen believed blue eels to be agents of fate.

Branson briefly considered whether the eels might be leading him straight to hell, but he really didn't care. He decided instead to concentrate on the immediate matters at hand.

THIRTY-NINE

Lights danced on the horizon, and sent flickering tendrils across the ocean. With the help of the eels, Branson guided the dory toward them. As he came closer, the outline of a flotilla took shape. It was a patchwork made of a variety of watercraft, strung together by rope and timber. The Pacificans' home base rose and fell on the ever shifting sea like a lumbering ancient city. White smoke rose from steeples built on well-weathered yachts, pleasure boats and scows, billowing overhead like a mushroom cloud. Music blared, tribal drums rattling and voices shouting and singing, a mixture of '60 rock and roll, Southern Baptist repertory hymns, and Native American song.

Branson released the throttle to let the engine idle. A host of eels circled between his dory and the flotilla. Sometimes they broke the surface, either individually or in groups, like porpoises. The splashing and flapping of their bodies added a complex counter-beat to the Pacifican's strangely musical rhythms. The greatest accumulation of eels was massing under the boats, countless fireflies on a watery meadow.

Branson could faintly make out the outlines of glowing men and woman aboard the flotilla. They drunkenly danced and swayed. The light emanating from their bodies blurred them together, obscuring their individual shapes. Only Pacificans at the outer edges sometimes showed themselves, and every one of those was either exceedingly thin, or obscenely skeletal. It was impossible to guess how many. Fifty? A hundred? *Five* hundred?

The pistol held six shots.

In grade school, Branson felt sympathy for the Hessian soldiers who died at the Battle of Trenton. In daydreams, he imagined them asleep in their barracks, still warm and drunk from their Christmas celebration and oblivious to fate, as the Continental Army bore down from the west. Washington's men cut them down. It wasn't a fair fight, and it seemed to Branson anything but heroic. Being himself direly outmanned and outgunned changed his mind about that. Branson decided to wait until the party was ended, then raid the floating compound. He hoped the majority of Pacificans would be too wasted to fight back. He no longer saw any shame in killing those who might be too drunk to resist. In fact, the thought of such easy prey brought a smile to his face.

A shot came from the deck of one of the larger boats, and Branson instinctively ducked down before realizing that someone had merely fired a shotgun into the air in celebration. The report echoed over the sea. Six more followed, then a dozen in answer until, with volley upon volley, the roar became almost volcanic, and the quick muzzle flashes threatened to turn night into day.

Branson figured the Pacificans were unlikely to spy him in the dark, at distance. But only a few hours remained before daylight and easy detection. He hoped the party would die down by then and the revelers retire to their beds. It was all desperately uncertain, but the best plan he could think of, and at least it'd worked for Washington at Trenton.

An unmistakable splash sounded near a patchwork vessel that might once have been a cabin cruiser, but was by then little more than a half-deconstructed, shoddily rebuilt, and decidedly lopsided raft. A large number of glowing Pacificans were assembled there. Some clapped, while others waved torches in time with the music. A line of smaller figures stood motionless at the very edge of the vessel. The water beneath it glowed with the combined light of thousands of eels. Millions, maybe. Standing above that maelstrom, and at the precipice, were the children taken from the Fontainebleau. One of the Pacificans leaned forward, and pushed a child over the edge. Branson turned his head. Then came another splash. And another. Each was in time to the beat of the music. With horrible clarity, Branson realized that the party would continue until the Pacificans ran out of children.

Had *that* happened to Madeline?

Raw fury spread heat through Branson's chest and set his jaw rigid. He couldn't wait for morning to act. If he stood by and let them sacrifice the children, then he'd be no better than his tormentor Woost, the angry cop more intent on prosecuting a suspect than in saving that suspect's daughter.

Another child hit the water.

Branson leaned on the throttle. The powerhead jerked up as the engine came to life with sudden strength. A blanket of fine mist drenched him, seawater soaking his clothes, matting his hair to his scalp. He set the dory on a direct course for the flotilla. The little boat cut across the surface of the ocean so keenly, to Branson it felt like falling.

As the dory raced towards the flotilla, the eels in its path gave way, some to the left or right, and some diving straight down to the depths, where a dark cleft opened on an illuminated sea, as if struck by the staff of Moses. And with that, the Pacificans noticed Branson.

He withdrew the pistol and tried to level it at the scarecrow of a woman standing over the children, on the dilapidated cruiser closest to the bow. Branson's mouth tasted of salt, and a little of his own blood, too. He steadied his arm to meet the rhythm of the ocean, and drew a bead on the Pacifican woman. Gun-toting celebrants ran to the cabin cruiser, leaping over the gaps between vessels where there were no planks. From all over the flotilla, glowing people took notice. The first shots not fired randomly at the heavens peppered the sea around Branson. The woman at the bow stepped back, and as Branson raced closer she looked like a frightened animal on unfamiliar ground.

Fuck you all, the Mortician hissed in Branson's head as he fired his weapon. A spindly man next to the woman fell to the deck in an explosion of blood.

Armed Pacificans rushed to the rails of the cruiser, pushing the children out of their way. A few of the kids toppled into the water. The rest remained where they'd been pushed, obedient and still. The Pacificans' first volley missed Branson by a wide margin but scattered the eels swimming close around him. Then three shots in rapid succession hit their mark. The dory started to leak, and its engine sputtered.

Branson got off a shot but hit no one. A shotgun blast pelted one side of his boat, which rocked the thing near to terminal stability. The dory self-corrected, spun to port, then came to a rough idle parallel to the flotilla. A single rifle shot tore into the engine, setting loose a plume of white smoke. The motor uttered a mechanical, cacophonous death rattle as it died.

Branson stood ready to do the same, but first he swung his gun upward and fired off three quick shots into a Pacifican holding a shotgun. The man stopped glowing as he crumpled.

A shotgun blast sent a geyser of seawater over Branson. The waterlogged dory dipped, and when the stern reached the water line the ocean invaded, plunging the vessel forward and down with enough force to tear boards from its deck. Water rose quickly to his hips, and so Branson abandoned his position.

He stowed the pistol in his waistband, took a deep breath and dove over the sinking transom, into the sea.

On the cruiser, and all along the rails of the flotilla, glowing men and women stood above Branson, weapons relaxed at their sides, as they stared down at him with keen fascination.

The circle of eels closed around Branson. Their sleek, slippery bodies surrounded him in a whirlpool of slime and scales. The force of their movements pulled him down. He tried to push and kick his way free, but each movement was matched by corresponding movements from the swarm, twisting around his arms and legs as he flailed, keeping him enveloped in a slithering, skin-tight cocoon. Branson was about to scream, but slammed his mouth shut when one of the creatures tried to invade it. His teeth snapped down on the eel and it fluttered violently until he released it in a trailing line of eel's blood— the instant effect of which pummeled Branson. Panic overrode all sense of reason or control. He became spastic and reactionary, no more controlled than the impulse to snatch one's fingers away from sudden open flame. The eels sensed the change and swam together in a tight, geometric pattern around him. Through his haze of terror, Branson recognized the same pattern as the scars written across the body of the Boy. Somehow, that was almost calming.

The eels rubbed against him. Then simultaneously, the texture of their bodies changed, as if the direction of their scales had reversed. Their soft bodies went rigid and were as rough as sandpaper. Bits of

Branson's clothes and skin surrendered without resistance, sloughing into blood-streaked water. They'd shave him down to particles unless he found an escape, and soon. His lungs ached and throat convulsed. Even if the eels didn't grind him down to skeletal remains, in short order he'd drown anyway and be just as dead. Branson bent his knees, took hold of his legs, and curled. Then he uncurled, and with a powerful thrust, propelled himself through the glowing funnel. The farther out he went, the less dense became the swarm. Once he was able to extend himself, he swam with graceless urgency past the fleshless remains of a child caught swirling in the maelstrom. Fragments of flesh and bone circled in the eel's wake, as if in the winds of a tornado.

Branson broke into open sea. A few of the eels followed, but individually they seemed more curious than anything. His ears popped from the pressure and his muscles ached, but freedom gave him the burst of energy needed to finally break the surface. Branson gulped in a great balloon of air just before he'd been set to burst and sink. The rush of oxygen to his brain was almost as intoxicating as eel's blood. He swam as best he could towards the hulking flotilla. If anything, the Pacificans had redoubled their celebration in reaction to the sinking of the dory and Branson's apparent death. A total victory, they thought. At the rusted hull of a trawler, Branson struggled to climb the mesh of a fishing net that rested over the side. He grappled his way up the net like an animal, and lost the gun to the water below in the bargain. There was nothing to be done about that. On gaining the ship's deck, he slithered like a mollusk under the guardrails. Flat on his back, Branson waited for his pounding heart to settle. When it didn't, he pulled into a fetal curl and wrapped his arms around himself for warmth. Body heat was slow to return, but as it did, that resurrected his senses as well.

The Pacificans continued to party. No depraved oligarch on the Fontainebleau pier ever had anything over them in that regard. Branson crept behind a wall of metal oil drums to watch them dance. If not for the line of children arranged at the rail of the main vessel, it could've been a New Year's Eve party.

Branson needed better clothes and a weapon. Szymon Kazanjian's pistol lay somewhere on the ocean's floor, along with Branson's shirt and most of his pants. Crouching down along the rusted metal barrels, he came to an open door that led to the trawler's cabin. It was dark, and Branson ducked inside. He took a quick survey of the bridge, found nothing of use, and proceeded to the other side of the cabin.

FORTY

The stairs leading down from the bridge to the deck of the trawler were a perfect hazard comprised of uneven, moldy planks with toothy splinters, coated in slick algae and crystalized brine. Branson climbed down with his arms outstretched, toes testing each stair. Halfway down, a vile stench brought tears to his eyes. It was rotten fish for sure, and something danker. A thick, uncomfortable scent, like stewing mushrooms gone bad. At the bottom he ducked beneath a blackened beam and through an open doorway. An oil lamp of the sort once used by railway men burnt softly on a table at the center of the room. The pallid yellow light didn't reach as far as the walls. The floor moaned beneath him as he made his way to the lamp. Branson ran his thumb over the wick control at its base. The flame rose, and he lifted the lamp.

Warm light revealed a large room. Hundreds of tiny, shriveled fetal bodies stared back at him. They were held to the walls by hooks and clamps, rope and netting. Grotesque and distorted, their stretched faces warped into expressions of absolute suffering.

None of the bodies seemed fully formed. Bulbous heads topped emaciated torsos, diminutive arms ended in elongated, spidery fingers, while winding umbilical cords swung placenta like pendulums from distended abdomens. The children's eyes were primitive black pebbles set deep in wide, alien craters. Stranger still, many of the bodies featured ridged foreheads, webbing between their arms and ribs, and horribly misplaced, lipless mouths.

"They're salt cured."

The glowing woman who'd seemed in charge on the Fontainebleau pier stood in the doorway. Her iridescent skin, beneath the flowing lace of a ceremonial gown, cast almost as much light as the lamp. Though unnaturally thin, she could have served well as an object of desire for most men, and the envy of many women. She smiled at Branson as she entered the room. His knees went weak.

"They're beautiful, don't you think?"

"No."

"No, I suppose you wouldn't. Few people ever care to see the ugliness in their own sons and daughters, but it's easy to see it in the children of *others*." Her smile turned wicked, and it burned Branson. "It doesn't matter. It was our mistake to think pure children would survive in a world so corrupt. Once, we were naive. Now we know better."

Branson countered each step she took with one of his own, edging away. He didn't dare take his eyes off her.

"Why so many?"

"Fate takes our babies from us." Her face filled with reverence as she spoke, but her tone remained even. Conversational. "Our pregnancies are... difficult. We've lost so many sisters over the years."

"You abduct children—"

"We rescue them. From society. From *you* ." She pointed a slender finger at Branson, one that had no fingernails and maybe no fingerprints, as if she'd evolved beyond the need for either. "It's the greatest gift we can give them—a chance to live free from the shackles of a filthy, patriarchal society that celebrates depravity."

"A chance?"

She raised an eyebrow. "Whoever gets anything more?"

Branson eyed the door.

"Please don't run. It's a dangerous ship. You're confused and most likely suffering from hypothermia. I think you're quite likely to get yourself hurt." She drew a hand up her profile, a knowing smile letting him know it amused her to watch his eyes follow. "Fate has entrusted you to us. I'll help you, get you some clothes, keep you safe. My name is Holiday. You should trust me."

Branson didn't think that likely.

"What's yours?" she asked.

It was like looking into a doll's eyes. Branson remembered her on the dock, demanding that he cut the Boy's throat. Still, he felt a strange compulsion to answer her.

"Branson." It was a whisper. Again, the glowing woman smiled. This time, she lit the horrid room with it.

"Good to know you, Branson."

"I just want my daughter back."

"As do I." She petted one of the misshapen fetal heads on the wall. "She was my first, but fate took her. It was hard. So hard that I no longer desired to live. Then I surrendered myself to the will of nature. You must consider doing the same."

"Like *hell* I will." Branson dropped the oil lamp and ran. He slipped on the slimy floor and slid into the doorjamb, cracking his shoulder and spinning off his feet. He crashed down hard onto the floor, but kept himself in motion. He galloped out the door on all fours, then up the stairs like an animal, until he burst onto the bridge and his feet found purchase. He stumbled to the far exit and threw himself out, falling to his knees just outside the door, where a dozen or so armed Pacificans awaited him on the deck. They surrounded Branson and greeted him with jubilant smiles, even as they sharpened their aim. He raised his hands in abject surrender, which prompted from his captors a chorus of howling laughter, mixed in with a few cat-calls, and a smattering of applause.

Holiday emerged from the bridge, and a tall, bald Pacifican handed her a full-length sealskin coat. Holiday gently draped that over Branson, then helped him to his feet. With the garment's warmth, raw instinct took over and he drew it tight around his shivering body.

"Do you know why we're happy to see you?" she asked.

"No." Branson shook his head.

"Fate showed us in a vision that you'd come." Holiday nodded to a young man in the glowing crowd. He dropped a bundle of white clothes at Branson's feet then slid back into the crowd, to the cold comfort of its collective light. "You think you've made the choices that brought you here. It's understandable that you'd think so. But free will is an illusion. You could have made a million different choices and would still have ended up here, with us, right now. Do you understand what I'm saying, Branson?"

"No," and he meant it.

Holiday lifted the bundle of clothes off the deck and handed them to him. They were warm. "I suspect," she purred, "that you will, in time."

"Let me talk to Benedict Shallcross." Exhausted and confused, Branson just blurted it out. Again the Pacificans laughed and jeered.

"Soon," Holiday answered.

"No," Branson said. "*Now.*"

Holiday seductively ran one hand through Branson's wet hair, then grabbed a handful of it and pulled him roughly to her, face-to-face. She grinned, revealing a full set of undersized, yellow teeth. "First, there's something else you need to see. Then you must rest, it's been a long journey. After that, I'll take you to see Dryhten."

Branson wanted to protest, but there was no doubt who was in charge. Instead, he nodded limply and Holiday released his hair.

She led him through the crowd, over rickety wooden ramps between ships, and finally to the long, open deck where Branson had seen children lined up as if for a firing squad. She led him to the rail at the edge, and Branson followed her gaze down to a fathomless sea. The eels were only now dispersing, groups breaking apart and diving down into the darkness, like lightning as seen from above a storm cloud. The eels cut the water in intricate patterns, and the sheer number of visible creatures diminished, dropping to thousands, hundreds, and finally no more than a few dozen. The last of the eels skated along the surface of the sea, zig-zagging with shocking precision, before they too disappeared into the depths.

Holiday turned to a Pacifican standing at the wheel of a great winch. At the far starboard side of the flotilla, another man stood at another station. Holiday raised on arm, then let it fall.

"It's time."

The men cranked the handles on their wheels. A massive set of hemp ropes retracted, which pulled a huge dredging-net up from the sea. The sound of the rusted gears turning reminded Branson of the music made by *The Telegraph's* printing press, a strangely rhythmic crescendo of grinding and clattering noises. As enormous nets rose out of the water, Branson could just make out squirming shapes amidst the tangles of seaweed and debris.

Naked and white as snow, three children were pulled from the nets. The Pacificans yanked them aboard and dropped each one in turn onto the deck. Their bodies convulsed and were adorned with a familiar pattern of deep bruises and cuts. Holiday's face filled with reverence.

"*These* are the children that fate has chosen to join us."

FORTY-ONE

Detective Susan Woost sat with legs crossed on a wooden bench that reminded her of high school, and of times spent waiting outside the principal's office for her turn to receive discipline. She'd spent the entire day today ignoring her cell phone. At first she'd turned off the ringer, then the vibrate function, and finally powered down the phone itself. She knew the story. Her time had run out. It was over.

The state police trooper who'd pulled Woost over on Interstate 5 reminded her of Roy, back before the cancer stole the ruddy color of his face, and the chemotherapy took away most of his jet-black hair. Maybe that was why she'd offered no resistance when the officer insisted she follow him to the station to wait for Commissioner Gideon. Or maybe it was simply that exhaustion had finally taken its toll, and in her heart of hearts she'd welcome being compelled to walk away from the Turaco case once and for all. Woost just couldn't manage to do that on her own. Things felt... unfinished.

Flanked by a pair of troopers, a couple of suits from the Governor's office, and a handful of local reporters, Commissioner Gideon strode into the room.

Woost stood up and snapped to attention.

"You're wearing *sneakers*?"

"Converse All-Stars," she said meekly. "I was in a hurry and they're comfortable. Had I known..."

"Get used to those shoes, Woost."

Gideon turned to the troopers and, referring both to reporters and bureaucrats, growled, "Get these people out of here," which the state troopers promptly did, even though Gideon was not their boss. The doors closed behind them, and the Commissioner softened, slightly. He motioned for Woost to sit.

"I'm fine standing, sir."

"Suit yourself," he said, sitting on one side of the bench and pointing. "My shoes, I'm afraid, are not quite as comfortable as yours. Or maybe I've just been on my feet too long, trying to clean up your mess. Have you seen the papers?"

She had, in passing. The headlines weren't pretty. One stuck in her head, a single word in the largest print she'd ever seen on a newspaper: MASSACRE. She shrugged. "I get most of my news from the internet."

"The Governor's office has filed charges against you."

"For what?" she asked.

"Everything that his lawyers can shoe-horn into your size-six Converse All-Stars, I'd imagine. They'll scrutinize the warrants, weapons procurement procedures, man-hour requests. There are always errors in those kinds of things. Usually, no one cares. I assure you, this time they care." He crossed his ankles, leaned an elbow against the wall, and rested his head against his hand. "You won't be able to afford the defense team that it would take to clear you. It depends on the judge, but you may face prison time."

She shook her head. "For trying to save children."

"What children?" he asked.

"Laurie Felston, for one."

"We'll get to that," he promised. "First, though, I'll take your badge, gun, and ID. There's paperwork, too, but you can fill that out in the morning. To be clear, this is unconditional suspension without compensation. All benefits are frozen."

She expected to feel something when the other shoe dropped—sadness, disappointment, resentment—but instead, she felt nothing. She handed over her shield, weapon, and swipe card without blinking. Setting them aside, Gideon seemed relieved at the lack of fireworks.

"How long have you been chasing Branson Turaco?"

"Five years."

"Why him?"

"Roy Faune and I found numerous inconsistencies in his statements. He reported that he last saw his daughter when she went to bed at eight-thirty, but then later he said that he might have checked in on her before he went to bed himself. In another interview, nine o'clock was Madeline's bedtime. Then it was his wife, not him, who checked on her. All over the place." She could've named dozens of contradictory statements, but understood that Gideon wasn't interested in case history. He didn't even really want to understand her position. He had asked the question not to hear her answer, but to allow himself a chance to speak. She let him.

He started with a long, drawn-out exhale. "You know, I once worked a case, a credit union robbery that got outta hand. The whole thing was on video from eight angles, not an inch of lobby hidden from view. A horrible thing to watch, and I had to watch it fifty, sixty times. These bank customers and a teller got shot up in the crossfire. Close range bullet hits. Nasty stuff.

"So, I knew that crime backwards and forwards, literally. I could tell you—shit, I probably still can—what every one of the victims and witnesses were wearing, where they stood, what kind of purses the women had in their hands. So, we interviewed the witnesses. And it's a funny thing. An old man with early symptoms of Alzheimer, the one standing the farthest away from the action, he described the events perfectly, down to details I had to go back to the tape to confirm. The college girl at the back of the teller line? She gets most of it right, but there's things that I know from the tape are just dead wrong.

"But the customers closest to the gunfire? They can't even get the description of the assailant right. They have him wearing a jacket on a muggy ninety-five degree day. One says he wore glasses. Another has him black. The next one says Spanish. None of them were good witnesses.

"Here's the thing: sometimes the people closest to a crime have the worst perspective on it. Maybe it's some kind of natural defense mechanism or something, but the best witnesses are never the ones right in the midst of the action. It's always the guy on the outskirts, looking in from a distance. He's the witness you want."

Gideon paused. "Branson Turaco was closer to the crime than anyone else. You look for mistakes in his statements, you'll find them. I'd be worried if you didn't. You ask a man his favorite color enough times and you'll eventually get a different answer, just cause he's tired of answering the same way."

Shaking her head, Woost said, "No, it was more than that. Roy—"

"Roy is exactly what this is about." The Commissioner uncrossed his ankles and reached into the inner pocket of his sports coat. "I know what he meant to you. It wasn't a well-kept secret then, and now it's accepted history. I don't care, mind you. Lots of guys can't talk to their wives about the job. Hard to connect after a time. Not saying I agree with it, but I can understand it. So, Roy dies and he leaves you with this. We all have a case that we just can't let go. This was his. And you feel you need to close the case for him. I get it."

Woost started to say something, but stopped. She had no idea what she could say.

"What happened to Roy was a terrible thing. It shouldn't have happened. But you need to let it go, because you're not chasing a suspect, you're chasing a ghost."

Gideon withdrew an evidence bag from his inner breast pocket and handed it over to Woost. The name on the badge inside read, *Branson Turaco*.

"What is this?" Woost asked.

"Press credentials."

"No, sorry." Woost turned the thing over in her hand. "I know what it is. I mean, why do you have this and how did you get it?"

"Late last night, a little girl came in and gave it to a desk clerk at this station." Gideon stood and gestured towards an office door at the end of a narrow hall. Woost sprang from the bench and hurriedly made her way to the window in the door as Gideon followed behind. Inside, a little girl sat motionless in a plush leather chair.

"That's *Laurie Felston*."

"Yes, it is."

"How..."

"She says God gave her the badge to give to us. She says He saved her, and the nine other kids who walked in with her, from the men who killed her parents and took her."

"Did... did she describe God?"

"She did indeed. Then we took things a bit further and ran a fingerprint off the badge."

"And?" Woost faltered.

"Seems that God is Branson Turaco."

FORTY-TWO

Branson awoke flat on his back in the middle of a scream. He rolled over onto his side, fell off the cot and retched until his midsection could take no more. He pounded the floor with his fist, then lay back and waited to stop shaking. An hour later he did, just in time for fresh waves of nausea that sent his head spinning into a migraine that rattled inside his head like broken glass. Caked with vomit, his throat and eyes burning, he clawed at his chest and squirmed on the floor. Branson was unable to concentrate on anything besides the pain and nausea for more than a few seconds at a time.

Hours passed in much the same manner.

In his occasional lucid moments Branson wondered where the sustenance he puked up came from. He'd no memory of food or eating it, or of anyone bringing him anything. But he continued to vomit and stay hydrated, and as wretched as it was, somehow, he still lived.

No one came to clean Branson's squalor; of that there was no doubt. He lay in his own filth on the floor, amidst a heady mixture of urine, excrement, bits of regurgitated food, and blood. Sometimes he'd even try to stand, but that was like walking a tightrope, what with the motion of the ship, the mess on the floor, and his own miasma undermining his legs. More than once he fell to the floorboards and just lay there, as if dead.

From the beginning, he tried to keep track of time. It seemed important for reasons he couldn't quite grasp. The cabin's single porthole was barricaded from the outside, but enough space remained between the boards for Branson to tell the difference between day and night. He counted days by scratching lines with his thumbnail on the wall next to his simple cot. The marks of the first week were messily scribbled, and he couldn't be certain he didn't miss a day or two, but the second week's scratches were straighter. Branson took that as progress, a good sign.

By the middle of the third week, his handwriting was sure, and so was his head. The hypothermia, profound exhaustion, and madness of the basic situation had mostly receded. Plates of food were delivered, he discovered, in the morning and at night, through a slot in the door two inches off the floor. Fish, mostly.

Recovering and reasonably alert, Branson found himself alone with his thoughts. Sometimes the Mortician's cynical voice mocked him, but other times he daydreamed of Madeline, and even Candice, in their cozy home at Christmas with thick red ribbons and shiny green boxes. Or of bedtime pillows with lost teeth underneath them, waiting to be swapped out for coins while Madeline slept. Or birthday parties when her friends and schoolmates would run with foil pinwheels held high in the wind.

Over time, Branson came to understand how death row inmates sometimes choose suicide rather than simply awaiting their fate. As strong as the fear of death could be, it didn't compare with the horror of the past, which could neither be redeemed nor resurrected. Branson's memories hurt him too much to relive, and now he'd never make any new ones.

He sprang from his cot when the door to his prison opened. He took a quick, careless step, lost his footing on the slick floor, and found himself on his knees when two glowing Pacificans entered the room. They each took up a position at either side of the door, then Holiday stepped through between them. A third glowing man came in behind Holiday, carrying a large bucket of water and several hand towels, which he set on the floor in front of Branson.

"Clean up," Holiday commanded. She turned on her heel to leave. Branson shot off his knees and stood tall. The Pacifican guards tensed, but all Branson did was shout.

"You said you'd take me to Benedict Shallcross."

"Not with you covered in shit," Holiday said, as she left without looking at him.

The door slammed, someone threw the lock and again Branson was alone. He paddled over to the bucket, and was stunned by his reflection in the water. He'd grown a ragged brown beard streaked with white. His shriveled face was pale and sunken, his bloodshot eyes barely visible in their dark sockets, and fresh age lines at his temples.

Your face was hairier when I saw you in his trailer.

Branson sat before the bucket, cupped his hands, lowered his face, and started washing away accumulated grime. He tossed his ruined white shirt and pants to a corner. As he washed himself down, he thought of that night in the motel, when Abriella had cleaned his wounds. He wondered if she was near, maybe locked away in a cabin like his. It was strange to wish it, but Branson hoped she was. He didn't dare let himself consider where she'd be, otherwise.

The water in the bucket first went clay red, then murky brown, and finally all but black. He felt not just refreshed but reborn, as if wearing newborn skin. Branson didn't sit on the cot; it was too dirty.

Two Pacificans entered, handed him new clothes, scooped up the bucket and soiled towels, then left. Branson pulled the shirt slowly over his head, the better to nestle into the fabric and absorb the fresh wool scent. When he slid into the pants, he realized for the first time just how much weight he'd lost. The tattered remains of his size 38 jeans, wherever they were, wouldn't have fit him now. Branson cinched tight the drawstring of his new pants around his severely diminished waist.

Before too long, more Pacificans came, and Holiday with them. The men carried two buckets this time, along with a sponge, and several over-sized towels. They put the buckets on the floor, draped the towels over Branson's shoulders like a cape, and handed him the sponge. Holiday swept one hand through the air.

"Clean this room. After that I'll take you to Dryhten." Then they all left.

He cleaned, without rest. Absorbed in his work and his thoughts, Branson didn't bother looking up when the door clanged open again. He'd hoped for a fresh set of buckets and towels. Light footfalls slipped into the room behind him, then the door closed quietly.

A young woman had entered. Her glow was less intense than the others, and besides the slight glimmer of her skin, she seemed normal. She was pretty. Branson stumbled to his feet. The girl regarded him with distrustful eyes.

"I've just come for the laundry," she said. And with that, a trip hammer replaced Branson's heart.

He took a step towards her and she retreated.

"Madeline?"

Her distrust was replaced by confusion. "Who?"

"Madeline. It's me. It's Daddy."

Branson reached for his daughter and she recoiled. But when he relented, she merely crossed her arms while shifting her weight from one foot to the other.

"My name's not Madeline. I'm Petal. I do laundry."

"No," Branson whispered, as much to himself as to her. "Your name is Madeline Jeanne Turaco." He could still make out the gentle child's lines in her face and her eyes, those eyes he'd know anywhere, even though they were largely vacant. "Don't you remember? It was only five years ago."

"Petal."

Branson recalled how the Boy had only remembered *his* mother under duress, and even then the memory of her was vague. Branson wondered just how much damage the eel's blood had done to his daughter.

"I love you," he said. Madeline flinched as if he'd sprayed her with cold water. "I'm going to take you away from here. Take you home to your mother. We'll all be happy again."

"I don't think so." She crinkled her brow.

"These... these *people*, they're bad. They kill. And they steal children away from their parents. They're monsters."

Madeline bent down and scooped up the pile of towels. Her eyes never left Branson. Standing, she turned to leave.

"My name is Petal and I do laundry. That's who I am."

Petal went out the door, closed and locked it behind her, and Madeline was gone again.

FORTY-THREE

Over the next few days, Branson cleaned. Holiday visited each evening to evaluate the work and bring more buckets and towels. With a frown, she'd direct him to an unclean corner, a smear on the wall, or a smudged fingerprint on the porthole windowpane. He'd come to realize that the buckets were meant for more than just housekeeping. They were his daily bathwater at the start of the day, and his toilet whenever the need arose.

The towels, he noticed, were identical every day: plain white, washed, dried and refolded for the next day's use. In his boredom he'd experimented, marking the tag on one with a vertical tear. The next day, the same towel returned. Resources, he realized, were limited aboard the flotilla.

Each morning when the wash arrived, he held the clean towels up to his face and inhaled deeply, hoping to catch a whiff of Madeline's scent. Eyes closed as he breathed, he imagined her at work in a laundry room somewhere, her hands on the fabric where his face now rested. It was the closest he'd been to her in five years.

The cabin was spotless.

Branson had barely finished marking the new morning on the wall when the deadbolt sounded and the door opened. The two Pacifican guards sauntered in and let Holiday pass between them, the same as they had every morning for at least a month. Her eyes scanned the room. Instead of dropping the new buckets, she nodded.

"I'll take you to Dryhten now."

Branson's chest tightened.

"There are rules," Holiday said. "He'll listen to you, but you're not enlightened, so he won't answer. Don't waste his time, say what you have to say and nothing more." Holiday led Branson toward the door. "Speak softly and clearly. Show respect. And above all else, never approach him."

The flotilla was a flurry of motion. Easily a hundred Pacificans or more scurried over the various decks of the ships, crossing on planks between the vessels as need be. They rushed through their workday much like anybody else who ever punched a clock. Some fished for food off the sides of the smaller, lower boats; others carried the fresh catches away in large wicker baskets. Overhead, women hung bedsheets and other things from a maze of clotheslines. Branson couldn't spot Madeline among them. The deck of an immense oil platform rose at the center of the flotilla. The other boats Branson could imagine the Pacificans stealing. How they got hold of such an industrial remnant, he couldn't fathom.

Like the other Pacificans Branson could see, Holiday's skin lost almost all of its luminescence in the sunlight. Hopping onto a connecting plank, she led Branson and his minders onto a massive yacht. Six guards greeted them there, each carrying a shotgun. Identical in all ways, they had knotty, bald heads, severe brows, double chins, and they regarded Holiday with obvious respect. Branson half expected them to salute. Following a lengthy run of brass railing, they continued to the inner deck, and then ducked into the bridge. As Holiday entered, the idle Pacifican with his ankles crossed atop the console jumped to his feet. She ignored him, and led Branson to a hallway, then down a short flight of stairs, where they stopped before a heavy mahogany door.

"Remember the rules," Holiday said. Then she knocked three times, and it opened as if they'd been expected.

Branson stepped through the door. Holiday crept in behind him and shut it, which doused the weak strand of light the open door had provided. Holiday swept past Branson in the dark, her clothes brushing against him more loudly than he'd have expected, accompanied by little sparks of static electricity that ran down his bare forearm like lightning at night across a distant prairie. He raised both hands and took a couple tentative steps forward, but his bare feet sunk into something soft and smooth, yet with an inlaid texture that sucked at his feet like a moist sponge. Branson stopped and stood where he was. Everything was still.

When the sudden, blistering light went on, he staggered back and threw his arms over his brow. He squinted to try and see. Branson was in a ballroom. A ballroom on a boat. A boat fit for the Gilded Age. As his eyes adjusted, Branson lowered his arms and saw a strange figure seated atop a raised platform at the far end of the long room. The man was enveloped in a light so intense it was impossible to look at him for long. Holiday stood just behind him, one hand on the man's shoulder, her own shape reduced to hazy silhouette. Her voice lost no authority when it carried across the hall.

"Kneel."

Benedict Kendrick Shallcross was godlike. As in religious paintings from the Renaissance—intense, haloed beings with flaming robes and impossible grandeur. Branson went to his knees freely, but he wavered, and when his hands touched the floor for balance, what Branson's fingers told him, his brain didn't want to know.

"You demanded to see Dryhten," Holiday said. "So, *speak*."

Branson had rehearsed his demands a hundred times, but now, given the opportunity to press them, he couldn't remember a word. He'd prepared himself to face down a man. A man can be reasoned with. Persuaded, if need be. Even killed. But not *this*. Branson was not prepared for this.

"I... want... my daughter. I've come for Madeline," was everything he could manage.

Branson remained on his knees, awaiting some sort of response, even just an acknowledgment that he'd actually spoken, but nothing came, as Holiday said it wouldn't.

Shallcross dimmed, gradually, until his glow disappeared entirely. Branson felt Holiday's hand on his shoulder, urging him to his feet. The only light left in the room was her glow. It was warm and comforting.

"Time to go."

"No." Branson's fear was burnt away in the light of Benedict Shallcross. Holiday's expression shifted from controlled poise to sudden uncertainty. Before he could consider the consequences, Branson threw caution to the wind and knocked Holiday to the floor.

He ran the length of the dark hall, bare feet on human skin, in the general direction where Shallcross sat. Branson slipped only once, briefly. Holiday called for the guards, and just as Branson reached the platform, they entered. But then the light from outside revealed a shadowy figure who now sat where Shallcross had been. With nothing to stop him, Branson leaped onto the platform and took a good, hard look at this silhouette of a man.

Benedict Kendrick Shallcross was nothing but a statue, though he was a statue made of flesh. Branson tentatively pressed one thumb into the face of the thing in front of him, and his thumb sank straight through.

"Stop," Holiday screamed.

Holiday motioned the guards to stand down then cut through the light's path to join Branson on the platform. She ran one hand over the hole he'd poked in Shallcross' cheek. Without even glancing at Branson, she said, "Close the panel."

"Why... *this*?" Branson asked.

Holiday reached past him and slid the panel closed. She disappeared in darkness for only the moment it took his eyesight to adjust to her skin's gentle glow. She motioned to the guards to take hold of him, which they did.

"Dryhten was a cruel man who came to believe he was a god. The eel's blood revealed to me the truth, that fate provided Dryhten to us only as a light to draw us here and begin our new lives. He was never meant to rule us."

Shallcross' face wore an expression of exquisite sadness, as chilling as medieval paintings of Christian martyrs.

"We're changing. I know you've noticed. Changing into something new. We will bridge the destructive void that man has built between himself and the conscious universe. One day, we will return to the humans, not led by one man, but all of us as an army of gods. Dryhten's ego placed him in the way of fate."

"What did you do?"

"We killed him. Then we made him a god for the interim, so we never forget that none of us are more than the whole."

"But now *you're* the leader."

"No." Holiday's solemn mouth broke into a wide smile. It was like the sun that breaks a retreating storm. "I'm a caretaker. The eels all have a head and a tail, but one can't be distinguished from the other. When a tail is cut off, it regenerates. But should its head be severed, the eel dies. As we no longer have a head, we cannot be killed."

FORTY-FOUR

Restless and agitated, Branson spent the next week locked in his cabin, sleeping and eating and defecating into buckets, a schedule so bland and routine that the anxiety of being held captive gave way to stupefied boredom. He moved from the cot to the floor, paced for hours, stood and sat, tried new sleeping positions. Flipping through his memories like a deck of well-worn playing cards, he dealt out his best recollections of a day in Madeline's life, and tried to relive it in his mind. Sometimes the images emerged in startling detail and clarity, while just as often the pictures were incomplete or faded, and he was forced to invent. Her first birthday. The Halloween she dressed as a cartoon mermaid. Stepping onto the school bus on the first day of kindergarten. The tears he tickled away when she lost her first tooth.

Every day he waited for Madeline to return for his laundry, but she didn't. Instead, a different Pacifican came each day, and none ever said a word when they retrieved his dirty clothes. Branson asked once why Petal didn't come back, but received no reply.

He no longer felt his prison rock back and forth with the tide, and began to suspect he wasn't at sea—that perhaps he was in the psych ward of a local hospital. Branson wondered if he'd seen his daughter at all, or whether she'd been merely delusion born of desperation and sickness. Maybe none of it had happened at all. The days ran together and with that, hope lost currency. Then Madeline returned.

When she entered his room, Branson wept. He no longer cared if she was real, or whether he was simply insane. Branson jumped to his feet, wrapped his arms around his daughter, and held on for dear life. Madeline trembled in her father's embrace. Holiday and two guards stood just inside the door.

"Petal tells me you believe she's your daughter," Holiday said. "I'm unconvinced. Petal remembers nothing about her life before coming here. She doesn't remember *you*. Can you be sure you're not just seeing what you want to see?"

Branson released Madeline and glowered at Holiday.

"Maybe *fate* brought us back together."

"Exactly my thought," Holiday purred. "Let's find out."

"Find *what* out?"

"If you really believe." The guards took Branson by the arms and herded him out the door. He didn't resist. Holiday and Madeline followed several paces behind. On deck, a crowd of Pacificans stood in a circle around a recessed pit, a top-loading equipment bay floored by gigantic metal doors. The Pacificans murmured and tittered in conversation until they caught sight of Branson. At that moment, they fell silent and watched with keen eyes as he was brought to the edge of the pit. Branson gazed down the steep decline to the rusting metal base, and he realized that climbing out would be impossible. He expected the guards to push him in, but instead, they held him upright and clamped their hands down with force on his arms. He wasn't going anywhere.

Holiday held Madeline's small hand in hers to guide the teenager to edge of the pit. She looked kindly at the girl.

"Do you have faith, Petal?" Madeline nodded, as solemn and honest a gesture as Branson had ever seen. It was heartbreaking.

Holiday's hand tightened and Madeline winced. With a quick, violent swing, the caretaker threw her charge into the pit. Madeline screamed as she fell, and hit the metal doors at the bottom with a loud metallic crash.

Madeline lay at the bottom of the pit, and Branson was certain the fall had killed her. Then she shuddered, curled up, and cried. Branson wept with his daughter.

"You're gonna die for this," he said to Holiday, who blew him a kiss through pursed lips in response.

"If so, it's already written and nothing we do here today will change that. Have a bit of patience, and I'll show you."

Two guards bullied their way through the Pacificans and came up beside Holiday. Between them they carried a semi-conscious woman. It took Branson a moment to recognize her through the dark purple bruises, and without her glasses. Inflamed, her right eye was no longer parallel to her left, her features distorted into an asymmetrical nightmare of knotted flesh. She'd been beautiful when he first saw her. No more.

"Abriella," he whispered.

A single tear raced down her cheek.

"Let her go. Let them *both* go. Do what you want to me, but—"

"No." Holiday's tone was firm, and commanding. "She's the key to your understanding fate. Understanding *us*. She's told us a great deal about you. Two people from such different backgrounds, there's no reason the two of you should ever have met. But you did. That wasn't chance. It was fate that brought you together, so that you could then come to us." The gathered Pacificans answered that with a call and response typical of a congregation in the throes of religious ecstasy.

"Did you notice Abriella's wrists, or were you too wrapped up in your own misery?"

Branson hadn't. That embarrassed him, considering all they'd been through together and everything Abriella had done for him.

"My guess is that she's been cutting herself since childhood. Why do you think she was so eager to go with you? Why would she put her own life in danger? Did you really think it was all about you, or didn't you care?"

Abriella raised her head and stared at him. The dark circles under her eyes glistened with fresh tears. Branson couldn't look her in the eye.

"Fate chose you for her, her for you, and the two of you for us. And now here we are together, as it was always meant to be."

A tall, male Pacifican placed a bucket filled with eel's blood at Holiday's feet. Holiday took a handkerchief and dipped one end into the bucket. She spread the fabric across her extended fingers and dangled it over Abriella's face. Abriella whimpered and shrank from the cloth as it descended like a shroud.

"Please..." Branson said to Holiday. "...just, I'm begging you, please don't—"

"Shut up, Mister Turaco," Holiday snarled. Releasing the handkerchief, she turned in a fury to face Branson square. "You're not in control here. None of us are. There's no such thing as free will. What happens now *must be*." She paused for a second before adding, "Unless..."

Abriella screamed as the eel's blood on the soaked cloth streamed down her neck. Her hands convulsed. Her arms flailed. Knees buckled.

"*Anything*," Branson offered. "I'll do anything."

A guard slid the butt of a handgun into Branson's hand. Branson stared down in astonishment at the weapon originally provided him by Szymon Kazanjian. The Pacifican held Branson's hand tight around the gun, preventing him from raising it.

"It was found in one of our fishing nets," Holiday told him. "Yet more intercession by the hand of fate. A single bullet remains. Since you believe in free will, fate has provided you with a chance to prove it. Shoot Petal, strike her dead, and you may leave unharmed with Abriella."

Branson couldn't believe what he'd just heard. The guard forced his index finger over the trigger, then raised Branson's arm just enough so that the gun pointed at Madeline.

"The choice is yours," Holiday said.

"No," Branson whispered.

"I thought as much. In that case..." Abriella was released. She tore the handkerchief away from her face and took a stumbling step towards Branson. With a shove, Holiday sent her over the edge and into the pit. Abriella tried to wipe the eel's blood from her face as she fell, and hit the metal doors at the bottom with a sickening thud. She attempted to raise herself but failed, and lay face first against the floor.

Madeline stared at Abriella with wide, innocent eyes. Even at a distance, Branson could see the empathy and worry on his daughter's face. She'd always cared deeply for others, especially those who were hurt or sick, even to the point of disregarding her own wellbeing. Holiday peered down at Abriella in the pit.

"The offer you just refused? Your freedom for your daughter's life? I offered it to your friend down there first. She rejected it, too. Shall we find out if she's changed her mind?"

A Pacifican passed Holiday a common butcher knife and she held it up for Branson to see. She dropped the glittering blade into the pit.

"You've tasted eel's blood. You've seen glimpses of the future and so has she. Your girlfriend knows what's about to happen. Let's see what choices she makes to try and change it."

The knife had fallen between Madeline and Abriella. For a moment, neither moved.

Abriella gazed up at Branson through bloodshot eyes. She trembled and cried, her arms wrapped around herself. They connected on a primal level, as if the horror of the moment bridged the distance between them. Branson shared Abriella's pain, her fear, her confusion. His heart broke.

Not making a sound, she mouthed the words, "*I'm sorry.*" Madeline's expression went from concern to outright fear when Abriella dove for the knife. Branson screamed.

"*NO—*"

He struggled against his captors, but their grasp on his arms was too strong and he couldn't break free.

"Settle down. Enjoy the show," Holiday said. "Or of course, you can stop it any time you choose."

The guard kept Branson's aim squarely centered on Madeline's head, even as she leaped from the spot where she crouched, her body colliding with Abriella as the darker girl scrambled for the knife. They were a flurry of motion as they grappled, a blur of arms and elbows, knees and legs. Abriella, flat to the metal floor, came to a rest underneath Madeline, hands snapping up to take hold of her neck. With a quick flash of teeth, Madeline bit down on Abriella's wrist, drawing blood and a scream.

"Please," Branson begged Holiday.

The woman merely shrugged. "I can do nothing. It's your fate to choose, not mine."

Down the barrel of the gun, moving from one combatant to the other, he watched the girls fight, their hair tossing and fists swinging. The knife rested less than a foot from their entangled bodies. Madeline broke free of the violent embrace and kicked away, tumbling and rolling across the metal doors. She jumped to her feet and wobbled, holding the blade in her shaking hands.

Abriella pulled her bruised knees up to her breasts, slammed her hands down on either side, and rolled onto her feet.

On her feet and retreating, Madeline raised her arms and outstretched her palms, offering a peaceful surrender. But Abriella ignored the plea and rushed in, sidestepped the knife, and plowed into the smaller girl. The metal doors rumbled as they collapsed to the floor.

"Don't do this. You said you're a caretaker. Don't let this happen…"

Though the Pacificans were gathered around the edge of the pit to watch the spectacle, they remained strangely impassive—observant and mildly curious perhaps, but not personally invested, and nothing like entertained.

Abriella grabbed a handful of Madeline's hair and used it to slam the girl's head against the metal doors. A second blow quickly followed, then a third. Madeline fell limp, and her eyelids fluttered.

Abriella tore the knife from Madeline's hand and raised it high.

"ABRY— NO—" Branson screamed.

Abriella looked up at Branson. Tears flowed down her battered face. She ran the back of her wrist roughly across her face. A sniffling, strangled cry floated up from the pit.

"I'm sorry, Branson."

"No," Branson whispered as he raised the gun of the Polish farmer who'd died in the fight against tyranny. The gun felt heavier now.

In one trembling hand, Abriella held the knife poised to strike. With the other, she pushed Madeline's face to one side, to reveal a pale, terribly vulnerable throat. The move was almost gentle, and Abriella drew a breath.

Branson pulled the trigger.

It was the loudest sound he'd ever heard. So loud, it seemed to blast away existence. Nothing had weight or substance anymore. As in a fever dream, the voice of death-delivered was at once the center of all attention and utterly meaningless.

Abriella lay dead, as peaceful as during a warm night's sleep in her own bed, in her own home. Branson sank to his knees and whimpered. He didn't even know Abriella's middle name.

"Why?"

Down below, Madeline rolled away from Abriella's body. She came to a rest on her stomach, propped herself up on her elbows, and heaved.

"That's the only question there is, really." Holiday settled down beside Branson and coaxed the empty gun from his hand. "This was always your fate. This is who you are. You came hunting monsters. But what have you done? You coaxed a young woman from her father's house by taking advantage of her good nature, her resourceful mind, even her body. When her usefulness was exhausted and she became an obstacle, you killed her."

Branson had no reply.

In the pit, Madeline cried out.

"So Mr. Turaco, you tell me, who's the monster?"

"*You* did this." Branson said, then wept.

Holiday smiled benignly and patted him softly on the head.

"You know better than that."

FORTY-FIVE

He thought of Abriella's father at home waiting for his daughter to return. When she never did, would he believe she'd run away from him? Then he'd also have to believe he'd failed her as father. And if not, would Abriella's father come to hate whomever took away his little girl, just as Branson had? Would he never rest, until he ferreted out the truth?

Branson's numbness became all encompassing. He'd spent the first day after Abriella died scratching his makeshift calendar of hash marks off the wall, digging down until nothing remained except bare wall. He'd no idea how much time had passed since then. Days? Weeks? There was no way to know and little reason to care.

From outside Branson's prison rose a sudden flurry of noise. There was a wild scramble of feet across the deck, a quick shout, an aggressive grunt, a wounded masculine scream followed by the heavy thud of a body hitting the floor and, after a few muffled moans, dead silence.

The deadbolt was thrown back and the door cracked open. The first thing Branson saw was a dead Pacifican, face down on the floor. A bright pool of blood spread beneath him as the man's glow faded.

Sidestepping the blood, the Boy came into view. His white shirt and pants were spotted with fresh red blotches. In one hand he held a thin bone knife, which dripped.

The Boy entered, and Branson craned back his chin, offering a clean path to his neck. He'd no longer condemn the Boy for the death of Marius Spiegler. Branson was no better.

The Boy sat in front of him, legs crossed. Once Branson realized death wasn't imminent, he lowered his head and stared at the Boy. Everything about him had changed. The leering, bestial boy was gone, replaced by a scared child with sad, regretful eyes. Twin tears traveled down his face until they met, and dripped from his pointed chin.

"Mommy- was- pwetty," he said, sobbing. "But- I- don't- 'member-like- that. I- 'member- ugly. 'Cause- she- never- came... She- never-came- save me."

The Boy turned the knife around and slid the hilt into Branson's palm. When he failed to take it, the Boy drew Branson's fingers closed over the knife.

"*You* came." It was the first time he'd ever heard the child speak without stammering.

Suddenly, Branson saw the boy's story differently. Every scar on his body had robbed a little more of his innocence and replaced that with distrust. With every abuse, hate swelled and, propelled by survival instincts, evolution took over, until finally a child was gone but the Boy remained. That wasn't an act of cowardice, or of weakness. Nor did it represent moral defeat. The child changed himself through strength. And against the most daunting of odds, the Boy managed to survive.

As Madeline had.

"Take me to Madeline," Branson said. The Boy smiled and got to his feet.

"Follow."

By the time he stood up, the Boy was already out the door. Branson did his best to keep up, but the kid's erratic, skittish movements were disorienting. He'd make a quick shuffle in one direction, pivot, and scamper off in the opposite. The path he took was unexpected. Rather than take Branson up to the main deck the way Holiday had, the Boy navigated a labyrinth of metal corridors and grated stairs. The place echoed with the metallic beat of their progress. Rust blanketed the walls in places. A dank odor came and went, something in the final stages of decay. The overhead lights were spaced farther and farther apart, leaving stretches of darkness.

Branson paused to retrieve a fire ax from inside a metal box that was riveted to a large wall plate. When he caught up to the Boy, he didn't seem at all impressed by Branson's new line of defense.

The Boy led them into an industrial laundry. Dozens of washing machines lined the walls in various states of disrepair. Some looked functional; others were apparently being cannibalized for parts. Drying clothes hung from a complex web of hemp rope at the center of the bay, which blocked any clear view down its length. Uneven, crossing rows of identical white uniforms fluttered in an artificial breeze created by massive fans rotating slowly overhead.

The Boy threaded a path through the maze of clothes, his erratic movements matched perfectly to the shifting garments. Branson lost sight of him several times, but then he'd catch a fleeting glimpse of a quick blur of white splashed with red amidst the fabric. The noise of the rotating fans drowned out the sound of his steps. Quickening his pace, Branson reached out blindly and managed to catch the Boy by the shoulder. Now leashed to Branson, the kid moved slower, but with no fewer jerks and starts. It was like walking a schizophrenic dog.

The scent of fresh linen brought to Branson an overpowering sense of lightheaded calm. His anxiety dissipated. As he pushed through the layers of white cloth, the lighting intensified. After the uniforms came a sea of bedsheets billowing like clouds.

Branson followed the Boy between two sheets, where he caught sight of a slim silhouette moving beyond a layer of sheer cloth. He released the Boy's shoulder, pushed past, and yanked down the last sheet in his path.

Madeline stood frozen at the sight of him, clutching the corner of a pillowcase with one hand and a clothespin in the other. As Branson came closer, she dropped both.

"Maddy-" A look of uncertainty passed over his daughter. Then he finally heard what he'd remembered so well.

"Daddy?"

Madeline fell into her father's embrace. He pulled her close and shut his eyes tight. He inhaled deeply of her hair, and basked in its sweet scent. Then she raised her arms and wrapped them around him in return. Branson cried. Good tears, for once.

"I'm gonna take you home," he whispered to his daughter. "Right now."

Taking Madeline by the hand, Branson led her through the hanging laundry, tearing down sheets and white uniforms as he went, to clear a direct path. It wasn't until they'd reached the exit from the laundry that Branson realized the Boy hadn't followed. When Branson turned to look, he found the Boy standing perfectly still in the middle of the room, linens fluttering on either side. He was smiling.

"Come on—" Branson urged the Boy on. The child only shook his head in response.

"Can't. Something- else- to do." Madeline tugged at Branson's arm.

"We should go."

Branson looked to the Boy a moment longer. He wanted to remember him as he was just then, emaciated and covered in scars, yes, but seemingly at peace. Then Branson remembered something important and called out to the child.

"What's your name?"

Somehow the Boy's answer managed to reach Branson despite the din of the overhead fans.

"Mark- Clausen." Branson nodded.

"Thank you, Mark."

A great sheet blew in a pale breeze and obscured the Boy. When it retreated, he was gone.

"We should go *now*," Madeline urged. And then they were running, hand-in-hand, out of the laundry and into the metal halls. At the first turn Branson realized that without the Boy to lead him, he was lost. Madeline never missed a beat and took the lead, guiding him this way and that as they raced through corridors and clambered up staircases. The cold industrial corridors gave way to wood paneling and tile.

They passed through a wide doorway.

"What is this place?"

The great round room featured a dozen open doorways, one for every hour on the clock. Ceremonial art hung from the walls depicting the Pacificans' history with the eels. One piece in particular drew Branson's attention. The brothers, St. Abaddon and Benedict Shallcross, stood back to back, a long blue eel coiled around them both.

At the center of the room stood an eight-foot tall, six-foot wide aquarium carved from a crystalline substance as clear as glass. Inside, a single blue eel swam in lazy circles. Easily six feet long, its segmented body was armored by thick plates of what looked like exoskeleton. A bulbous head capped its tubular body. The thing had four tiny black beads for eyes, and a single long proboscis dangled from its chin above a whiskered, star-shaped mouth.

Madeline tried to pull Branson along. "This is the breeding room. She's very old. The ocean wasn't safe for her anymore, so they brought her aboard. Her weakest offspring are sold to the mainland."

Rather than heed his daughter, Branson could only stare.

And it stared back at him. Its mouth undulated, as if articulating words in an alien language. Its eyes blinked in quick succession.

"Face to face with fate, I see."

Though Branson was unable to break the eel's gaze, he saw Holiday's approach from behind him as a strange, wavy reflection in the glass. Her glow refracted off the aquarium, and tiny shards of prismatic light blinded him. He forced his concentration to her light, away from the monster behind the glass. With a hard blink, he was free. Branson stepped away from the aquarium and faced Holiday.

Like swarming insects, Pacificans poured in from every doorway until they filled the room, closing a circle around Branson and Madeline. Madeline wrapped her arm around one of his and held on tight. The glow radiating from the Pacificans muted all color. Black became gray; gray became white.

"Just let us go," Branson said.

Holiday ran one hand along the side of the aquarium as she circled it. She traced strange, lighted patterns on the glass, and the eel turned its attention from Branson over to those and followed Holiday around the tank. It looped through the water in mesmerizing patterns.

"Go where? Anywhere but here and the police will be waiting for you. What will you tell them, about Abriella? You belong with us now, here." As Holiday came around the tank and back towards Branson, he flinched at the sight of Szymon Kazanjian's gun in her hand.

"This?" With genuine affection, she turned the weapon over. "This spoke to me. Its purpose is not yet fulfilled. Don't worry, I reloaded it. It's ready to fulfill its destiny."

Branson turned from the eel and from Holiday and from Szymon Kazanjian's gun, to address the crowd of Pacificans in the room.

"It's you that have no choice, not me. You *must* let us go."

Holiday chuckled.

"We must? And why's that?"

"Because I've seen that you do." A low mumbling sped through the room. "Under the influence of eel's blood, I saw myself driving home with Madeline by my side. You believe in fate, don't you? You have faith, right?"

"He's lying," Holiday said through clenched teeth.

"No, I'm not."

Holiday gestured to three exceptionally large Pacificans. They came forward at her command.

"We've heard enough of your blasphemy."

Branson offered no resistance. The Pacificans took hold of him and slammed his face against the aquarium glass. The eel pressed its pink, segmented mouth to the glass from the inside with such puckering force as to threaten to turn the creature inside out.

"Dump him," Holiday commanded with a sneer.

The Pacificans hoisted Branson over their heads. The crowd cheered. The eel's face broke the surface of the water, mouth agape, before diving back down to the bottom of the tank. Branson screamed.

"You can't do this. I saw—"

In the tank, the eel swam in ever tighter circles, which turned the thing into a perfect spiraled spring, as if ready to leap from the water, wrap Branson in slimy blue coils, and drag him home.

"Do it now," Holiday said.

The Pacificans grunted as they adjusted Branson for the throwing. Below him the tip of the eel's tail tittered back and forth like a rattlesnake.

"*No.*"

The Pacificans froze with Branson poised to die.

"He's right." Madeline turned to the crowd and raised both hands in a gesture of unity. "During the last offering celebration, I had the same vision. We were together in an automobile. My father was taking me home."

A deep chorus of confused whispers stirred the crowd.

"Petal?" Madeline took a step towards Holiday.

"Madeline," she said simply. Branson's body dipped closer to the water as the men's grip faltered. "What he said, it's true."

"Don't betray us," Holiday said.

"I'm not. It's you who'll betray us, if you do this."

Fleshy appendages around the eel's mouth twitched in a frenzy. Translucent lids shut tight over all four of its eyes. It was primed. A young female Pacifican in the crowd spoke up in a cautious, uneasy voice.

"I saw something, too, during the celebration."

Madeline spun towards the girl. "What did you see?"

"An explosion. Tonight."

That got Holiday's attention.

"Where?"

"Here, right here. On the rig." Holiday shook her head.

"Don't do this. Don't lie."

"She's not," Madeline said.

Another voice sounded from deep within the crowd, this one male and older and much more self-assured.

"Yes, thunder, then fire and heat. From the fuel stores in the generator room."

The Boy, Branson thought. *Mark.*

"Just next door," someone blurted out.

The port side wall erupted with a roar that hurled shrapnel through the room, and through every Pacifican in the explosion's path. Those left standing either scrambled for the remaining exits or fell flat to the floor.

Branson fell into the aquarium amidst the terrible conflagration that ensued. The terrified screams of cultists were quickly reduced to a muffled chorus of end-times cinders.

The eel struck a forceful blow to Branson's neck and latched on with prejudice even as he hit the water. Liquid filled Branson's lungs as the eel wrapped him in a coil of blue.

A shard of something smacked through one side of the aquarium and out the other, leaving a fizzy trail in its wake. The glass spider-webbed, then couldn't hold and shattered, releasing Branson and the eel together, along with a wave of bloody salt water. Water hissed and steam filled the air as the immediate flames succumbed. Branson and the eel thrashed and wrestled across the deck, each in turn arching off the smoking floorboards as needed.

Its sleek body seemed impossible to escape. The eel blocked every route with a coil of its body. Thrusting him against the floorboards, it shook him back and forth. Branson struggled, punching at its sides with no effect.

With the last of his strength, Branson snapped his head down and bit deep into eel flesh. A jolt spread from his gums and then straight through him, which felt like it tore the roof out of Branson's mouth along the way. He and the eel's consciousness blended. Colors and sounds gained shape, shapes became shapeless, smells were visible in the air. He saw an alien world and a long, painful journey. Death. Rebirth. And children, so many children, both eel and human.

At the same moment that Branson came to know the eel, the eel came to know him. He felt it recoil from his anger and pain and frustration. It heard the Mortician's voice, and it feared him.

The eel released Branson, and squirmed away from him. Branson backpedaled on his heels and elbows like a crab. Scooping aquarium water off the floor, he rinsed his mouth and spat. The psychic link was broken.

The room was rocked by a second explosion. The portside floor upended and the bodies of dead and dying Pacificans slid across it. From somewhere deep below, metal shrieked. The entire place tilted, and Branson understood it was no effect of eel's blood. The remnant foundations of an oil platform long removed from its host rig were failing. Branson added his own shrill scream to the building cacophony.

"Madeline."

With a hellish roar, the floor under his feet tore back and a fireball emerged, throwing Branson onto his back. A chasm opened, revealing deck after deck below on fire. He turned, searching for Madeline, but with no success.

He struggled to get back on his feet. Rising from the edge of the fiery pit, Holiday snatched Branson's ankle and he collapsed back onto the deck. The right side of her face was charred down to the skull, yet still she lived. Then she was on him. With a blackened fist, Holiday thrust Szymon Kazanjian's pistol to Branson's chest. She tried to pull the trigger, but her scorched index finger snapped off and fell to the floor, followed a moment later by the gun.

Branson snapped it up and held it to Holiday's temple.

"It doesn't... tell you... everything," she moaned. Then she was dead.

The ceiling on the far side of the bay buckled, then failed, burying half the room and the Pacificans in a smoldering pile of rubble. Branson wobbled to his feet, and found the eel. About half its length was stuck fast beneath flaming debris, and in fury the creature repeatedly thudded its heavy head hard against the floor.

Branson put one foot on the eel's neck, placed the muzzle of a dead Polish farmer's pistol right in the middle of its four beady black eyes, and pulled the trigger.

The eel became still. A line of eel's blood raced down the sloping floor toward the widening hole between decks.

Standing straight, Branson turned towards the only exit still not consumed by fire or debris. Madeline stood there, dusted by soot, waiting for him. He rushed through the floating embers and wrapped his arms around her. She clung to him.

Another blast from below rocked the flotilla. The platform tilted. Thrown off balance, they fell against the descending hallway wall. Pulling Madeline up, Branson pushed her forward, away from the growing inferno. They ran, dodging falling ceiling beams. They leaped over a pile of charred bodies. At the end of the hall, they pushed through a door that hung limply from a single hinge, and escaped out onto the deck.

Pacificans scattered, running for the smaller boats moored to the sides. Branson took Madeline's hand and led her across gangplanks and drawbridges onto smaller and smaller crafts. He kept his gun drawn. The Pacificans steered clear of him.

Spotting a small motorboat docked to the port side of the final yacht, Branson raced across the deck as another explosion rippled through the flotilla. He helped Madeline aboard, the quickly unwound the mooring rope. Leaping inside, he rushed to the outboard motor, thumbed the choke, and pulled the cord. The engine came to life. He yanked the tiller hard away from the yacht. The motorboat pulled away from the flotilla.

They were free.

He pulled Madeline close to his side and looked back over his shoulder. What remained of the flotilla tried to pull itself apart. A few smaller vessels were already broken free and sailing away, but only a few and those were scattering on the open sea. On what remained of the oil rig platform, Pacifican lives were snuffed out one by one, their glowing bodies failing like candles before a stiff wind. A single figure stood on the bow of a vertically sinking yacht, still and unmoving. An enormous wave crested, and when it subsided, Mark Clausen was gone.

When the oilrig collapsed into the ocean, it would drag everything still tethered to it straight down to the bottom.

Once at a safe distance, Branson pulled Madeline close to his chest and held her there.

It'd still be a long journey. But that'd be like no time at all, when considering how long it'd taken for Branson and Madeline to get so far from home.

FORTY-SIX

Susan Woost, retired, sat in a chair on her porch and watched the house across the street. The teenage girl there paced the yard and chatted at her device, one hand gesturing wildly as she did.

Woost couldn't remember the last time she'd felt that carefree, and she didn't want to, because that would inevitably lead to Roy, and soon after, the half-empty bottle of vodka waiting atop her refrigerator.

A beater Chevy rolled up the street and into her driveway. For the first time in years, Woost didn't make a mental note of the plate number. An older man, age and description unimportant, stepped out of the car and joined her on the porch. An empty chair stood beside her. She nodded. He sat.

"Les Franklin," he said, holding out a hand.

They shook.

"I'd ask how you found me—"

"—I wouldn't be much of a cop, retired or not, if I couldn't." He had an easy smile and a grandfatherly charm. She could see why Roy liked him. "But what made you move all the hell of the way out here?"

"Friends in the neighborhood," she said. The old man nodded and smiled.

"I was happy to read in the papers that they dropped the charges."

She'd copped to lessers and accepted probation on condition of early retirement. Gideon didn't hesitate to sign the paperwork.

"Why'd you come all the way out here, Les?"

"Maybe I'm just checking in on a friend of a friend. Making sure you're doing all right." He eyed the shotgun propped up against Woost's chair. She smiled.

"Think I might take up duck hunting. If I had a dog. And a pond. And ducks."

"Yeah, okay…" Les reached into the breast pocket of his coat and withdrew a folded piece of paper. "There was this, as well. I've got friends, you know, still on the job." Les handed Susan the paper.

"The Donne case?"

"You'd know it as the Turaco case."

"The *Turaco* case?" Woost visibly flinched.

"The inventory of Donne's trailer turned up a big box of receipts. Serial killers aren't generally known for being charitable, but they say there's an exception to every rule."

She unfolded the sheet, but it trembled too much in her hand to read it.

"He had a thing for kid's hair, I guess we both know. Took a lock from each victim. Souvenir."

Woost raised an eyebrow.

"But here," Les pointed to a line on the paper. "You see *that*? Donne supported a local cancer event every year. You see these? Children cut their hair and auctioned it off. It was all supposed to go for wigs for chemo patients, but they always attach a single lock to the thank-you letter."

"He *bought* her hair," Woost whispered.

"Which means Bruce Donne didn't kidnap Madeline Turaco." Les paused. "You don't seem surprised."

Woost sat forward in her chair and looked toward her neighbor's chatty daughter through the refreshed eyes of a predator.

"The person closest to a crime is *always* the worst witness."

FORTY-SEVEN

Maxine the cat purred contently in Madeline's lap. They'd stopped home just long enough to pick her up from Hal Norcross. Branson looked at his daughter and smiled. It was exactly as he'd seen in the vision. Madeline and he in a car, on a long drive, together. He had smiled a lot over the last few days, maybe more than he could ever remember.

Madeline's slight glow was invisible beneath the amber sunlight. Even at night it seemed to grow dimmer a little more each day. Soon, he hoped, it would be gone for good.

At last they pulled into a long driveway that led to a simple split-level ranch with painted, non-functional shutters and a one-car attached garage. It was exactly the sort of home Branson once had, and wanted again. Killing the engine, he took Madeline's hand and squeezed.

"You ready?"

She nodded, but even through the winsome smile and adoring dimples, he could tell she was nervous.

"Don't worry. Everything's gonna be fine now."

"Okay," Madeline said.

They got out and together headed to the front door. Holding Maxine against her chest, Madeline fell a cautious step behind. Her hair blew down over her face.

Branson rang the bell.

It took a moment, but patience was rewarded when the door opened. Candice stepped up. A framed portrait hung on the wall behind her—Candice and her new husband, no doubt. All smiles.

"The police came here looking for you. What're you doing, Branson? You can't just come out here and—"

Branson nudged Madeline toward Candice. He exhaled a breath he'd held for a very long time. Tears clouded his vision, but Candice didn't seem impressed.

"Who? Who's this?" she asked.

"Can't you see?" Branson took Madeline by the hand and pulled her to the doorway. "It's our daughter, Candy. It's Madeline."

"Oh, Bran..."

He'd expected exaltation. Candice seemed only frightened and sad.

"It's our... it's *Madeline*."

"No," Candice answered, "it's not." Branson's ex-wife shook her head in a slow, deliberate manner. A second figure appeared behind her, a teenaged girl with a cellphone pressed to her ear. The girl looked at him with uneasy recognition, and put the cellphone away.

He recognized the girl, even with the added years. His eyes shot over to the Pacifican girl at his side, the one called *Petal*, then back to his daughter. *To Madeline.*

"I don't—"

"You put me in the *hospital*, Bran. What was I supposed to do, wait for you to put *her there too*? I was already seeing Andrew. I sent Madeline out here to protect her. You can understand that, can't you? I didn't know what you'd do if—"

"Don't move," a voice called from behind him. He glanced over his shoulder.

"*Blonde* again, Detective?" Branson said.

Woost leveled the shotgun at Branson's back. "Drop to your knees and raise your hands over your head."

Branson didn't.

"You shouldn't have lied to me," Susan said to Candice. "None of this had to happen. I could have protected you better."

"I'm sorry Sue, really I am. But when this started I didn't know you or Roy well enough. I didn't know whether you—"

Petal's eyes glazed over and she took a slow backward step. She knew exactly where she was. She'd seen it.

"Am I under arrest?"

"That's not my job," Woost said. "Not anymore."

Branson slid his hand into his waistband and felt the handle of the pistol stashed there. He'd been told all along that his journey would end badly, and he'd ignored it. He'd chosen to believe he could escape fate. That he needn't be a criminal. A kidnapper of children. A liar, a man of violence, a murderer. He'd been wrong.

The Mortician was right all along.

A gentle laugh drifted through the stillness, innocent and carefree. With childlike glee, Petal snapped Maxine's neck. The cat's body slipped from Petal's hands like a broken plaything. A fierce glow surged from her skin.

Branson reached for his gun. It used to belong to Szymon Kazanjian the rebel and before that, to a Polish farmer. But that day it belonged to Branson.

Then Woost did what she had to do, Branson Turaco did what he had to do, and what happened, happened.

Other Cutting Block Books Titles

+Horror Library+ Volume 1
+Horror Library+ Volume 2
+Horror Library+ Volume 3
+Horror Library+ Volume 4
+Horror Library+ Volume 5
Best of +Horror Library+ Volumes 1-5
Butchershop Quartet I
Butchershop Quartet II
Tattered Souls
Tattered Souls 2

Coming Soon

Cutting Block: Single Slices